"*The Vicar's Wife* is gorge̲̲̲̲̲̲̲̲̲̲̲̲̲̲̲̲̲̲ ly
moving story of two lives that echo each other across time,
and a stunning exploration of finding one's way home, no
matter what the heart thinks it wants. The perfect book to
lose yourself in!"
- Megan Crane, author of *Once More With Feeling* and
I Love the 80s

....

"An absorbing and captivating tale that kept me on the edge
of my seat. Heart-warming, dramatic, and impossible to
put down, *The Vicar's Wife* is the new book from Katharine
Swartz's immensely talented pen."
- Julie Bonello, CataRomance Reviews

....

"Katharine Swartz skillfully weaves together two stories in
this engrossing tale. A warm, wonderful emotional read."
- Sarah Morgan, USA Today bestselling author

ABOUT THE AUTHOR

After spending her childhood in Canada and then three years as a diehard New Yorker, Katharine Swartz now lives in the Lake District with her husband, an Anglican minister, their five children, and a Golden Retriever. She enjoys such novel things as long country walks and chatting with people in the street, and her children love the freedom of village life – although she often has to ring four or five people to figure out where they've gone off to!

She writes women's fiction as well as contemporary romance for Mills & Boon Modern under the name Kate Hewitt, and whatever the genre she enjoys delivering a compelling and intensely emotional story. Find out more about her books at www.katharineswartz.com.

THE VICAR'S WIFE

Katharine Swartz

LION FICTION

Published by Lion Fiction
an imprint of
Lion Hudson plc
Wilkinson House, Jordan Hill Road,
Oxford OX2 8DR, England
www.lionhudson.com/fiction

ISBN 978 1 78264 070 7
e-ISBN 978 1 78264 071 4

First edition 2013

Acknowledgments
Scripture quotations taken from The Authorized (King James) Version. Rights in the Authorized Version are vested in the Crown. Reproduced by permission of the Crown's patentee, Cambridge University Press.

A catalogue record for this book is available from the British Library

Printed and bound in the UK, September 2013, LH26

To the lovely people of St Bees,
who made the village feel like my home.

Acknowledgments

Many thanks to all the people who helped with the writing of this story: my editor Shirley Blair at *The People's Friend*, Alison Hull and Tony Collins at Lion Hudson, and the many people of St Bees who unknowingly provided inspiration – just remember this is fiction!

CHAPTER ONE

....

Jane

It started with a shopping list. Jane Hatton had been painting the second pantry; it seemed ridiculous that there were two, but then this huge, rambling monstrosity of a vicarage was ridiculous.

A month ago she'd been in New York City, playing with the children in Central Park and touring the Met, trying to forget the fact that she was about to move countries, that she had, albeit rather passively, agreed to her husband's long-held dream of finally returning to the land of his birth and living in the middle of nowhere.

Now there could be no avoiding it. The wind rattled the kitchen windowpanes and Jane could feel the draught from under the back door, unforgivingly raw even though it was only early September. In New York City, Jane had checked that morning, it was a balmy twenty-three degrees. In Cumbria the thermometer hovered around a miserable ten.

"Stop moaning," she told herself as she took out the old, weathered shelves of the second pantry in preparation to paint the walls. When she did a thing, she did it properly, which was why she'd started with the second pantry. The formal sitting and dining rooms with their fourteen-foot-high ceilings and long, curling strips of old, peeling paint were far too overwhelming. The pantry, and the second one at that, she could just about manage.

"You agreed to this," she reminded herself, her voice ringing out through the stone-flagged kitchen. "You did. There's no use complaining about it now."

And even though she knew there wasn't, she could not keep from feeling painfully homesick for the city's bright lights and frantic energy. She'd been born there, and after a childhood stint in the suburbs had lived her whole adult life there. She'd raised their three children there. They'd liked New York, liked the verdant expanse of Central Park, the traditional outings to Radio City for Christmas, to the Natural History Museum the day before Thanksgiving to watch them blow up the floats, the buzz and excitement of living at the very centre of the world.

Just the thought of all the things they'd done, the *life* they'd lived, made Jane close her eyes, a shelf still held in her hands. She missed it so much. There was nothing to do, among these barren fells and morose sheep. *Nothing*.

Natalie, her oldest child at fourteen, had already given this scathing indictment three days ago. Jane had, somewhat doubtfully, cajoled her children to play in the garden, even though the sky was heavy and grey with lowering clouds and a freezing wind – it was *August*, for heaven's sake – came straight off the sea.

She'd watched them from the dining room window as they mooched around the expanse of overgrown grass, looking bored and even bewildered. It was, she had told them in a too-cheerful voice, quite an *interesting* garden, surrounded by high stone walls, and with plenty of overgrown borders and intriguing nooks – Merrie, their youngest, had found a stone bench built right into the hillside and covered in mulchy leaves.

Still, it wasn't familiar; it wasn't New York. There was no modern Swedish-designed climbing equipment, no ice cream and balloon vendors, no towering rocks to climb on like in Central Park. After three minutes Natalie folded her arms and sat in a plastic chair – their only one – while she glared at Jane still standing there hopefully by the window.

When she'd finally ushered them all back in – it had started to rain, *again* – Natalie had turned to her and hissed, "There is *nothing* to do here."

Jane had stayed silent, mainly because she agreed and did not want Natalie to know.

Maybe things would be different now, she thought as she reached for another shelf. Today was their first day of school, and surely they'd all feel differently once they made friends. Even her.

Sighing, Jane eased the next shelf off its braces. This one was slate, and very old; its heaviness surprised her and she almost dropped it. When Andrew had bought the former vicarage last spring – Jane hadn't even seen it – he'd raved about all the period details, cornices and fireplaces and an ancient Aga in the kitchen. Tucked up in their Upper West Side apartment with its double-glazed windows and air conditioning, Jane had been vaguely charmed.

"And the pantry has a slate shelf," Andrew had said happily. "You know – a cold shelf, to put meat and milk and things on."

"Well, I hope we'll have a fridge," Jane had replied with a little laugh, but she, like Andrew, had liked the idea of it. It all sounded very charming, sort of like living in a period drama. Next she'd be churning butter.

The reality, however, was that the house was a mess of peeling paint, warped floorboards, and dodgy electrics. It was freezing even in summer and the slate shelf she held now was ridiculously heavy. With a sigh she placed the shelf carefully on the floor – she really didn't feel like picking up a million pieces of shattered slate – and that's when the yellowed piece of paper fluttered off it. It must have been stuck to the back, trapped against the wall, and with a flicker of curiosity Jane picked it up.

It was just a scrap, torn carefully from the corner of a larger sheet, and the writing on it was a spidery kind of cursive no one seemed to use any more. Jane squinted to read the few lines.

> *Beef joint for Weltons, 2 lb, 2s/3d*
> *Potatoes, 5 lb, 6d*
> *Tea, 1/4 lb, 4d*
> *Mint Humbugs for David, 1d*

Jane read it through again, slowly, trying to make sense of it. It was a shopping list, obviously, but she didn't know what the *d* stood for. And who were the Weltons? And David?

She sat back on her heels, intrigued enough for her own homesickness to abate for a moment. She had no idea how old the shopping list was, but by the crackly age of the paper and the spidery writing she guessed at least forty or fifty years. And it had been stuck behind that slate shelf the whole time.

"I don't suppose anyone wanted to move that heavy thing," Jane murmured. She stood up, wincing at the cramp in her legs. She hadn't even started painting yet, but she felt due a coffee break. She put the kettle on and stared out the kitchen window, the sky heavy and grey, the wind battering every tree and shrub in the garden into woeful submission.

They'd arrived in Goswell on a beautiful sunny day two weeks ago. It had been mid-August, warm although not hot, and the sunlight had bathed everything in a mellow, golden light. Jane had climbed out of the rented estate car and blinked up at the stately old vicarage in wary surprise. It was a place, she'd felt, that had a huge amount of history and she could not quite imagine becoming a part of it.

"It looks like something out of an Austen novel," she told Andrew, who was already hurrying towards the door with the big, ridiculously old-fashioned iron key he'd picked up at the estate agent's in Penrith.

"It should do," he called back. "It was built in 1819, right around the time she was writing."

The children had tumbled out of the car like puppies, racing around the huge garden, and Jane was heartened to hear their cries of delight upon the discovery of an old wooden swing in a horse chestnut tree.

Breathless and red-cheeked, eight-year-old Merrie had run up to Jane and tugged her sleeve, her eyes wide with rapture. "There's a horse in the field over there – *right next door!*"

Jane had smiled. "Is there, sweetheart? Maybe we can find a carrot to feed it." Even Natalie, persistently and determinedly sullen ever since the move had been announced, had sloped around the garden, looking begrudgingly interested. Ben, eleven and full of manic boy-energy, was romping and whooping like a joyful savage.

Jane had felt a wave of relief. Perhaps it was going to be all right after all. They'd make a home here, find a kind of bucolic life for themselves. It would be, as they'd told themselves over and over again, good for the children. David opened the door.

The first thing Jane had noticed when she stepped inside was how musty the house smelled.

"Look at that Victorian tile," Andrew enthused, pointing to the intricate pattern of coloured tile on the floor, blood-red and army green. It looked, Jane thought, like something out of *Oliver Twist*. Victorian orphanage decor.

The children pushed past them and raced upstairs, and Jane could hear them laying claim to the best bedrooms.

"How long has it been empty?" she asked, taking another step inside. She could not deny the gracious, soaring space of the rooms was both imposing and beautiful, if a little overwhelming. The entry hall alone was bigger than their sitting room back in New York.

"A year or two," Andrew replied with a shrug. "The last vicar left and the diocese decided to sell it, buy a modern bungalow for the next incumbent."

"I see." And frankly, staring around at the huge, musty rooms, Jane could see the appeal of a smaller, warmer house with a fitted kitchen, an electric cooker, and central heating. She let out a long, slow breath. "Well, let's see the rest of it."

"You'll love it," Andrew assured her. "It was a complete bargain – we'll have to do it up slowly—"

As he took her through the house, clearly brimming with excitement, Jane knew she could not say or do anything to dampen his enthusiasm. She remained mostly silent, taking in the period details Andrew had raved about – fireplaces in all six bedrooms – as well as noting the flaking paint, rotten floorboards, and rattling windowpanes. It was a beautiful house, and it hadn't been cared for properly in years. And they were meant to be moving in tomorrow, when their things arrived from the States.

"Let's go to the kitchen," Andrew said after they'd toured the whole house and decided which bedrooms everyone would take. "I'll put the kettle on and we'll all have a cup of tea."

"There's a kettle?" Jane asked dubiously, and Andrew grinned, excited even about that.

"Yes, a huge brass one – it must be almost as old as the house. I instructed them to turn the Aga back on before we came, and I've brought a packet of tea and mugs." He grinned again, clearly pleased with himself, and Jane smiled weakly back.

Even after sixteen years in New York, Andrew had not lost the British belief that a cup of tea made things better. Jane was not so sure. Even after a mug of English Breakfast the house would remain in all of its unkempt glory. They would still be living in a tiny village in Cumbria, having given up everything in New York. The pre-war, full-service three bedroom they'd saved and saved for. A circle of gracious if busy friends. Places for all their children at some of the city's best private schools. And a job – a calling, managing a nonprofit for disadvantaged women – that she'd dearly loved.

She knew there was no point thinking about it now. They'd discussed it all, the pros and cons, the possibilities, five months ago, when Natalie had been suspended from school for two weeks after being busted for drinking at a friend's party.

Jane had been furious, because several other girls had weaselled out of a proper punishment since their fathers were on the Board of Trustees. The Hattons didn't have that kind of pull, and so Natalie had paid.

Andrew, of course, had seen things differently. Natalie had done wrong; Natalie deserved what she got. And the whole episode, unfortunately, had served as a wake-up call to him that he did not want to raise his family in New York City.

Jane still remembered the shock that had trickled icily through her as Andrew sat across from her on the sofa, the children in bed, her laptop on her knees. She'd been going over donor figures for the end of the year and she hadn't been in the mood for a deep conversation.

"I've been thinking," Andrew had said, his face worryingly earnest, "about moving out of New York."

Jane stared at him blankly, for the first thought that had crossed her mind was that Andrew meant he would move by himself. *She* wasn't about to leave the only place she'd thought of as home.

"Moving," she repeated, noncommittally, and Andrew nodded, wrapped a hand around her bare ankle.

"Yes. Somewhere where the children have more space, more freedom."

She wrinkled her nose. "You mean New Jersey?"

He gave her a small, patient smile. "No, Jane."

Thank God. "Connecticut?"

"No." Andrew let out a little sigh and squeezed her ankle. "I mean back to England. You know I've always wanted to live there again, let the children see where half of their family comes from—"

Still she refused to understand, some stubborn part of her insisting on confusion as the safer option. "You mean a trip."

Andrew shook his head, still earnest. "No, Jane. I mean a move." He took a breath, his fingers tightening around the fragile bones of her ankle. "There's a position at a technology park near Keswick. The kind of engineering research I've always wanted to do—"

"A job in *Keswick*?" Jane shifted, slipping her legs away from Andrew, her feet firmly on the floor. They'd gone to visit his mother in Keswick nearly every year since they'd been married, and although decidedly quaint it was not a place she'd ever considered living in. It was five hours from London, for heaven's sake. Not even near the motorway.

"It's not in Keswick. It's about half an hour away, near the coast."

"Farther away than Keswick."

Andrew gave her one of his endearing, crooked smiles, the kind she'd always loved. "Farther away from what?"

Everything. Jane just stared at him blankly. Nothing, absolutely nothing, had prepared her for this moment. Oh, Andrew had made noises about wanting to move back to England one day, but that's all they'd been. Noises. Jane had, on rare occasions, entertained an extremely vague notion of retiring to some delightful thatched cottage in the Cotswolds, near enough to London and with plenty of culture and sophistication.

And now Andrew was talking about moving to the remote northwest corner of England, near *nothing*, and raising their children there? It was inconceivable.

"I'm surprised," she finally said.

"I know."

"I didn't realize you were actually thinking of moving." She'd meant to sound neutral, but it came out like an accusation.

"This whole thing with Natalie has really made me think."

Jane kept her temper with effort. She already knew they disagreed about "this whole thing" with Natalie. She felt it was a blip on the radar; Andrew thought it was huge. A wake-up call – but to what? "So," she finally said, "you think kids don't drink and go to parties in Cumbria?"

Hurt flashed across Andrew's face and Jane looked away. He could be such a little *boy* about some things. So innocent, so eager. It was at least in part why she'd fallen in love with him back when they'd both been students at Columbia – Andrew visiting for a term – but twenty years later, almost all of them spent in the city, she would have thought he'd have developed some hard city gloss. She wished, in that moment, that he had.

"Of course I don't think that. But I'm tired of life here, Jane. I'm tired of snarling with cab drivers and shoving my way to work on a crowded pavement. I'm bored with my job teaching over-entitled college students who are even more bored than I am and trekking seven blocks to Central Park to kick a football with my son. I don't want this any more."

She heard the urgent sincerity in his voice. She felt it. And she remained silent, because she knew in that moment that all the arguments she'd been poised to launch like missiles would fall crucially short of their target. Andrew had sacrificed the kind of life he'd wanted to live so she could live the kind of life she wanted, and he'd done it for sixteen years. It was that simple. She'd had her turn, and now he wanted his.

Tit for tat. It was about what was fair, what was right, even if it felt completely unjust in that moment. She got that, even if she didn't want to.

"OK," she said. "I'll think about it."

She tried not to think about it and yet it constantly occupied her thoughts. It seemed as if every few seconds her mind broached the terrifying possibility, only to back away from it with panicked speed. Andrew had applied for the job, got the interview. He asked Jane if she wanted to accompany him, and she'd made excuses about needing to stay with the children. She knew she should go, she should see what this life of theirs might be like, but she was too afraid. Some childish part of her psyche insisted that if she didn't go, if she didn't *see*, it wouldn't happen.

Andrew got the job. It was time for another serious and earnest discussion, and in a panic Jane conducted countless frenzied internet searches on the region – West Cumberland – and found it all incredibly depressing. The local schools' OFSTED reports – Jane wasn't even sure what those were

– seemed mediocre. The hospital was overcrowded and the unemployment was one of the highest in the country.

"If you reduced Manhattan to a bunch of similar statistics," Andrew told her, "it would be worse."

Of course Jane knew that. Manhattan's statistics would be much worse, and yet it didn't make her feel any better. Andrew, however, seemed remarkably placid about the whole thing, seemed irritatingly certain that they would all thrive – his word – in this new environment. As if they were houseplants.

"Do you know," she told him once, "there are only four Starbucks in all of Cumbria? One in Carlisle, and three in the Center Parcs."

Andrew had smiled and patted her shoulder. "We're not moving so we can be near a Starbucks," he said. "We're moving away from them."

"And no take-out places." She thought of the vast array they had on their doorstep; take-out was often an easier option than cooking, and her children had learned to dial and order for themselves – all part of a Manhattan childhood.

"Thank goodness," Andrew answered lightly. "I'm ready for some home-cooked meals."

She'd reared back then, struck by the awful possibility that this move wasn't just about changing lifestyles, but changing her.

"I'm not going to turn into Betty Homemaker," Jane warned him and Andrew just chuckled.

"I'm not asking you to, Jane. I just want an easier pace."

Yet despite Andrew's wish, things seemed only to pick up speed, decisions made faster and faster, so Jane felt like a spectator in her own life, everything a blur of activity around her. Even as Andrew accepted the job, even as they sat down and told the children, even as they put their gorgeous apartment up for sale, and she cried the first time someone came in and looked at it, turning their noses up at the granite countertops in the kitchen – *"but they're not marble"* – even as he went back to look at houses and Jane stubbornly refused to accompany him, still in some kind of outrageous denial, she'd felt removed from it all, like it wasn't really going to happen. It wasn't going to happen to her. It *couldn't*.

And now they were here.

"More tea?" Andrew asked cheerfully and Jane took her mug to the huge, stained sink. It looked as ancient as the rest of the house, and the depth of it was sure to give her backache.

"No, thank you," she said. "I'm going outside."

She stood on the crumbling front steps and shivered. It was a beautiful day, but it was still cold. It was *freezing*. Directly outside the house was a horse paddock, and beyond that a sheep pasture. Besides the animals all she could see were a few miserable, terraced cottages, the woebegone rail station, and a plume of smoke curling up to a greying sky.

She swallowed, sniffed. She'd already done her grieving for the life they'd left in New York, or at least she thought she had. She'd cried, alone in the shower, and presented a determinedly cheerful if rather brittle front to her friends.

She had accepted that Andrew needed this, that the children probably needed this. And she'd told herself that maybe she needed this too, because she'd been pulling sixty-hour working weeks and juggling childcare while pretending she didn't get migraines or ulcers – and that was no way to live your life, right?

Right, Jane told herself as she stared out at the verdant hills, the trees fringing the crest a dark green smudge, the whole world silent and empty around her except for the relentless howl of the wind and the mournful bleating of the sheep. Right.

Once their things arrived the next day she was kept busy enough not to dwell on all the things she didn't like about their new home, such as the fact it was on the church grounds, basically in the middle of a cemetery, with no neighbours to speak of. Or that the nearest supermarket was a fifteen-minute drive away, the only takeaway available was a kebab place with an extremely limited menu, and the silence at night rang in her ears, kept her from sleeping, and just about drove her mad.

She was not going to be a snob about things, she told herself. She had plenty of friends in New York who thought Brooklyn, never mind anywhere actually out of the city, was the back of beyond. Most of them had been shocked when she'd announced she was moving to a tiny village on the coast of one of England's least populated counties.

"It will be so atmospheric," they'd cooed, as if enthusiastic or even envious, but Jane saw the look in their eyes that they couldn't quite hide. *Better you than me.*

And she'd tried not to agree with them, tried not to want so desperately to stay in New York, to keep everything just as it was.

And here she was, two weeks in, the children off to school, alone in this great big rambling place. The house seemed to stretch in every direction, empty, endless, unfriendly. Their furniture filled all of three rooms.

She had not met anyone in the village beyond a cautious hello when she'd walked to the little post office shop for a newspaper. The only person she'd had an actual conversation with – if she could call it that – was the postman, when he'd delivered their post. He'd engaged her in a lengthy discussion in a West Cumbrian accent so thick Jane had not understood a word. She'd clutched their first telephone bill to her chest and made what she hoped were appropriate noises of interest until the man, giving her a look as if he thought her a complete idiot, had taken himself off in his little red van.

She felt, she finally admitted to herself as she took a sip of coffee, the pantry shelves lying all around her, quite unbearably lonely and homesick, without purpose or happiness. Tears threatened, and she blinked them back. She had not cried once since they'd moved here, and she wasn't about to now. Crying alone in this great big house would only make her more miserable. Drawing a shuddering breath, she stared down at the aged shopping list once more.

Beef joint for Weltons, 2 lb, 2s/3d
Potatoes, 5 lb, 6d
Tea, 1/4 lb, 4d
Mint Humbugs for David, 1d

She wondered what woman – for surely it was a woman – had written the little list, and if she'd ever felt as lonely as Jane did right now.

CHAPTER TWO

Alice
Cambridge, 1931

"You remember David James, don't you, Alice?"

Alice Mobberley wiped her floury hands on her apron and wished she'd thought to crimp or at least brush her hair. She was wearing her oldest house dress because she'd been baking – Father did always like his scones – and she hadn't expected visitors, and certainly not a handsome young man like David James.

"Mr James," she said hesitantly, for her father, a tutor in Theology at Trinity College, had had many young men troop through their house, and sit in the study with cups of tea precariously balanced on their knees, arguing quite passionately about church doctrine or who actually wrote the book of Hebrews.

"I'm sure you don't remember me," David James said, smiling. He had sandy brown hair and friendly, hazel eyes, and he held his hat in his hands. "I was a student here ages ago."

"Not that long ago, surely," her father protested with a genial laugh. "It seems only yesterday…"

Alice didn't bother to listen as her father began one of his long-winded reminisces about being David James's tutor. The way Peter Mobberley talked, every student who came through the door of the tall, narrow house on Grange Road was his favourite and most gifted. And perhaps, in her father's mind, he was; Peter was affable and generous, if a bit absent-minded, by nature.

"Would you like a cup of tea, Mr James?" Alice asked, as she always did when one of her father's old students happened by, yet even so she wasn't quite prepared for the rather pleasant tingle of awareness she felt when David James swung his bright hazel gaze towards her.

"If it wouldn't be a terrible bother?" he asked, not perfunctorily, the way most people did, but as if he meant it and was waiting for her answer.

"Of course not," Alice replied. "I'll just put the kettle on."

"And you must call me David," he said to her retreating back, making Alice falter slightly in her step. "I always think of Mr James as my father."

"Come in, come in, my boy," her father entreated, and led David into his study, surely the warmest and most comfortable room in the house.

Alice hurried to the kitchen to make the tea. She put several fresh, hot scones on a tray with a generous pat of butter and the pot of blackcurrant jam their housekeeper, Mrs Chesney, had brought over yesterday morning. Then she whipped off her apron, washed her hands, tidied her hair, and even pinched her cheeks to give them just a bit of colour, although it was hardly necessary. Just the thought of David James set her to blushing.

She thought she would have remembered such a friendly face, but she didn't. She wondered how old he was; he surely couldn't be more than twenty-five or -six? And she was nineteen now, which would have made her twelve when he started at the university. The kettle whistled shrilly, and Alice hurried to pour the tea. Silly even to think how old David James was! It hardly mattered; he was just stopping by, and she most likely would never see him again.

Still as she brought the tea things into the study, she felt another little tingle of pleasure when David turned to her with a smile. He did have such a nice smile, so honest and open. She trusted that smile.

Her father remained in his usual frayed armchair by the fire, rubbing his hands together in anticipation as Alice brought in the tray, but David sprang from his chair and took the heavy tray from her, leaving her pleased and flustered and not quite sure what to do with her hands. She hid them in the folds of her dress.

"So where are you now, my boy?" Peter asked. Alice started to pour the tea.

"I don't know if you remember, but I'm originally from Keswick, up in the Lakes," David said, and Peter nodded genially, although Alice doubted her father remembered. He couldn't even remember where he'd put his pipe most days. "I did my curacy in Penrith," David continued, "and I've just been appointed vicar of a little church on the coast – a small village called Goswell."

"Goswell," Peter repeated, nodding, although Alice knew he couldn't have ever heard of the place. "Lovely."

"It is, actually," David replied, and to Alice's surprise he turned to smile at her. "It's a pretty little village – right on the sea. A bit windy, though."

"Do you mind the wind?" she asked as she handed him a cup of tea. Her voice sounded too high-pitched to her own ears, and she turned back to the teapot.

"I like it when I'm tucked up in my sitting room with the fire going and the wind blowing everything to pieces outside," David told her. She could hear a laugh in his voice, and she liked it. "I feel quite cosy, then."

"Yes, I imagine so." It sounded cosy. Cosier, perhaps,

than the rather dour drawing room of her father's house; the fire was never lit and the room was always freezing, with the heavy dark drapes drawn across the windows.

The kitchen and her father's study were the most comfortable places to be in the house, and Alice usually found herself in the kitchen, the high, narrow windows letting in a greenish light as they were covered with ivy.

"But I don't particularly enjoy walking through a gale to a Parish Council meeting," David continued, and when Alice looked up again his eyes seemed to glint with humour. She felt herself blush a second time and looked away.

"I should leave you two to chat," she murmured after she had handed her father his cup of tea. She didn't really want to go, but she knew she had no reason to stay. Her father liked his little scholarly chats with former students.

Peter waved a hand in both thanks and dismissal, and David gave her another smile. He really was a rather smiley person, Alice thought. She quite liked it; her father was dear, but he was so absorbed in his books and papers that he often forgot to look at her when he was speaking, much less smile.

Still, David and her father would have their chat, and then he would go on his way, all the way back up to windy Goswell, and she would never see him again. The little twist of disappointment she felt at that thought was absurd, considering she didn't even know him. She just liked his smile.

She was surprised, therefore, when David poked his head in the kitchen an hour later. Startled, Alice jumped up from the scrubbed pine table where she'd been reading a rather silly romance novel which she hurriedly hid under her discarded apron.

"Oh—"

"I'm sorry to startle you," David said. "I just wanted to inform you that your father has very kindly invited me to stay for supper, and I've very happily accepted." He raised his eyebrows, no doubt taking in her look of surprised dismay. "That's far more trouble for you than a cup of tea, isn't it?"

"Oh no, it's not that," Alice said, trying not to stammer. She pulled the apron to conceal the unfortunately lurid cover of her novel. "It's only – all we're having for supper is half a cold game pie Mrs Chesney left, and it wasn't even very good to begin with." She felt her cheeks flush so deeply it felt as if her face had caught fire. What a thing to admit to a guest. And now he probably wouldn't want to stay, and she knew suddenly that she very much wanted him to.

"Well, then," David said easily, "it's a good thing I like cold game pie."

Alice let out a startled laugh. "Do you, really?" she asked. "You couldn't." *No one* liked cold game pie; it was greasy and awful.

"It's my favourite," he said solemnly, and then stepped into the kitchen and looked around. "How can I help?"

"You mustn't *help*—"

"But I want to," David said simply. "I see a bag of potatoes there. Shall we have boiled potatoes with the pie? I'm quite adept at peeling them."

Shocked into silence, Alice just shook her head. Not one of her father's students had ever ventured into the kitchen, much less asked to help make a meal. She didn't know whether to be appalled or pleased. It certainly felt strange.

"Please," David said, and Alice wondered why she was resisting. She imagined standing at the sink together, peeling potatoes and chatting, and found she quite liked the image, unfamiliar as it was.

"If you insist," she said, and went to the drawer to get him a knife. "Mrs Chesney usually does the cooking," she explained. "She doesn't come in on Saturdays or Sundays, though, which is why we only have the pie."

"Half a pie," David corrected cheerfully. "I presume you ate the other half yesterday?"

Alice nodded. "I quite like to bake, but I'm afraid I haven't managed too many meals." She felt as if she had to explain this deficiency, how at nineteen she could make bread and scones and a decent cake, but putting together an entire meal was quite beyond her. She supposed, if her mother had lived longer, she might have taught her to cook. Perhaps Alice would have been an accomplished housekeeper herself then, rather than just learning the bits she liked, such as baking and polishing the silver. She couldn't iron, didn't sew, and much preferred reading to doing anything else. She wasn't housewife material at all.

Not, she told herself rather quickly, that she was looking to become a housewife, or a wife at all. Yet even so her gaze slid sideways to David, and she thought how nice it was not to be alone in the kitchen.

After that lovely evening when they had eaten cold game pie and boiled potatoes and David had even helped with the washing up, Alice hadn't expected to see him again. He was surely going back to his dear little Goswell, after all, and wouldn't return to Cambridge for who knew how long.

Yet as they'd both stood by the old stone sink in the kitchen and he dried the last plate, he turned to her suddenly, his expression surprisingly intense, and said, "I'd like to see you again. May I?"

Alice had stared at him, completely flummoxed. In all her nineteen years no boy – much less a *man* – had ever asked to see her the first time, never mind again. She'd completed a perfectly satisfactory but rather uninspiring education at The Perse School for Girls, and had been managing her father's house – well, more or less – in the three years since then. Her marks, alas, had not been high enough to consider university even if she'd wanted to, and with no real need for money she'd never tried for a proper job the way some girls had, in a shop or an office. In that moment when David looked at her, his face so earnest, Alice realized what she'd really been doing for the last three years was waiting. Waiting, perhaps, for this.

"Yes," she said, and she knew she sounded as earnest as he looked. "Yes, you may."

The very next day he took her punting on the River Cam, and Alice felt rather languidly grown up as she sat in the boat and trailed her fingers through the water while David somewhat inexpertly navigated them along the river, the college Backs awash in crocuses and daffodils.

Afterwards they had tea at a little shop on King Street, and David asked her all about her life, the subjects she'd liked in school, and the books she liked to read. Alice answered shyly, for under David's friendly yet intent gaze it was hard to keep two thoughts in her head, much less answer sensibly.

She felt silly and schoolgirlish, telling him she didn't like depressing novels or poetry that didn't rhyme, and how she hardly ever went to the cinema because she found it all too loud.

"I did like art in school," she said, wishing she could find one thing about herself that was noteworthy or even remotely interesting. "I won the 'Most Improved' award in third form."

As if that wasn't the most ridiculous and childish thing to say! She blushed and stared at her crumb-scattered plate and David chuckled and said, "I'm afraid I'm rather rubbish at art. Stick figures only."

She looked up, blinking rapidly. "I must seem so… silly to you," she said impulsively and David looked, to her gratification, completely surprised.

"Silly? You seem like just about the least silly person that I know."

That she could not credit. "But I'm not serious or smart or even particularly thoughtful. I mean, you know, I don't think important thoughts. Weighty things."

David smiled and touched the back of her hand lightly, with just the tips of his fingers. Even so Alice felt her skin buzz as if a bee had landed on her, only far more pleasant, of course. A little sting of pleasure.

"You've been spending too much time with your father," he said. "I have quite enough of weighty things and serious subjects in my life already. I like how you take pleasure in small things, Alice, and how every thought shows on your face."

Her eyes widened and her hands flew to her cheeks. "*Do* they?" she said, so clearly horrified that David burst out laughing.

"Perhaps not every one. But trust me, Alice, I enjoy spending time with you." He glanced away, and Alice certainly didn't think his thoughts showed on his face. She wasn't sure if she could believe him at all. "I like it very much," he said quietly, and the sincerity in his voice gave her another little sting.

They talked then about his childhood on a farm outside Keswick, and his years at theological college. He mentioned a sister, Rose, who had died from pneumonia when he was seventeen, and how Alice's smile reminded him a bit of her. And of course he talked about Goswell, which Alice liked best of all: the sweep of sea, the dramatic fells, the little village with its steep, winding high street and the parish church at one end, with the vicarage right next to it, in the churchyard.

"It's a grand old place," David said, sounding a bit wistful. "The kind of place you could have a half-dozen children in." And then he, for once, blushed beet-red and Alice, also flushing, took a hasty sip of tea and burned her tongue.

Afterwards they walked home through the spring sunshine and David bought a bag of mint humbugs which they shared, and once their fingers brushed as they reached into the paper bag at the same time. Alice yanked her hand away as if burned, flushing yet again, but David just smiled and popped the humbug into his mouth. She took care after that to make sure he withdrew his hand from the bag before she put hers in.

At her door he told her he wouldn't come in, which was a bit of a disappointment, but she was glad they'd spent the whole afternoon together. "I return to Goswell tomorrow on the eleven o'clock train," David said, and Alice felt her heart free-fall towards her toes. She tried to arrange her face into a suitably composed and interested expression and must have failed, for David laughed softly and said, "I wish I didn't have to."

Alice couldn't look at him as she answered in a low voice, "So do I."

"May I write to you?" David asked, and she nodded quickly. "And may," he continued with a new hesitancy, "may you think of those letters as – well, as something important? I don't mean important of themselves, but that they might speak of – of a deeper feeling." He blushed as he said this awkward little speech, and it took Alice a few seconds to realize what he might be hinting at.

"Yes," she whispered. "Yes, I'll – I'll think of them like that."

"Good." He smiled at her, and Alice knew this was goodbye. She held out her hand, and to her stunned delight David brought it to his lips. "I'm returning to Cambridge in the autumn," he said. "May I see you then?"

She nodded, her skin still tingling from where he'd barely brushed it with his mouth. "Then farewell, Alice, but only for now," he said softly, and releasing her hand, he turned and walked down Grange Road.

CHAPTER THREE

Jane

On the Saturday after school started, Andrew drove them all to Keswick to visit his mother. Jane half-dreaded this visit, for she'd never got along with Dorothy Hatton, having been the reason her only son stayed in America for eighteen long years. They'd visited Dorothy once a year while they lived in New York, and it had been a vaguely pleasant memory of the beautiful Derwentwater and Keswick's quaint, narrow streets that had softened Jane's feelings somewhat towards this move. Goswell's streets, she observed morosely now, weren't nearly as quaint.

In the three days since she'd found the shopping list – and *not* painted the pantry – her homesickness had not abated. If anything, it had grown worse. Even Merrie's delight in school had only cheered her a little. That first afternoon she'd walked up the steep hill to the little primary school where Merrie went, half-hoping she might meet another mother, *anyone*, and in fact there were plenty of parents standing by the school gate. The problem was they all seemed to be waiting in tight little knots, so Jane felt she couldn't elbow in even if she'd wanted to, or they gave her what felt like such stony looks that she was quite unable to offer a smile, much less a cheery hello.

Surely, Jane had told herself, she was just being paranoid, yet even so she couldn't seem to dredge up a single piece of chitchat to start a conversation. She didn't even want to and so she'd stood by herself, hands shoved in the pockets of her winter coat, her head lowered against the wind.

Then Merrie had come tumbling out of school, her plaits flying behind her, looking very sweet in her grey pinafore and red cardigan, and Jane's heart squeezed with a sudden softening of love.

"How was it, sweetheart?" she asked as Merrie threw her arms around her waist.

"It was wonderful," her daughter breathed, her eyes alight with rapture. "Do you know what we had for lunch? Roast chicken!" Since Jane had always sent her to school with the kind of packed lunch that came directly from the refrigerated aisle and was encased in plastic, she could see why this was quite impressive. "And," Merrie continued, "do you know what dessert was? Except they call it pudding, even though it isn't really a pudding." She turned to face Jane, her eyes wide and round as she proclaimed, "Chocolate cake *with* chocolate cream inside *and* chocolate sauce on top!"

"Goodness," Jane murmured. "That's a lot of chocolate." She'd half-heartedly tried to catch someone's eye as they started walking back down towards the vicarage, to give some kind of smile of solidarity, but no one seemed to notice. Or perhaps they were avoiding her – the strange, brash American who'd put the vicar out of his house. Either way, she completed the school run without talking to anyone but her daughter, and in truth Merrie did most of the talking.

An hour later Ben and Natalie had slouched into the house, having taken the bus from Copeland Academy, the local comprehensive a few miles away in Endsleigh, the nearest market town. Jane had striven for a casual tone as she asked how their day went, trying not to show her anxiety about how Natalie in particular had settled in.

"Fine," Ben said, cramming a bun into his mouth, and Natalie just gave one of her annoyingly aloof one-shoulder shrugs and disappeared upstairs.

"Come have something to eat—" Jane urged, and heard her daughter grunt back:

"Not hungry." Then a door slammed.

The next two days had been depressingly similar to the first, from Merrie's exultation to Jane's increasing sense of isolation, to Ben and Natalie's reactions. Once, tentatively, Jane had asked Natalie if she'd made any nice friends, hoping she didn't sound too concerned.

Natalie had simply given her one of those looks only teenaged girls could manage, a combination of incredulity and disdain that had Jane, a 42-year-old woman, curling her toes in a kind of motherly mortification. Then her daughter had slouched off to her room without a word, never mind a courteous reply.

Was this their life now, Jane wondered. This silence and loneliness and *emptiness*? She sat at the kitchen table after the children had all gone to school and longed with a desperation so intense it made her feel physically sick to be back at her desk in New York, a *vente latte* by her elbow, a full day of work ahead of her, and the sun – the damn *sun* – shining outside.

Hardly anyone had been in touch from New York, which depressed her. It had only been three weeks, but still. *Still.* Claudia, her former PA, had sent a few tersely worded emails asking basic questions about the running of the office, and Jane had spent the better part of one morning composing a three-page essay in return. Overkill, she got that, but she couldn't help it. She needed stimulation. She craved it.

As for her other friends… they'd left a few "thinking of you" messages on her Facebook page, but those had tailed off quite quickly and after one agonizing morning when Jane had trawled through their pages and seen the cheery updates – *First day of school celebration at Serendipity 3, frozen hot chocolates all around!* or *Barney's sample sale! My favorite time of year!* – she'd clicked the browser window shut and vowed never to look at Facebook again, at least not until she had just as cheery an update to post.

And now they were off to Keswick, and Jane knew she could look forward to a few of Dorothy's thinly veiled barbs about how Andrew was *finally* back in his homeland after *so* long away, and how Dorothy had missed so much of her grandchildren's upbringing. All this said, it seemed, to make Jane feel guilty without appearing to do so.

Sighing, she leaned her head against the car window. It had started to drizzle. How, she wondered, could things have fallen into an unwanted pattern after just a few weeks? Did she need to make more of an effort with the house, the school run, her own children? She wasn't sure she knew how, or even if she knew, if she could.

Dorothy met them at the door of her rambling, 200-year-old farmhouse; its semi-dilapidated state was probably why Andrew had been so keen on the vicarage. As always, she looked fit and well, dressed in a fleece and jeans. Although in her seventies, Dorothy jogged, gardened, and walked her two ancient Labradors with the kind of brisk vigour that made Jane feel like a slouch. In the past she'd had her career to buoy her or at least give her an excuse for not exercising or doing much of anything else, but now that was gone and she was still spinning in a void of inactivity.

Before they'd moved Andrew had told her this change could be "the best thing for her", a bit of prescriptive advice Jane had noncommittally agreed to but inwardly resented.

Andrew obviously hadn't seen any need to give up his job.

Not, she acknowledged with a sigh, that she could imagine actually working here. Any kind of job was scarce in this part of the country; almost everyone was employed in government services or by the nuclear power plant ten miles away, neither of which appealed to her skill set or her interest.

"Andrew!" Dorothy cried joyfully, and embraced her son. She'd been helping Andrew's sister Trisha move house down in Lancashire when they'd arrived in the country, so it had been almost a year since they'd last seen each other. As Andrew hugged her back, Jane couldn't help but notice that while still fit and toned, Dorothy looked just a little frailer, her hair a bit more white. The realization made her feel bizarrely guilty.

"And you three!" she exclaimed, turning to the children who were standing by the car, shuffling their feet. Merrie, as usual, started forward first and gave her grandmother a warm hug.

"I get puddings at school," she said, which clearly was a highlight of their move to England.

"Do you? You must tell me all about it." Dorothy hugged each of the children before turning to Jane. "And Jane," she said, a note of finality entering her voice as she pressed her cheek to Jane's without quite touching her. Jane was used to this; she never got hugged by Dorothy, and she'd learned not to care, or at least act like she didn't. Now she stepped back quickly and Dorothy turned back to the house.

"Come inside, come inside," she said, and ushered everyone indoors, the dogs trotting amicably behind.

Dorothy soon had everyone settled in the sitting room, a fire blazing merrily away. Tea things, including a large, gooey chocolate cake, were already laid out. Ben and Merrie rushed forward, and Natalie sat in the corner of the sofa, her arms crossed over her chest. She hadn't wanted to spend her whole Saturday with her grandmother, which had made Jane feel both aggrieved and guilty, since she didn't really want to either.

"So tell me about your new life in Goswell," Dorothy exclaimed as she cut into the cake. "You must have masses of space. Not like that little flat in New York." Jane tensed at this implied criticism of their life in the city – *back home* – but Andrew just nodded as he accepted a large piece of cake.

"Masses," he agreed, "and the garden as well. It's huge, isn't it, Ben?"

"It's a graveyard," Natalie muttered, and Jane felt a pang of sympathy. The house did have a private garden, but there could be no denying they were surrounded by headstones on three sides, and the church was just a few yards from their front door. On Sunday Jane had drawn all the curtains, feeling a bit like a prisoner, and peeking out, had seen about two dozen people, most of them over seventy, head for the church doors.

"We'll have people knocking on our door at all hours," she'd told Andrew, not quite half-joking. "Asking us about christenings and weddings and who knows what else."

Andrew, as usual, had been affable. "I could do my best, I suppose, but I think they'd cotton on pretty quick that I wasn't the real thing." Jane wasn't so sure. Although he loved his new job as a researcher in physics, she thought with all that cheerful bonhomie he'd make quite a good vicar. Perhaps that was what had drawn him to the vicarage.

"It is a large garden," Dorothy agreed now. She'd given everyone cake but Jane and even though she didn't want any, Jane inwardly seethed. "Do you know I've actually been in that house? My cousin married a man from Goswell and she did the housekeeping for the vicarage for a little while. She invited me up once, and I had a look in. It was quite an imposing place."

Curious despite her intention to remain as aloof to Dorothy as she was to her, Jane asked, "When was that?"

Dorothy almost looked surprised that Jane had spoken; she did tend to keep silent during these family gatherings. "Oh, ages ago now. Back in the mid-fifties, perhaps. I met the vicar then – lovely man, although he rattled around in that place. Never married."

Jane thought of the shopping list she'd found in the pantry. She hadn't told anyone about it, yet she'd found herself thinking of it surprisingly often, and wondering about the woman who'd written it. Silly, perhaps, but she felt more of a connection to the unknown woman who'd written that list than to anyone she'd encountered in Goswell so far. No, that wasn't silly; it was sad. Sad and pathetic. She didn't even know who that woman was.

"Do you know what *d* stands for, perhaps in money terms?" Jane asked abruptly, and everyone stared at her in complete bewilderment. She let out a little laugh. "Sorry – I must sound strange. It's only I read something somewhere, and I wondered."

"Well, *d* stood for pence," Dorothy said after a moment. "Before the money changed over, back in the early seventies. Shillings were marked with an *s*, and pence by a *d* for some reason."

"Oh, I see," Jane said. She realized how off her question must have seemed. "Thank you."

"What did you read with a mention of shillings and pence?" Andrew asked, and Jane just shrugged. She had no idea why she didn't want to share the shopping list with anyone, yet she knew she didn't. It was hers, and telling anyone else about it would both spoil and trivialize it.

"Just a mention of it, somewhere," she said vaguely, but Dorothy had already turned to Merrie and was asking about the puddings at school.

No one spoke in the car on the way home, a drizzle obscuring the fells with mist and streaking down the windows.

"That went well," Andrew finally remarked, turning on the windscreen wipers, and Jane turned to stare at him.

"Do you really think it did?" she asked before she could think better of it, and Andrew frowned.

"What do you mean?"

She glanced behind her at the three children crammed in the backseat. Natalie had her headphones on and Ben was drawing shapes in the condensation on the windowpane, but Merrie was all bright eyes and listening ears. She turned around to face the front.

"Nothing. Only that it went about as well as it always does, which isn't very well at all."

Andrew glanced over his shoulder at Merrie, still frowning. "I'm not sure where this is coming from, Jane, but we can talk about it later."

She folded her arms across her chest and wondered if she was trying to pick a fight. "Fine."

They ended up not discussing it until Sunday evening at nearly eleven o'clock, when Jane had spent the evening cleaning a roasting pan that had been left in the Aga with a thick, hardened crust of fat all over it, and then running around the huge, freezing house, searching for Ben's PE kit (in a spare room in the attic – why on earth had he put it up there?) and making sure Merrie had her money for milk and had filled out her reading diary in painstaking joined-up writing, so different from the elegant cursive she'd been learning back in New York.

"So what's this about my mother?" Andrew asked as he pulled on his pyjamas, which was not, Jane thought, the most neutral way of starting a conversation.

"Nothing," she said, shivering as she slid into her nightly wear: yoga pants, a long-sleeved tee-shirt, a fleece, and thick socks. In September.

"It's not nothing," Andrew said in a tone so reasonable Jane wanted to slap him. Not the nicest of wifely impulses. "You brought it up earlier, after all."

Jane peeled back the duvet and huddled underneath, trying to generate some warmth. "Earlier," she said, "not now, when I'm exhausted and it's nearing midnight."

"That sounds like we need to have a proper conversation about it," Andrew said, his tone still so even and reasonable that Jane was goaded into beginning a conversation she had not wanted to have now if at all, and her opening gambit was about as neutral as Andrew's.

"Oh Andrew, you just don't see it. You're blind when it comes to your mother. I suspect most men are."

"Probably," Andrew agreed, clearly refusing to be ruffled, "but what is it about my mother in particular?"

Jane pressed her head back into the pillow and closed her eyes. Why had she brought the whole situation with Dorothy up now? She'd been living with it for so many years, and after one awful Christmas early on in their marriage, when Dorothy had refused – politely, of course – to eat the Christmas pudding Jane had painstakingly made because it had American ingredients (raisins, rather than currants), Jane had chosen quite deliberately to let it go. She gave up on making headway with Dorothy, and accepted that Andrew would never see the problem (*"You can't really have California raisins in a proper Christmas pudding, Jane, and my mother's always been a purist..."*)

Yet here she was, having been married for sixteen years, about to have a conversation she'd studiously avoided for so long. Perhaps it was because they were now, geographically at least, so much closer to Dorothy, or maybe it was just she felt lonely and vulnerable and rather hard done by – none of which, she knew, this conversation would alleviate.

"Your mother's never liked me," she said flatly, and Andrew turned to her in the bed.

"Why do you think that?"

Jane suppressed a groan. She could tell Andrew was going to approach this conversation, this whole concept of Dorothy not liking her, as a three year old would. *Why is the sky blue? Why do birds fly and people don't? Why? Why?*

"Because it's obvious, Andrew. It's always been obvious."

"To you," Andrew said after a moment. "Obviously."

"Yes, to me. She would have rather you married some British girl, I suppose, some *Cumbrian* girl who would breed Labradors and raise Herdwick sheep and who knows what else—"

Andrew chuckled, a rich, indulgent sound that made Jane grit her teeth. "You think my mother wants you to raise sheep?"

"Don't patronize me. You know what I mean."

"Honestly, Jane, I don't. And I'm not as blind as you think, you know. I've never thought my mother didn't like you, but I have wondered if *you* liked *her*."

Jane absorbed that for a few seconds and then she flipped onto her side, away from Andrew. "Great," she said. "Lovely."

"Why are you so angry?"

"I'm not angry—"

"You seem it."

She kept her back to him, her whole body taut with yes, anger, and even hurt. "If I seem angry, it's because you've turned this conversation around to me. If there's a strained relationship between your mother and me, it's *my* fault."

"I wasn't blaming you, just stating an observation—"

"That I don't like your mother? Has it ever occurred to you that if I have a problem with your mother, it's because she first had a problem with me?" Jane heard her voice rise shrilly and she felt her body shake.

This was why she didn't want to have this conversation now, or ever. She was tired and emotional and overwhelmed, and talking about Dorothy didn't help. At all.

"Jane, I'm sorry." Andrew laid a conciliatory hand on her shoulder; she felt her muscles twang with tension, like a wire. "Clearly this whole thing has upset you, and has probably been upsetting you for some time. I should have realized."

"Let's just drop it, Andrew. There's no easy solution, and I've learned to get along with your mother as she has with me, and that's about the best we can say about it. I'm sorry I brought it up today. I've just been feeling a bit…" she fished for a word that would not cause more conversation and acrimony, "… tired."

Andrew removed his hand from her shoulder. "I'll leave it for now," he said. "But I still think we need to talk about it. Now that we're living here, we'll see a lot more of Mum. We can't let these things fester."

Which felt, Jane thought, like a threat even if she knew Andrew hadn't meant it as one. She nodded from underneath the duvet which she'd drawn up past her chin and after a moment Andrew rolled over onto his back, let out a sigh, and within minutes – seconds – he was snoring.

Jane remained huddled on her side, staring into the darkness, a misery she couldn't even begin to explain to Andrew swamping her soul.

On Monday morning Jane told herself she would tackle the house. Find someone to wash the outside windows, finish painting the pantry, maybe look at paint colours for the rest of the downstairs. Something bright, perhaps, for the sitting room, which was painted a dark green and felt positively cavernous.

She felt weirdly reluctant to finish painting the pantry, though; finding that shopping list had made her unwilling to change anything about the little room, and after a few minutes' consideration she put all the shelves back where they were, and the paint tins away.

Yet the dire state of the rest of the house left her paralysed with indecision. They'd unpacked all the boxes and arranged all their furniture, but everything looked small and lost in the reception rooms with their grand proportions, and they hadn't yet put any pictures up or added the kind of touches that made a house into a home. Really, Jane thought as she surveyed the nearly empty dining room, she wasn't sure this house would ever feel like home. It always seemed to yawn about her, so empty and silent, almost accusing. And cold.

The sun was shining weakly for once and she decided to leave it all behind for a bit and go for a walk. She hadn't explored any of the village except for the short jaunt to school, and the cluster of terraced houses huddled against the rolling hills that were dotted with sheep and cows looked friendlier and more appealing in the sunshine. The fells provided a gloriously stark backdrop, a steep and jagged line of dark green and brown on the horizon.

Her shoes crunched on the gravel as she walked down the curving lane that ran between the old vicarage and the church. Gazing round the church gardens, the sunlight gilding everything in gold, she felt a sudden, uncomfortable pang of guilt about her bad attitude. She was being so grumpy and unimpressed by everything, and yet at that moment she couldn't help but see how beautiful their new surroundings – and house – were.

In New York they'd had an apartment the size of a shoebox (admittedly a very nice shoebox), and the nearest green space had been a ten-minute walk away. Yet here they had a huge, if overgrown, garden, a lovely, if rather dilapidated, house, and the fells and lakes and sea all close by. She was living in paradise, even if she acted like it was a prison.

She'd meant to take a stroll through the village, but she hesitated by the church entrance. It looked like a very old church, with an arched doorway with elaborate stonework in wind-worn sandstone. Andrew had mentioned something about Vikings, but surely the church couldn't be that old?

Both curious and hesitant, Jane pushed open the nail-studded door and stepped into the cool, dark interior. She hadn't been in a church in a long time, although she and Andrew had always meant to take the children, at least on the major holidays.

"No excuses now that it's on our doorstep," she murmured, and then nearly jumped out of her skin when someone seemed to materialize out of the gloom.

"May I help?"

A sandy-haired man in his fifties, wearing an old wool jumper and a pair of worn Chinos, smiled at her. Jane stammered her apologies. "Sorry – I didn't realize anyone was here. I was just talking to myself. Bad habit."

"A useful one, I'd say," the man replied. "Are you visiting?"

"Oh no, just moved here—" She felt herself flush. "Into your old house, actually, I think."

The man looked confused for a moment, then his face cleared. "Oh, you mean the old vicarage! I'm afraid I never lived there. I was appointed last year and moved straight into the bungalow up on Vale Road."

"Oh, right."

"It's a lovely place, though, isn't it?" he said kindly. "From the outside, at least."

Jane wondered if she should offer to tour him round the inside, but then the thought of him seeing all of its unpainted shabbiness made her just give a smiling nod of agreement instead. "So this church – is it very old?" she asked, wincing at the ridiculousness of such a question. Of course it was old.

"Nearly a thousand years," the man answered cheerfully. He stuck out one hand. "My name's Simon Truesdell, by the way."

Jane shook his hand. "Jane Hatton."

"Yes, legend has it that the church was founded by an Irish princess fleeing a marriage with a pagan Viking. But there are quite a few churches with that legend, although I think this church has a bit more to back up its story than others." He gestured to a well-appointed corner with posters and guidebooks on display. "There's a little history exhibit there, if you're interested."

"Oh, thanks." She was probably taking up too much of his time, Jane realized with another one of those guilty pangs. He needed to get on with his vicar duties, whatever they were. "Thanks," she said again. "I'll have a look."

She wandered over to the corner, and read with surprising interest about the ancient history of the church, and how it then became a monastery that was dissolved during the Reformation. There was nothing specific about recent times except for some minor bomb damage during the Second World War, and she knew that was what she was interested

46

in. She wanted to find out who had written that shopping list, silly as it seemed. Silly and sad.

She browsed through the bookstall and read the notices on the board, knowing she was simply postponing the moment when she had to return to the house and face the endless tasks that awaited her. She saw with a flash of surprise that the village had quite a lot going on – Cub Scouts and dance classes, a historical society and a writing circle, lectures on art history and a big band concert down at the hotel by the beach.

If they wanted to, she and her family could become involved in a whole variety of ways here, start making that bucolic life for themselves, start actually feeling a part of things.

If they wanted to.

That, Jane thought with a sigh, was the rub, wasn't it? At this point in time she could not remotely imagine becoming involved in any of those things. She could not even imagine wanting to.

She was just heading back out into the sunlight when the vicar met her by the door. "Come again," he said with a wave. "Even on a Sunday."

Jane was about to wave back when she suddenly stopped. "Do you have a list," she asked, "of all the vicars here? I mean, in the past?"

Simon Truesdell looked a little surprised by the question, but he took it in his stride. "There is a kind of register," he said. "It's kept in the vestry. Would you like to see it?"

"Would you mind? I know it seems odd, but I'm curious about who has lived in our house."

He chuckled as he led her to a room carved out of a corner of the church with wooden partitions. "A whole lot of people have, I should imagine," he said.

It only took a few minutes for Simon to find the book, and Jane peered over his shoulder at all the neatly written entries. "The vicar before me was here for thirty years," he said. "And the one before that was here for ten." He tapped another entry. "Is there a particular period you're interested in?"

Jane thought of the shopping list. *Beef joint for Weltons, 2 lb, 2s/3d.* With Dorothy's information she'd deciphered that *2s/3d* must mean 2 shillings and 3 pence per pound of beef, but when had beef cost that much – or really, that little? She had absolutely no idea. Sometime before the decimalization of currency in 1971, she supposed. "The 1950s?" she hazarded a guess. "Or before?"

Simon scanned the list and turned a page. "Here we are. There was a vicar from 1944 to 1956... a Reverend Ian Hawkins."

Could the list have been written by his wife? "Was he married?" Jane asked, knowing her questions must seem very odd.

"I can't tell from this register," Simon told her. "But I could do some research for you, if you like. I'm sure the information is around somewhere."

"I don't want to put you to any trouble—"

"No, no, I find it quite interesting," he reassured her with a smile. "These are my predecessors, after all."

Jane thanked him and with a sudden burst of energy she left the church and returned to the house, tidied the breakfast dishes and did a load of washing before she took out the paint things. She'd tackle the downstairs loo today. That was manageable, surely. One room at a time, she could do it. Work her way through the house slowly, room by room.

She'd just finished the primer coat in the mid-afternoon when the doorbell rang. To her surprise it was Simon, a piece of paper in his hand.

"I found the information I think you were looking for," he told her, holding up a hand before Jane could even stammer her surprised thanks. "I was glad to do it. I like knowing who came before me." He handed her the piece of paper. "Anyway, here it is. Ian Hawkins, as it turned out, was a confirmed bachelor, but the man before him was married. He was in the post for quite a while – 1930 to 1943. David James. His wife's name was Alice."

Alice James. As Jane took the paper she felt an entirely unreasonable thrill go through her, the kind of otherworldly shiver that had no logical explanation. Had Alice James written that shopping list? What kind of woman had she been? Surely there was no real way for her to find out... and yet. Alice James. The name held some kind of resonance, like the name of someone she'd heard of, or even knew.

"Thank you, Simon," she said, and she'd just closed the door, still thinking of Alice James, and shillings and pence and mint humbugs, when her mobile rang and a number she didn't recognize glowed on the screen.

"Hello?" she answered cautiously, and a woman spoke with brisk efficiency.

"Mrs Hatton? This is Diane Davis from Copeland Academy. I'm afraid your daughter Natalie has not reported to school today."

CHAPTER FOUR

Jane

"She didn't come to school today?" Jane repeated, the words seeming to echo in the taut silence created by the woman's pronouncement. Her fingers ached as she clenched the phone. "What do you mean?"

"I mean," the woman – Diane, she said her name was – replied patiently, "Natalie was not present during register, and has not been seen at all since. Were you aware of her absence?"

"No," Jane admitted, a bit reluctantly. What kind of parent couldn't keep track of her daughter less than a week into the school year? She still couldn't get her head around it. She'd waved Natalie off to the bus that morning; she'd seen the bus lumber up to the lonely intersection of the high street and the beach road, and she'd even seen Natalie get on it. The bus went directly to Copeland Academy, stopping only to pick up more pupils. How could Natalie not have shown up at school? Where had she gone? "I – I don't know where she could be," Jane confessed.

"This will be considered an unexcused absence," Diane warned. "We take truancy very seriously here, Mrs Hatton." She paused, her tone gentling. "If Natalie is having difficulty adjusting, we could have her speak to one of our counsellors. We'd like to help ease her transition."

"Thank you," Jane murmured. She felt a prickly heat spread over her, a rash of embarrassment and fear. *Where* could Natalie be? "I'll certainly consider it."

"Please do. We want Natalie to have a successful career at Copeland."

So do I. Jane hung up the phone, stared into space as her mind spun. The bright bathroom walls seemed to mock her now; strange to think only a few moments ago she'd been painting, feeling almost cheerful. Now dread pooled icily in her stomach. She tried to imagine Natalie getting off the bus, sneaking away from the school doors and doing what? What on earth was there to do in a tiny market town whose highlight of the year was a livestock auction?

She swallowed and tried to marshal her thoughts. She should phone Andrew, of course, yet she was hesitant to do so because they'd disagreed over Natalie's school issues before. Jane had a feeling they might disagree now, and after last night she couldn't face an argument. She wished, suddenly and desperately, that she had a friend. A proper friend, the kind you could moan to or run round to for a cup of coffee and a chat.

Tears stung her eyes as she sank onto an unopened tin of paint. She'd never had that kind of friend, not even in New York. Her career had made her too frantic and focused, and all her friends had been the same. When they'd run into each other, harried and rushed, they'd just moaned about how busy they were and hurried on. And none of them had been in touch besides those few brief messages since she'd moved.

Still, she couldn't be bothered with that now. She needed to think of Natalie. What if something had happened to her, something worse than skipping school? Jane launched herself upwards, scooping up her keys before heading out to the car. Endsleigh was little more than a high street and a market square; surely she'd be able to find Natalie on her own.

Please let her be all right.

Ten minutes later Jane had parked in the town's one public car park and was hurrying down Endsleigh's high street, peering into the rain-fogged windows of cafés and charity shops, looking for her daughter as her heart started to thud with hard, painful beats. She checked the tiny library, even the waiting rooms of the doctor's surgery and the local vet, where a Great Dane glared at her balefully. She walked up and down the high street twice before she finally spied Natalie sitting in a tiny fish and chip shop. She was hunched in a plastic booth in the corner, sipping disconsolately at a can of cola and looking utterly miserable.

Jane stopped in the doorway, the breath she hadn't even realized she'd been holding released in a long, weary sigh of relief. "Natalie."

Natalie looked up, hunching further into her seat. Her hair half-covered her face but Jane still saw that flicker of mingled defiance and relief. Her daughter, she suspected, had had a wretched day evading the law.

"Come with me," she said, keeping her voice gentle. "I've brought the car."

After a long pause – with Jane praying her daughter would not make some awful scene – Natalie rose from her seat and followed her out into the high street. It had started to drizzle, with a gusty wind blowing the rain right into their faces. The weather matched Jane's mood perfectly.

"Come on," she said, and neither of them spoke again until they reached the shelter of the car. Jane turned the ignition on and glanced at the clock on the dashboard. She'd be late for Merrie now, she realized with a pang. She turned to look at her daughter, huddled away from her, face angled determinedly towards the window. Jane tried to think of what she'd read in the parenting how-to manuals. All the advice coalesced in her brain into a sludge of semi-coherent offerings: *don't be judgmental, really listen, try to find out what's really going on.*

Swallowing, she asked, "Do you want to talk about it?"

"No."

So much for that. "Why did you skip school, Natalie?"

"Because I hate it," she replied flatly.

Jane's hands tensed on the steering wheel. "It's only been four days," she said as mildly as she could. "I think you need to give it a chance."

Her daughter turned to give her an alarmingly hostile look. "I don't *want* to give it a chance."

Jane bit her lip. She could understand all too well how Natalie felt. Unfortunately, she felt pretty much the same. "You're only hurting yourself then, Nat." And she was probably hurting herself as well.

"Fine."

No parenting book could help her now, Jane thought wearily. Natalie had effectively closed the conversation down, at least for now. And Jane felt too tired and heartsick herself to press. She pulled into the gravel drive of the vicarage, everything silent and empty around them except for the spatter of rain on the windscreen. "Go inside," she ordered as she turned off the car. "And stay there, please. I need to get your sister."

With another glowering look, Natalie flounced inside and slammed the door of the vicarage with loud and clearly satisfying force. Jane watched as a slate tile fell off the roof and shattered on the drive below.

Jane waited until the children were in bed and Andrew was in a convivial mood, having made a fire in the cavernous living room, its flames dancing along the shadowy walls, before she broached the subject of Natalie and her missed day of school.

"That's quite nice, isn't it?" Andrew said as he rose from the floor in front of the fireplace, brushing the dust from his knees. Jane glanced at the little fire rather dubiously. It *was* nice, but it wasn't at all warm. All the heat was drawn straight up the chimney by the ferocious wind; she could hear it howling and rattling the windowpanes like Marley's ghost.

"Lovely," she said.

"Imagine when that was the only heat," Andrew said with a theatrical little shiver. Jane knew he loved this house, loved its history and its *potential* – that was the word he kept using, although Jane didn't really see it herself. "It must have been freezing in here back in the day."

It *was* freezing in here, Jane almost pointed out, but decided not to. The storage heaters that the diocese had put in about twenty years ago didn't provide much warmth. She thought suddenly of the woman who had written that shopping list, perhaps even this Alice James. Had she stood in front of this little fire and held her hands out to its meagre warmth? Had she been happy, standing in this huge room, living in this little village? Jane tried to picture it.

She realized she had not asked the current vicar, Simon, what had happened to the Jameses, both during and after the war. David James, she remembered Simon telling her, had left the parish in 1943. Where had he and Alice gone? Had they had children, filling the rooms upstairs? Had the sound of laughter and chatter rung through these huge rooms, so unlike now, where everyone had disappeared upstairs in a morose silence?

She'd tried to talk to Natalie before bed, but her chummy tone was unlike her and sounded false. Natalie had glared at her through her too-long fringe and said, "I know you're just going to go downstairs and tell Dad all about it, and then he'll ground me, as if I care." She'd rolled her eyes. "As if there's anything to do here, anyway."

"I do have to tell Dad," Jane had answered evenly, "but I'm not sure punishment is the answer here, Nat. I want to know what's going on with you. What were you hoping to accomplish by skipping school?"

"What did I hope to *accomplish*?" Natalie had repeated, her voice sharp with sarcasm. "I'm not in one of your board meetings, Mom. I just didn't want to *go*." And then she'd flopped on her bed, tucking her knees up to her chest, her back to Jane.

Jane had sat there for a moment gazing at her daughter, the knobs of her spine visible under her pyjama top, her hair as dark and silky as it had been when she'd been an angelic toddler. You didn't think of toddlers as angelic normally, but when compared to teens...

She'd sighed and risen from the bed. "I want you to be happy here," she'd said quietly, and Natalie hadn't answered.

Now she turned from the meagre warmth of the fire and stared resolutely at her husband. "Andrew, we need to talk about Natalie."

Andrew glanced at her, eyebrows raised, and with a deep breath Jane plunged in, telling him what had happened. It wasn't a pleasant conversation. She had expected that, had known Andrew would fume for a bit before coming down hard and insisting that Natalie be grounded until she was about sixteen. It was how he'd reacted when she'd been busted at a friend's party for drinking; it was how he predictably reacted now.

"There's no point in grounding her," Jane said wearily. "She doesn't have anywhere to go."

"No email, then. No Facebook, no internet—"

"That's not fair," she protested. "Email and internet are the only ways she can keep in touch with her friends in New York."

"And some friends they were," Andrew snapped. "Getting her into all sorts of trouble, suspended from school—"

"It was a party, Andrew, not an orgy."

"She was drinking alcohol at fourteen! Do you really want to excuse that?"

Jane felt the beginnings of a headache. She did not want to dredge up this old argument. "I'm not excusing anything. I'm just saying she's paid the price for that, and I think it was an aberration."

The truth, Jane knew, was that Natalie had wanted to impress some of the popular girls in her class, but Andrew would take an even dimmer view of that. He didn't understand the pressure girls and women faced from their peers, even their friends. He didn't realize what a balancing act life was, between work and home and family, trying to please everyone—

OK, this was *not* about her.

"How about this," she said. "I'll drive her to and from school, make sure she goes in the building—"

"That seems like a reward rather than a punishment."

It was certainly a punishment for Jane. "She's unhappy, Andrew," she said quietly. "I think we need to deal with the unhappiness rather than the truancy."

Andrew swung away from her suddenly, seeming strangely deflated, which surprised her. He was the most optimistic person she'd ever known. Even in moments like this he was determined to make a plan and see it through. Positive action, always going forward.

He'd certainly been relentlessly cheerful about everything to do with their move, and it was only now when he looked a little – *defeated* – that Jane realized she might actually miss his optimism. His cheerfulness annoyed her, made her feel like he didn't care about her feelings, and wasn't even aware of what she was going through. Yet if he became as moody as she obviously was, she didn't think she could take that either. Clearly, she was a mess.

"It's how she deals with the unhappiness that matters," he said after a moment. "And in any case, she just needs time to settle in, give life here a chance." He paused, meaningfully. "We all do."

Jane stilled. Was he talking about her? He turned around to face her, his gaze grim and yet determined, and she knew he was. She felt the stirrings of an uncomfortable, prickly guilt as well as burgeoning anger. Something else that was her fault.

"We also need to give each other time," she said, just as meaningfully. "Settling in here isn't going to happen overnight, Andrew."

"I know that. I'm not pretending this is easy, Jane."

"It seems easy for you," she pointed out in what she hoped was a reasonable tone but suspected was not.

He glanced at her, and he looked so weary she had to fight the impulse to go and comfort him. Yet why didn't she want to comfort him? Part of her, she knew – a bolshy, unreasonable part – wanted to make things difficult. Wanted him to feel just a little of what she was feeling. "I meant," he said quietly, "I know it's not easy for you."

"Well, at least you *know*," she answered, and heard how snide she sounded. She closed her eyes, took a deep breath. "I don't want to argue."

"I don't, either."

So why were they, then? How could two people who loved each other and didn't want to argue end up feeling so opposed, so angry? Sighing, she shook her head, started again.

"This is about Natalie, at least for now. We need to focus on what's best for her."

"I think what's best for her is to realize the consequences of her actions. She might be miserable, she might hate school, but she can't skip out of classes."

"I know that."

"So a punishment seems in order." He spoke mildly, yet with a determined edge Jane recognized. He wasn't going to give in, not about this.

"Fine. I'll drive her to school—"

"Something else, Jane."

"What?" she demanded. "What else could be a punishment for her, when already life is so—" She stopped, helplessly, shaking her head. Andrew stared at her.

"Life is so what?"

"Miserable," Jane said flatly. "It's miserable, Andrew. She's lost all her friends, everyone she knows—"

"She hasn't lost them. They're still there."

"And we're here."

He shook his head. "People move, Jane. People start over all the time. Why are you resisting this so much?"

"Because it's *hard*."

"I know it's hard, but I thought we'd agreed. I thought we were on the same page, only now it seems like you've closed the bloody book." His voice rose, so unlike him, and Jane wondered if the children could hear upstairs. She'd already noticed how noise carried in this house, voices echoing through the cavernous, carpetless rooms.

"I haven't," she said quietly. "I'm sorry. I'm just being honest."

"I know you are." Andrew rubbed his hands over his face. "All right, look. Drive her to and from school. Limit email and computer time to twenty minutes a night. I think that's fair."

"All right." It was a compromise, so that was something, yet Jane felt more unsettled than ever as she turned to leave the room, Andrew staring dispiritedly at the fire he'd taken so much pleasure in building.

The following day Jane drove Natalie to school as agreed, suffering her daughter's stony silence and Ben's vociferous complaints because he actually preferred taking the bus. Typically, Ben had made a raft of friends who accosted him the moment he climbed out of the car, while Natalie sloped towards the school door, a miserable, solitary figure. Jane stared at them both, wondering why it had to be so hard. Why couldn't Natalie, in a school of nearly 2,000, have found one kindred spirit? Why couldn't they pull together as a family in times of stress instead of, as it felt in that moment, pulling furiously and resentfully apart?

At least the sun was shining. She drove back to Goswell, her mood lifting a little at the sight of the sun gilding the fields in warm light and making the sea, a wash of blue in the distance, twinkle with golden glints.

Yet as she pulled into the vicarage's drive Jane felt that now-familiar dread. She couldn't face the huge, near-empty rooms, the ringing silence, the bathroom abandoned only half-painted, all of it making her feel so terribly lonely and purposeless. She had so much to do, and yet nothing to do at the same time. How could you feel simultaneously overwhelmed and bored? She decided to take a walk.

She hadn't walked much beyond the school run, although the fells beckoned enticingly in the distance, dark green and blurred blue. Half-heartedly Jane wondered how long it would actually take to hike up there before she decided to walk around the churchyard instead.

She made a sharp left down the old stone walk in front of the church, but instead of turning inside the house as she'd done before she kept walking, past the church and up a little hill, and then into the cemetery itself, a sprawling acre of velvety green studded with ancient, mossy headstones, half of them near to falling down.

She came closer to one and tried to make out the inscription, but it was too faded to read properly. Others were more legible, and with a flicker of curiosity she wondered if any of the previous vicars – or their wives – were buried here. Was Alice James? She felt quite sure now that Alice was the woman who had written the shopping list. The mint humbugs had been for a David, after all, and David James had been her husband. The deduction gave her an absurd little thrill, as if she were solving some age-old and even important mystery.

There were no Jameses that she could see in the churchyard, however, and Jane wandered through the cemetery, which spilled down a hill and through an untended wildflower garden before stopping, quite suddenly and surprisingly, at a little stone cottage. It was huddled in the very corner of the cemetery, right against the high stone wall, and had an uncared-for look about it.

Curious, Jane stepped closer. The windows were dark, with dingy net curtains drawn, and as far as she could see there was no sign of life from inside. A gate in the wall revealed a narrow lane, empty except for a tottering pile of cracked terracotta pots. The place, Jane suspected, was abandoned, just as the vicarage had been... until Andrew had bought it.

Sighing, suppressing another flare of curiosity, she turned away from the cottage – her nearest neighbour – and headed back through the churchyard towards her own house.

CHAPTER FIVE

Alice
Cambridge, 1931

Carefully Alice fixed the new cloche hat she'd bought a bit lower on her forehead. Did she look ridiculous, like a girl playing dress-up with her mother's clothes? Of course, her mother had never worn a cloche hat. She'd died before they'd even come into fashion.

Alice was afraid they might be out of fashion already. An old classmate from Perse had told her, quite firmly, that hats were meant to be "pert" now, and tilted to one side. Cloche hats, even ones made of red felt, were passé.

Sighing, Alice turned away from the mirror. It wasn't as if she wanted to dress up for David anyway, even if she hadn't seen him in six months. She still wanted to be herself. Even as she reminded herself of that she could not keep nerves from fluttering in her tummy like the autumn leaves the wind chased down Grange Road.

She might not have seen him for six months, but they'd exchanged letters regularly, lovely long letters full of news and anecdotes and little jokes. Letters, Alice would not tell anyone, she kept under her pillow tied with a hair ribbon.

From David's letters she felt as if she knew all about Goswell and the vicarage and the church; she could picture the steep, winding high street and almost feel the wind sweeping off the sea. She knew how the housekeeper, Mrs Sutherland, doted on David, and made sure he had enough to eat, so "I might roll into church by the time she's done with me!"

She knew that David had addressed the Women's Institute, thinking he was to speak on missions when in fact they'd been expecting a lecture on the history of the church building, but he hadn't learned afterwards because no one wanted to tell him he'd got it wrong. She knew he liked to walk up in the fells, but felt he really ought to have a dog to go with him. He'd asked Alice if she liked dogs, and she'd assured him that she did, although that wasn't quite true. She hadn't met enough dogs to know whether she liked them or not, but she thought she would, if she were ever given the chance.

And now, after six months of receiving a letter every week, and sometimes two or even three (well, *once* three, because the post had been delayed), David James was coming to Cambridge, and would be calling in at Grange Road in just a few minutes.

Her nerves fluttered again, swirling upwards just like the leaves, so Alice took a deep breath and pressed a hand to her tummy. It wouldn't do to be sick right before he arrived.

"Well, well!" Her father appeared in the doorway of his study, an open book forgotten in his hand as he blinked rather owlishly at her. "Don't you look smart. But what is the occasion, my dear?"

"Da— Mr James is coming," Alice said, fighting a flush. "He's taking me out to tea, you remember? He'll be here any moment, Father."

"I thought he was having tea here, with me," her father said, looking a bit bewildered. "As before."

Alice's hopes sank like a stone inside her. "Oh, did you? Well, I suppose he could – that is, we could—" She faltered, overcome with disappointment at the thought that they wouldn't be going out after all.

"No, no," her father said, and when Alice looked up she saw he was smiling. "I see how it is. Go out to tea, Alice, and enjoy yourself. Mr James can make an account of himself to me afterward."

Alice had no time to reply, for a knock sounded at the door, and she flew to answer it without thinking how forward or eager she might seem, flinging it open to greet David with a wide smile.

"You look exactly the same!" she blurted, and he answered easily,

"As do you, I'm happy to say. Good afternoon, Mr Mobberley."

Her father waved from his doorway. "Good afternoon, David. I shall see you a bit later, I'm sure, after you've gone out with Alice."

Alice blushed, realizing rather belatedly how childishly eager she must have seemed, but David didn't seem to mind. He held out his arm, and she slipped her own into it awkwardly, still so glad to see him but not sure if she should show it quite so much.

"I've been waiting for this moment for six months," David told her as they started down the road, and Alice turned to him in surprise.

"Which moment?"

"Seeing you again," he said simply, and her heart swelled ridiculously. She knew then it didn't matter how happy or eager she seemed to David, for, wonderfully, miraculously, he surely felt the same.

"I have too," she blurted right back at him. "Oh, I have too!"

In retrospect Alice could not remember all they discussed over tea and crumpets; all she remembered was how wonderful she felt, how gloriously alive. They spoke of silly things, weather and books, and David told some stories about Goswell, but it all passed her in a blur of happiness, a haze of joy.

On the way back to Grange Road David disentangled her arm from his, causing her a ripple of dismay, only to then take her gloved hand in his own. Alice's heart sang and she'd never felt so aware of her hand before – every finger, every joint, feeling the warmth of David's hand even through her glove.

He stayed for a week, and he saw Alice every day. They went punting and to the Fitzwilliam, and they walked to Grantchester for tea. The weather was glorious, and it felt as if God Himself had ordained their romance – for surely it was a romance?

It seemed silly to Alice that she might not actually know David's feelings for her. He had not, of course, taken any liberties. He held her hand on occasion, and he'd kissed it once when he'd said goodbye, but that was all.

Yet they talked. They talked of everything, and it seemed to Alice that talking held far more significance, more intimacy than any holding of hands or brushing of lips could have. David told her about growing up on a farm, his father's disappointment in having his only son take up the cloth rather than the crook.

"Did you ever think about returning to the farm?" Alice asked as they sat on a blanket in the meadows near Grantchester, the remains of a picnic spread out around them. "Doing what your father wanted?"

David sighed and nodded. "I did, and I certainly felt I should. I'm my father's only son and it's natural he'd want me to continue on. Since I haven't, the farm will be sold when he dies, or passed on to a cousin. It's surely not the same."

"No," Alice agreed quietly. She could almost feel David's father's disappointment, and David's own guilty regret. "But you had a calling, I suppose."

He smiled, his expression lightening. "Yes, I did, although it came to me rather slowly. I remember the first time I felt it, though. I was in church when I was about fifteen. It was absolutely pouring out, the rain just bucketing down like it only can up there. The wind too was howling. A dreadful day."

"And what happened?" Alice, her hands clasped around her knees, was enthralled by David's sharing of this important part of himself.

"I was feeling quite bored and discontented with life," he told her. "I didn't particularly like farming, and I couldn't imagine keeping at it. But I couldn't imagine doing anything else either." He smiled in reminiscence. "Then the rain stopped, and the wind blew itself out. I remember looking up and a single, fragile ray of light was coming through the stained-glass window, making a pattern on the floor. A pattern of a cross."

"Oh," Alice breathed, enchanted, and David smiled.

"I didn't take it as sign, actually. It wasn't as if a bolt of lightning hit me and I knew what I wanted to do from that moment on. It was more of a gradual awakening, like the unfurling bud of a flower. I looked at that cross and I thought about what it meant, and the verse about Jesus telling people to take up their cross and follow Him flitted through my mind. But then my mother poked me in the shoulder because I suppose I looked like I was falling asleep, staring at the floor, and I forgot all about it until my schoolmaster at the grammar school told me I should think about reading theology."

"And you did."

"I did," he confirmed with a smile. "And I knew I wanted to go back up there, to be near my parents and serve the community I had come to love, being so far away from it. But what about you, Alice? What have you wanted out of life?"

She felt herself flush because she did not want to admit that the only thing she wanted out of life right now was more time with him, more sunlit afternoons like these. "I don't know," she confessed, ducking her head. "I never thought of going to university, even though my father might have liked me to. I haven't got the brains."

"You sat your exams, though."

"My marks were barely average. I do love reading, but the rest of it escapes me. But I must admit I've never fancied working in a shop or an office, either." She'd seen the girls who worked in town sometimes when she was at the market, with their smart, belted dresses and heels and lipstick. They weren't much older than she was, yet she felt like a child next to them. A child with so little experience or even understanding of the world, who had spent most of her time sitting in the kitchen watching life happen from a distance. "I suppose I'm still waiting," she admitted with a shy smile, "for whatever I'm meant to be doing."

David gazed at her, his hazel eyes glinting intently. "And what do you think that is?" he asked quietly, and suddenly Alice felt quite breathless.

"I – I don't know," she managed. "But I hope I find out quite soon."

Two days before he was due to return to Goswell David

paid her father a visit. They were closeted in Peter Mobberley's study for nearly an hour, and Alice had no idea what they were talking about. She didn't think they were debating the author of Hebrews, yet she didn't dare hope they might actually be talking about her... or even David's intentions, which she couldn't quite let herself think about.

She stayed in the kitchen with Mrs Chesney, who bustled about with a knowing, cat-like smile on her face. "What do you think they're talking about, Mrs Chesney?" Alice finally asked, unable to keep the question inside any longer. "Do you think they're talking about theology?"

"Only if it's Genesis chapter two," Mrs Chesney answered smartly, which was no help at all as Alice couldn't remember Genesis chapter two. She had no head for Bible verses, which certainly couldn't be a good thing, considering David was a *vicar*—

"Therefore," Mrs Chesney intoned with a glint in her eye, "a man shall leave his father and mother and join unto his wife, and they shall become one."

Alice felt her eyes go round and her breath caught in her chest. "*Oh*—"

After an hour David came out smiling, and he kissed her hand before he took her leave. Alice's head was full of Genesis and she couldn't quite look at him as he said his farewells. As the door closed she glanced questioningly at her father, and saw, to her surprise, he had his old handkerchief out – she really must iron it – and was dabbing his eyes.

On his last day in Cambridge David took her out to dinner instead of one of their usual daytime pursuits. Alice wore her most grown-up dress – a slim-fitting frock in pale blue crepe de chine – and even put her hair up, with the help of Mrs Chesney.

"Do I look ridiculous?" she asked anxiously. "Do I look as if I'm trying to look glamorous or sophisticated? I know I'm not either, not a bit."

"You look," Mrs Chesney said firmly, "like a young woman in love."

Alice felt a hectic flush spread over her whole body. *Yes*, she thought, *that's exactly what I am*. She didn't know what would happen tonight, but she felt in her bones – in her heart – that something would. That something must. *A man shall leave his mother and father…*

David took her to a restaurant on Trumpington Street, a fancy one with candlelight and white linen tablecloths. Alice felt so nervous she hardly ate anything, and David seemed rather strained too, his gaze darting all over the restaurant. He'd clear his throat as if he meant to speak, and then fall into a rather morose silence.

Their paltry conversation was stilted and awkward, far more than it ever had been before, and Alice was awash with disappointment. What had happened to their comfort, their ease in chatting and laughing and simply being together? It seemed to have completely drained away and she did not know how to reclaim it.

They walked in silence from the restaurant, and Alice's spirits lifted just a little when David took her hand as they walked down Trumpington Street.

"Let's walk across the Backs," he said. "It's such a lovely night."

It *was* lovely, crisp and clear and cool, with a hint of winter in the air although it was only mid-September. They walked in silence through the Backs of Trinity College, the gardens cloaked in darkness, until they came to the ancient stone bridge arching over the river Cam and David stopped suddenly.

"Alice," he said abruptly, importantly, and every thought emptied out of her head. "Alice," he said again, and thinking he needed a response, she licked her lips and whispered,

"Yes?"

David turned to her, taking her limp hands in his as he gazed at her so very seriously. "Alice, I love you rather desperately. Will you – would you consider – giving me the honour of becoming my wife?" This little speech sounded both heartfelt and well rehearsed and it took Alice a good thirty seconds to summon the sensibility to speak.

"I will," she said, and she'd never meant anything more.

Then, with a boyish grin of relief, David drew her to him and whispered, "May I kiss you?"

Alice gave a jerky little nod and he brushed his lips against hers. This was her first – and surely sweetest – kiss. Her lips parted under his and she felt as if the whole world had suddenly burst to glorious life, as if the heavens themselves had opened up with choruses of angels and heralded this moment.

Lightly clasped in David's arms, his lips pressed now to her forehead, she knew in her bones – in her heart – that she had found her calling. She knew what she wanted to do, who she wanted to be.

David's wife.

CHAPTER SIX

Jane

"Are you Merrie's mum?"

Jane turned around in surprise at the sound of the cheerful voice. She was standing in the schoolyard, hunching her shoulders against the wind and waiting for Merrie to come out.

"Yes, I am," she said after a startled pause. A woman with a frizzy halo of ginger hair and bright hazel eyes stuck out her hand. "I'm Ellen, Sophie's mum."

"Sophie?" Jane repeated, rather stupidly, taking her hand, and Ellen smiled.

"Has Merrie mentioned? We'd like to have Merrie over for tea. Apparently she and Sophie are firm friends now."

"Oh… oh, that would be nice. Lovely," she amended, attempting to sound a bit more British.

"You're welcome to stop by for a coffee," Ellen offered. "Make sure we're not mad."

"Oh, I'm sure you're not," Jane said with a little laugh. She felt strangely discomfited by this exchange; it had been so long since she'd had a proper conversation with anyone outside her family. It felt amazingly good just to exchange pleasantries, to feel normal and noticeable again, an actual part of things instead of a lone figure standing at the school gate.

"Well, perhaps just a bit mad," Ellen allowed with a smile. "But let's set a date – Sophie really would like to have Merrie round."

Just then Merrie and a ginger-haired girl – Sophie, presumably – came racing out of school, arm in arm, discomfiting Jane even further. Why had Merrie never mentioned a special friend? Why had she never noticed? She'd been so wrapped up in her own homesickness and worries about Natalie and this simmering tension with Andrew that she hadn't given Merrie much thought at all, beyond a vague relief that she seemed happy. Now she felt a flood of both guilt and hope. At least Merrie was adjusting to this strange new life of theirs. She'd found a friend, which was more than Jane could say.

"Hello, sweetheart," Jane said, ruffling Merrie's dark blonde curls. "Would you like to go to Sophie's one afternoon?"

"Oh yes, *please!*" Merrie looked up, her eyes shining. She was already, Jane noticed, developing a bit of a northern accent. It gave her a funny little pang to hear Merrie sounding different.

"Would tomorrow suit?" Ellen asked and Merrie nodded rather frantically.

"Sounds good," Jane said with a smile.

"And there's a swish party at the village hall on Friday, if you'd like to come along to that," Ellen continued. Jane stared at her blankly.

"A swish party?"

"Yes, you know, everyone brings a few pieces of clothing they don't want any more, and you can exchange them for ones you like. Most of the school mums come along, and you can usually find something halfway decent." She glanced ruefully at Jane. "Although you're quite swish already, aren't you? You might find everything a bit tatty!"

Jane smiled, trying to absorb the slight sting of Ellen's words. She knew the other woman hadn't meant it unkindly, not at all, and yet it still hurt. Not only did she feel like she didn't fit in, but it seemed no one else thought she did either. She'd told Andrew she needed time, but at that moment she wondered if time would make any difference. Maybe she would never fit into this place. This world.

Back at the house she set about making dinner while Merrie did her homework at the kitchen table. Natalie and Ben trooped in from the bus – Jane had driven them to school and back for a week before she'd given up – and threw their rucksacks on the floor before slouching into the pantry, looking for food.

"Are there any biscuits?" Ben asked, and Natalie snorted.

"Biscuits? Don't you mean cookies?"

"I was just thinking you're all starting to sound a bit British," Jane said lightly. "It was bound to happen."

"I'm not," Natalie said flatly, her expression mutinous as she cracked open a can of cola. Inwardly Jane sighed.

"Well, I'm not either. We can be American together."

Natalie stared at her for a moment, and Jane wondered if she'd said the wrong thing. She didn't want to encourage her daughter to resist acclimatizing here, and yet... she certainly wasn't doing it herself.

"What shall we have for tea, then, dearies?" she said, putting on a fake and rather atrocious English accent, and was rewarded with a giggle from Merrie, a guffaw from Ben, and even a reluctant smile from Natalie.

"Don't you mean dinner?" Natalie said, and Merrie piped up.

"No, no, dinner is lunch. That's what they call it – school dinners."

"I hate school dinners," Natalie answered. "Fish and chips every Friday – ugh!"

"I could pack you a lunch," Jane offered, and Natalie just shrugged.

She leaned against the sink, watching them all mooch around the kitchen, opening cans of cola and packets of crisps, papers trailing out of their rucksacks onto the floor. She had a kilo of mince thawing on the counter for dinner – or tea – and for once the sun was shining, streaming through the tall sashed windows behind her. The moment felt, bizarrely and poignantly, normal.

More normal, even, than anything they'd had in New York, when Jane had been so frazzled and rushed that most evenings she'd barely asked how the children's day had gone as she pressed the phone to one ear and dialled for takeaway.

She'd missed this, Jane realized with a pang. She'd missed something she hadn't even realized she hadn't had. And yet even though she'd missed it, she wasn't sure what to do with it now.

"Why don't you start your homework, Nat," she said as she peered into the fridge for something to go with the mince.

"I did it at school," Natalie said and flung herself into a chair.

Jane turned from the fridge. "At school? When?"

"Lunch."

"You mean dinner—"

"Oh shut up, Merrie," Natalie snapped, and Merrie's face crumpled. She adored Natalie, sullen and sulky as she was.

"Don't," Jane said quietly and Natalie just slid further down in her chair. Jane turned back to the fridge. So much for that moment of family togetherness. It had lasted, what, fifteen seconds? She felt the sullen silence descend on the kitchen like a shroud. Even the sun had disappeared, as it was wont to do, and the kitchen had been thrown into gloom.

Jane took out some carrots and cheddar cheese and went to switch on the lights.

She glanced down as she crossed the kitchen, saw a crumpled paper trailing out of Ben's rucksack, with a very red "35" marked on top. She set the cheese and carrots on top of the Aga and bent to pick up the paper; it was an English test – or literacy, as they called it here.

"Ben?"

Ben barely glanced up from the Nintendo DS he was now playing with a kind of frantic intensity, despite the family rule that computer games were only for weekends.

"*Ben*." Jane yanked the device from his hands and he looked up mutinously.

"What?"

"What is this?"

He shrugged. "A test."

"An English test? You got thirty-five out of a hundred"

Another shrug.

"Why – why did you do so poorly?"

Ben had done well enough at the boys' school he'd attended in New York. He'd been comfortably average, at least. Jane couldn't believe that the work in a state comprehensive in a forgotten county of England was harder. Maybe that made her a snob, but she still believed it.

"I dunno."

"This isn't acceptable, Ben."

Jane saw her son's face harden into indifference and knew she'd said the wrong thing. *I don't know how to do this.* She hated how ignorant she felt, of her own children. What had she done in New York? She'd delegated, she knew. She'd farmed it all out, with afterschool care and extra tutors and so much scheduled activity that they never needed to talk or spend time together as a family at all.

She hadn't meant it to be like that, not exactly, but it was just how it *was*. Everyone in New York worked insane hours; you felt like a guilty slacker if you didn't. Everyone had help; Jane had had friends who communicated with their children mainly by text or through the nanny. She'd even felt a little self-righteous pride that she didn't employ a nanny. At least, not a full-time one.

Now she stared down at Ben's heavily marked test – so many crosses! – and realized she hadn't even asked to see any of the children's school-work. She'd felt noble for helping Merrie with her reading diary, and telling Natalie and Ben to do their homework before they disappeared upstairs.

I'm a terrible mother, she thought suddenly, painfully. *I'm terrible, and I didn't even realize it until now.* Swallowing, she put the test back in Ben's bag. "We'll talk about this later," she said and Ben just shrugged.

"Can I have my DS back?"

And Jane gave it to him before she remembered the electronics-on-weekends-only rule.

"Come in, come in."

Jane stood uncertainly in the doorway as Ellen – also known as Sophie's mum – invited her in. The house was one of the terraced cottages on the high street, up in the middle of the village, and as Jane stepped in she glanced around at the clutter of welly boots and raincoats, the children's drawings sellotaped to the wall, and the profusion of houseplants on the window sill, with a kind of envy.

"Sorry, it's a complete tip," Ellen said with a laugh as she ushered her into the kitchen, which was as cosy and cluttered as the rest of the house. "But I've put the kettle on. Coffee or tea?"

Sophie and Merrie had already pounded up the stairs, and Jane could hear their far-off giggles from the kitchen. "Coffee, please," she said, and with a smile Ellen reached for a jar of instant coffee.

"I suppose you're used to Starbucks and all that, living in New York," she said as she spooned granules into two colourful ceramic mugs.

Jane thought a bit wistfully of the large vanilla latte she brought to work every morning. She had not quite developed a taste for instant coffee. "I suppose," she agreed, "but instant is fine."

"Are you settled?" Ellen asked. "I know it takes time, of course, but you've got the boxes put away at least?"

Jane thought of the half-painted bathroom and the bookshelves she'd only partially filled so they looked like mouths with missing teeth. There were still boxes and suitcases stacked in the corners of rooms, and despite the emptiness of her days she could not motivate herself to unpack the last of them. "The important ones, anyway," she said, and Ellen laughed.

She was a cheerful sort of person, bustling around her little kitchen, taking out a plate and opening up a packet of store-bought biscuits, smiling and chatting all the while. Jane felt herself start to relax, just a little.

"Of course the weather's awful here," Ellen said as she handed Jane a mug of coffee. "Everyone knows that, it's practically a joke. But when you do get a sunny day – well." She paused, bracing one hip against the table as her face took on a wistful expression. "There's no lovelier place on God's earth, and that's a fact."

Jane just smiled. She wasn't sure she'd lived in Cumbria long enough to agree. Right now she thought the sunlight glinting off the Central Park Reservoir as she cabbed it to work was a far lovelier view than the mist-covered fells that greeted her every morning on her walk to school.

"Merrie said you have some older children?" Ellen asked, eyebrows raised. "Up at Copeland Academy?"

Jane felt herself start to tense. Just thinking about Ben and Natalie made her head throb. She hadn't talked to Ben or Andrew about the 35 Ben had got on the test, and Natalie seemed as morose and sullen as ever.

In the three weeks since school had started her daughter had not thawed towards school or life here in the least. And Jane still couldn't blame her. In all honesty she hadn't made much of an attempt to help Natalie settle in, although she didn't even know what that would look like. She had yet to meet a single parent from the school; she hadn't even met any of Natalie's teachers. Her daughter's life was eight hours of ignorance, as far as Jane was concerned.

Andrew kept saying they just needed time, but the days ticked by and nothing changed. Jane knew you needed more than time. You needed purpose, a strength of will she felt she – and Natalie too – was completely lacking. She didn't feel like explaining that to Andrew.

Despite his persistent bonhomie, she felt a tension from him and between them that hadn't been there before. At night, despite the chill, they stayed on their separate sides of the bed. In the evenings their conversation revolved around mechanics – usually requests for Jane to do things since Andrew was so busy with work. Find a dry-cleaner, a dentist, an orthodontist for Natalie, someone to mow the lawn, someone to service the Aga. She hadn't done any of it, although she'd written it all down, almost as neatly as Alice James had written her long-ago shopping list.

"Yes, Ben and Natalie," she replied. "Ben's in Year Seven, and Natalie is in Year Nine."

"She'll be thinking of her options, then."

Jane stared at her blankly. "Options?"

"For GCSEs. Don't worry, she's got plenty of time. But she can drop three subjects next year – the ones she doesn't like, usually." Ellen let out a merry laugh. Jane wondered how she managed to stay so cheerful.

"Oh, I see." She wondered if that news would cheer Natalie. She had a feeling her daughter would prefer to drop *all* of her subjects, and move back to New York. Just like she would.

"And how are they finding life here? Quite a change!"

"You could say that." Jane took a sip of her coffee. Ellen had made it with plenty of milk and actually, it wasn't that bad. Maybe she was developing a taste for instant coffee, as long as she didn't compare it to her vanilla lattes of old. "Ben is fine," she said, "but that's boys for you. I think I could parachute-drop him into the middle of the Sahara and he'd make a friend."

Ellen nodded sagely. "Girls have it harder, don't they? Especially at that age. I've a daughter in the lower sixth, and she had a tough few years, what with the cliques and the mean-girl rubbish going on. It sorted itself out eventually, thank goodness, but it's not easy."

"No," Jane said quietly, "it's not." She wondered if that was Natalie's problem. She didn't know if her daughter had made many – or any – friends at her new school, but suspected she had not. Certainly her solitude would make her experience of living here worse. Yet it was a vicious circle; the more Natalie disliked it, the less she would try, just as she'd said in the car. *I don't want to give it a chance.*

To Jane's surprise she felt Ellen put her hand on top of her own. She looked up, and saw Ellen gazing at her with smiling compassion. "I can't say I know what you're going through, because I've lived in this village my whole life, same as my mother and my grandmother and even her mother as well. But I do know what it feels like to wonder what on earth you're doing with your life, and why."

"Do you?" Jane asked. She couldn't manage anything more; her throat had suddenly become very tight and she felt a humiliating dampness stinging her eyes.

"I do. My older daughter is Sophie's half-sister. I was married before I had Sophie, but it didn't work out." Ellen made a face. "To say the least."

"I'm sorry."

Ellen sighed, cradling her mug between her hands. "I was young and silly, and I got Alyssa – that's my daughter – out of it, so I can't say I regret it. But there were moments when I wondered what I was doing – and why."

Jane said nothing; her throat was still too tight. She wondered what she was doing – and why – nearly every moment of every day.

"Jack – that's my ex-husband – was from Birmingham. He got a job locally so we could raise Alyssa here. It's such a good place for children, it seemed like the best thing to do. I certainly didn't want to move anywhere."

"And?" Jane asked, because she was curious as to how this Jack found Goswell after life in a large city. Had he experienced the same kind of isolation and loneliness that she was feeling now?

"And he hated it. He'd always lived in a city, and he hated the country. The silence, the one pub, even the smell of manure. It does stink sometimes, I admit." The smile she gave

Jane was rather crooked. "I met him when he came up here on an outdoor course with school – we were only seventeen." She took a sip of coffee. "But him not liking Goswell wasn't what ended our marriage. I think if we'd truly loved each other, it wouldn't have mattered where we were. He would have settled here, or I would have been willing to move to Birmingham."

She sighed, and Jane felt a lurch of something close to panic. *If we'd truly loved each other…* but she did love Andrew, and she knew he loved her. That didn't make it any simpler… but perhaps it should have.

"But the truth is," Ellen resumed, "we married too quickly and too young, and we really weren't suited at all." She gazed down into the depths of her mug, her expression becoming shadowed. "It became rather nasty towards the end. Jack ended up taking off for Birmingham when Alyssa was only two."

"Does she still see her father?"

Ellen sighed. "Once a year, if that. He hasn't been the most involved dad." She blew out a breath and shook her head. "But look at me here, telling you all these troubles. I meant to be asking how *you* are."

"You did," Jane said lightly. "You asked if I were settled."

"And you said you had boxes unpacked, but that isn't what I really meant." Ellen smiled. "Goswell is a friendly village, but it takes a while. Everyone knows each other, and we take so much for granted. But we mean well, honestly."

Jane just nodded. She was grateful for Ellen's warmth and friendliness, but she didn't think she could fully articulate just how far she felt from home, how lonely and isolated and *miserable*.

Ellen patted her hand. "It will get better," she said quietly.

"With time. I promise."

With time. Just like Andrew seemed to think. If only it were a matter of time, a matter of waiting and then suddenly everything would look and feel better. But Jane knew it wasn't – and never would – be so simple. She needed to change, too, and she wasn't sure she could.

"Why don't you come to the swish party?" Ellen suggested brightly. "You'll meet a whole load of mums there. And I'm sure we'll all be fighting over your fancy city clothes!"

Jane smiled weakly. She did not want to go to a swish party, but she knew to refuse now would be rude. "That's an idea," she finally said, and drank her coffee.

Three days later she decided she really ought to finish the bathroom. It looked absurd, with half of it a dull cream and the other half a canary yellow. She'd chosen the yellow because it looked cheerful and sunny, but now she wondered if it was too loud. Well, it was too late to change now, and it was only the bathroom anyway. With a deep breath she set to it.

She'd only just got everything out, the drop cloth and pan and roller, and was just easing the lid off the tin when the doorbell rang, surprising her. The only people who had rung the doorbell so far were the postman, when he'd been delivering a parcel that didn't fit through the flap, and the vicar.

Jane wiped her hands on her jeans and went to the door, her jaw nearly dropping in surprise when she saw who it was.

"Dorothy." She opened the door wider and stepped aside. "Have you come all the way from Keswick?"

"I had some errands in the area, and I thought I'd stop by. Unless it's inconvenient?"

"No, of course not. But I'm afraid I'm the only one here. The children are at school and Andrew is at work, of course. But he might be able to slip out for a little while—"

"It doesn't matter." Dorothy waved a hand as she stepped into the vestibule. "It's you I've come to see."

Jane's spirits flagged a bit at this news. As starved as she felt for company sometimes, Andrew's mother was not high on her list of hoped-for visitors.

"Would you like a coffee?"

"Tea, please, if you have it. I never drink coffee."

She'd forgotten that. Suppressing a sigh, Jane led the way into the kitchen and reached for the electric kettle. Andrew liked to use the big old brass one on the Aga, but Jane didn't see the point of lugging it to the sink and filling it for a couple of cups' worth of tea. And the electric kettle was much quicker.

"What an amazing place," Dorothy said. Jane watched her gaze round the kitchen in all of its dilapidated glory: the peeling paint, the streaky windows, the ancient drying rack hanging above the Aga. Jane had told Andrew she wanted to buy a tumble dryer, but they hadn't yet, and in any case there was no good place to put it. Ironic, really, that she lived in a house the size of a mausoleum and she had no place to put a dryer.

Dorothy sat down at the kitchen table. "So what do you think of it?" she asked, gesturing around the kitchen in a way meant to encompass the entire house.

"It's… big," Jane said, rather lamely. She knew she should summon some enthusiasm for the house, especially to Dorothy, because anything other than unbounded joy would be seen as criticism. Of course, any enthusiasm she summoned wouldn't be enough to satisfy Dorothy. It never was, so why bother?

"Very big," she agreed with a small smile. "I told you I'd been here before, when my cousin worked as housekeeper back in the fifties."

"Yes—"

"She showed me round the whole place, when the vicar and his family were out. A bit naughty really, but I did like peeking in all the rooms."

Jane had no reply to this; she could not imagine Dorothy doing anything a bit naughty. "What did it look like, back then?" she asked as she handed Dorothy a cup of tea and sat at the table across from her. She thought of Alice James, who would have left the vicarage when her husband moved on, in 1943. She'd asked the current vicar, Simon, if he had any more information on the Jameses, but he'd told her he didn't. Besides the record of when they started and finished the job, there was little documentation about the vicars of Goswell – or their wives.

"Well," Dorothy said slowly, looking round, "it looked about exactly the same as it does now." She smiled rather wryly, and Jane felt a sudden bubble of slightly hysterical laughter erupt out of her. Dorothy laughed too, and for some reason that made Jane laugh harder. She shook her head and wiped her eyes, trying to bring herself back to propriety with a sip of tea. She couldn't believe she was laughing with Dorothy, of all people. She must really be losing it.

"Sorry," she finally said when the laughter had thankfully subsided. "It's just that I don't think this place has changed in about a hundred years, except for maybe the electricity. I don't even know why I asked the question."

"I doubt it has," Dorothy agreed, smiling again. "And don't be sorry. I haven't had a good laugh in ages."

And certainly not with her. Jane didn't think she'd ever shared a moment of sympathy, never mind laughter, with her mother-in-law before. Yet within seconds of their mutual hilarity she felt the old unspoken tension return. "Well," she said, glancing around once more, "Andrew intends to do it up slowly. So perhaps by the time he's retired we'll have it in liveable condition."

"Perhaps," Dorothy agreed, rather doubtfully, and Jane almost started laughing again. "In any case," she continued after a pause, "I really came here to tell you how much I appreciate you agreeing to move back to England. I know it can't have been easy to give up your life in New York, and your career, and I want you to know I appreciate it… even if I don't seem like I do." Dorothy gazed at her steadily, and after a moment, Jane finally managed to reply:

"Thank you for – for understanding." Had Andrew talked to Dorothy? Was this her mother-in-law's reluctantly offered olive branch? Jane couldn't think of what else it could be. In sixteen years of marriage Dorothy had never spoken to her like this. She'd barely spoken to her at all.

"I know it can't be easy, adjusting to life in rural Cumbria," Dorothy said, her voice strangely stilted. "Most people in England would have quite an adjustment moving here, never mind coming all the way from New York."

"It is very different," Jane allowed. She didn't want to unburden herself completely to her mother-in-law, especially since Dorothy had spent her whole life in Keswick. And she had a horrible feeling that if she admitted how wretched she was feeling, she would say far too much. Dorothy might seem somewhat sympathetic now, but Jane had no illusions that she could use whatever Jane unadvisedly confessed now in an argument later.

"I just hope," Dorothy continued, her gaze turning steely, "that you'll give it a chance."

Jane stiffened. Ah-hah. So here was the sting in all the supposed honey. "What do you mean?"

Dorothy pursed her lips. "I know what life in a small village is like, Jane. People are friendly and welcoming, but they need you to make an effort."

"You don't think I'm making an effort?" Jane heard how prickly she sounded. She shouldn't really be annoyed, she knew, since she had already admitted to herself that she wasn't making much of an effort. Yet she acknowledged that she wasn't just annoyed; she was livid. How dare Dorothy come here and lecture her, all the while pretending to understand what she was going through? Andrew must have spoken with her. What had he said? Had he *complained*? And how on earth could Dorothy make these accusations, when she had never even visited here before?

"I think making an effort can be exhausting," Dorothy said carefully. "Especially when you don't know anyone, and everything feels unfamiliar."

It *was* exhausting, and she wasn't even making much of an effort. But she was still angry. "I'm doing my best, Dorothy," Jane said, her voice cold and stiff, "but clearly that's not enough for you – or Andrew."

"It's not me you need to satisfy," Dorothy answered sharply. "And Andrew has nothing to do with this. He doesn't even know I'm here."

"Why *are* you here?" Jane rose from the table and dumped her mug in the sink. It landed in the basin with a rattle of thick china but Jane wished it had broken.

"Because I want this to work," Dorothy said after a moment. "For all of you."

"If you think I'm going to move everybody back to New York, you're mistaken," Jane said. Yet she couldn't deny, to herself at least, that she had thought about just that. She could get her old job back; she hadn't been replaced. The children could slot back into school. They'd have to rent an apartment, of course, but their realtor had been amazing and they could probably find something serviceable relatively quickly – maybe go down to a two-bedroom from a three, but they could *manage*—

Good grief. Jane put her hands up to her face, not even caring in that moment if Dorothy saw. She hadn't quite realized just how much she'd thought about it, how much an insane part of her wanted this to be temporary, *not real*. There was no way Andrew would agree to move back to New York, not after three weeks. Not even after three months or maybe even three years. He loved it here.

"I'm not worried about that," Dorothy said quietly, and Jane drew a shuddering breath and dropped her hands. "But you all need to be happy here for it to work. I know this might be an old-fashioned sentiment, but a woman – a wife and mother – sets the tone of any home."

"And what's the tone of this home, then?" Jane heard how aggressive she sounded. What was wrong with her? She never fought like this with Dorothy. But then she'd never dealt with Dorothy so much before; week-long visits were easy to endure compared to this endless, ongoing reality.

"I think you know the answer to that question," Dorothy said with stiff dignity, and rose from the table. "Thank you for the tea."

"Thank you for your advice," Jane answered, and if she'd meant it to be some kind of peace offering, it clearly wasn't. Her voice had come out sharp and sarcastic.

Dorothy didn't answer as she collected her coat and handbag. Jane followed her to the door and she turned around, her hand on the knob. In the gloom of the entrance hall Jane couldn't make out her expression, but the weak sunlight filtering in from the stained-glass windows on either side of the door touched her hair in pale gold and showed the deepening lines on her face.

"I know we haven't always seen eye to eye, Jane," Dorothy said. "I really don't mean to offend you."

Jane just nodded, knowing there was more – and so there was.

"I just hope you'll consider what I've said." Dorothy slid on her coat and put her bag on her shoulder. "And now I should get on. I must go pay my cousin a visit. She's up at a care home just outside the village."

"Your cousin the housekeeper?" Jane asked with a sudden, sharp curiosity, and Dorothy raised her eyebrows.

"Yes, she's in her nineties now, but still in quite good health. She appreciates visitors."

Jane nodded slowly, diverted momentarily from her issues with Dorothy. She doubted a housekeeper from the 1950s would know anything about Alice James, yet what if she *did*?

Still, she could hardly go marching into the care home and start asking questions. Why did she even care who'd written a silly shopping list decades ago? It wasn't as if any of it actually mattered.

"Why do you ask?" Dorothy asked. "Are you curious about the house?"

It was close to the truth, and yet something kept Jane from confiding in her mother-in-law. Alice James and her shopping list still felt, strangely, like her secret. A pointless secret, and yet still, something that was hers. Besides, if she mentioned any kind of positive emotion about this house, Dorothy would take it as a personal success, and Jane was still feeling raw and yes, petty enough not to want that.

"It's nothing, really," she said, and ushered Dorothy outside.

CHAPTER SEVEN

Alice
Cambridge, 1931

Alice and David married quietly in a small ceremony at St Mark's Church in Newnham just before Christmas. Alice had invited just a handful of friends from school, and her father had invited a few of his work colleagues as well as his stern-faced sister Myra, who came from Colchester for the day and as usual tsked at the state of the house. David had a friend from his own college days as best man, but his family hadn't been able to leave the farm and travel all the way from Keswick.

"I hope you don't mind," David had said, "having it small. I just can't wait to take you back to Goswell."

Alice had assured him she didn't mind, which was mainly the truth. The important thing, of course, was that she was marrying David, not how it was done or how many people saw the ceremony.

The ceremony itself was quick and quiet, passing in a kind of surreal blur that made Alice feel almost as if it were happening to someone else. Someone else was standing here, speaking the words she remembered to say but couldn't seem to understand the meaning of any more.

When David took her hand to put her ring on, she was conscious of how cold his hand seemed in hers, or perhaps hers was the cold one. He smiled at her then, and the sight of that familiar, crooked smile with its wry humour and promise of shared secrets made Alice feel a little burst of relief.

This is happening to me.

When she turned towards the congregation after their vows had been said, she saw her father dabbing his eyes again, and her heart twisted because she felt so wonderfully happy and yet, in that moment, unbearably sad all at the same time.

They had a wedding breakfast back at Grange Road after the ceremony, a quiet affair put on by a beaming Mrs Chesney. Her father gave a rambling toast about David's days at Cambridge, and from her husband's – yes, her *husband's!* – bemused expression Alice suspected her father's remembrances were not entirely accurate.

David toasted his "lovely bride" and Alice beamed and flushed and felt as if her heart might burst as everyone raised a glass to her.

Then everyone was filing away and Mrs Chesney was hurrying her upstairs, for their train left in an hour. David had told her they would take the train to Doncaster, and then to Manchester, and on to Carlisle, and finally – finally! – to Goswell. David wanted to spend their first night as husband and wife in the vicarage. Alice had agreed, for she could think of no place she'd rather be – in her new home, as David's wife.

Yet as she changed from her wedding dress (a simple affair of ivory crepe chiffon, with capped sleeves and a narrow skirt that made her feel very grown up) into a more sensible travelling costume, she felt a sudden fear clutch at her and turn her breathless. This intensified when Mrs Chesney bustled up to her and adjusted her cloche hat, saying,

"You do know what to expect, Alice, don't you?"

Alice pulled the brim a little lower. "Expect?"

"I mean," Mrs Chesney said in a hushed voice, "what

happens between a man and a woman. On a wedding night."

"Oh." Alice felt her face go hot. "Yes, I mean, I think…"
She couldn't manage anything more. The thought of talking
about *that* with Mrs Chesney was appalling. Not that she
knew all the particulars about *that*. Girls had talked about it
in school, of course, and she'd read her romantic novels. She
knew, she hoped, the essentials if not the exact specifics, and
really, surely none of it bore talking about.

"You know what Mr James expects, then?" Mrs Chesney
prompted with a rather beady look, and Alice felt her face go
even hotter.

"Yes, of course, Mrs Chesney. I'm not a child."

Alice must not have sounded all that convincing,
however, for Mrs Chesney simply huffed and said, "When
you love someone, when you're married, it's a lovely thing,
even if it might seem a bit… odd at first. And that's all you
need to know."

That was quite enough, Alice thought, and let Mrs
Chesney lead her downstairs with a gusty sigh of relief.

David and her father stood by the door, both of them
looking quite sober. As she came down the stairs Alice saw her
father dab his eyes once more with his handkerchief, and felt
her own eyes begin to well up. He clasped her awkwardly to
him as she stood by her husband.

"It is so very far away, isn't it," he murmured, and Alice
realized then – and perhaps only then – just how far away she
was going.

"But you will visit, won't you, Father?" she said, smiling
into his dear, wrinkled face as she blinked back tears.

"You are certainly most welcome," David added. "There
is a spare room waiting for you whenever you wish to make
use of it."

"So kind, my boy," Peter said, and stepped back. Alice clung to his hands for a moment, aware then how old and frail he looked, with his white, wispy hair fluttering in the draught from the door. He had tufts of hair sprouting from his ears. She'd taken him for granted, she knew, with his rambling, rather doddering ways. She'd been exasperated by the way he stopped sentences in the middle, and forgot his pipe, and let his dinner go cold. She'd been annoyed at how he retreated into his study and closed the door, making her often feel as if she were alone in the house.

Yet in that moment as she clung to his hands and felt how swollen and knobbly his knuckles had become, she knew she loved him and would miss him quite desperately.

"You'd best get on," Mrs Chesney said, pulling Alice back by the shoulders. Alice hugged her, breathing in her comfortable, floury scent, savouring the warmth of her. She'd miss Mrs Chesney too, with her briskly practical tone and her awful cooking. She'd miss everything and everyone, for this was home even as she anticipated making another home, a wonderful home, with David.

Finally she stepped back, and David took her hand, squeezing her fingers as if he knew exactly what she was thinking and feeling. She turned to him with a rather watery smile.

"I'm ready."

With a final farewell they left the house in Grange Road and took a cab to the station, an extravagance to Alice but one David deemed necessary since they had two cases and a hatbox.

It took most of the day to travel to Goswell, with all the train changes, and it was dark before they left Doncaster. She spent the first part of the train journey looking eagerly out the window, watching as the flat fields and fens surrounding

Cambridge gave way to gently rolling countryside glittering with frost, and then later, as dusk settled, the far more dramatic, sweeping fells.

They'd eaten sandwiches Mrs Chesney had made, and it all seemed like such an adventure. Yet as the darkness settled around them and the train chugged relentlessly on Alice started feeling very tired, and very far away from everything she'd ever known. Sitting there, staring out at the unrelieved night, she had a sudden, mad urge to be a child again, a child with her mother, even though her own mother had died when she was only three and she could not remember her beyond a faint smell of rosewater.

How could you miss someone you've never known? She wondered then if perhaps the sharp pain she felt under her breastbone wasn't missing her mother, precisely, but everything. Everything familiar and safe and dear.

She felt David's hand touch her shoulder lightly, hesitantly. "All right, darling?" he asked quietly and she nodded and turned to him, and it seemed natural for her to rest her head against his shoulder, and then she fell asleep.

Some hours later he gently prodded her awake, so she blinked in the gloom of the compartment, the train still chugging on.

"We've just left Whitehaven. We'll be in Goswell in a few minutes."

Hurriedly Alice adjusted her hair and smoothed down her dress. It was nearing ten o'clock at night, yet she wanted to look fresh for her arrival in her new home. Excitement and just a little trepidation raced inside her at the thought of finally seeing Goswell.

Her heart beat hard as the train came into the station, yet there were no street lights and all Alice saw as she peered out the windows was a fathomless darkness relieved only by a few small rectangles of pale light coming from cottage windows.

She stepped off the train with the hatbox clutched to her chest, and David followed behind her, holding their two travelling cases. She'd sent a trunk of things – the rest of her clothes, her mother's Irish linen, and a set of Limoges china that had been a wedding present from her father – by post so they could travel lightly on the train.

Now she looked around, blinking in the darkness, trying to orient herself from David's many descriptions of the village. She hadn't expected it to be so dark. Or cold. Her good winter coat seemed thin indeed and she shivered as she stood on the platform and the train chugged resolutely away, towards Millom.

At that moment a gust of icy wind swept down the rail line and took Alice's hat – her smart new cloche – right from her head. She let out a yelp of dismay, watched as the wind bowled it along the station platform into the blackness.

"Never fear!" David called, and he set down their cases to chase after it. A moment later he presented the recaptured hat to her, a bit dusty and slightly crumpled, but altogether not too worse for wear. Alice took it with a small smile and fought the sudden and dreadful impulse to burst into tears. It was just a hat, just a gust of wind, and yet at that moment it was everything. She felt more homesick and heartsore than she ever had in her life, and she could not even fathom why. She was here, where she'd so looked forward to being, with the one person she loved more than any other. How could she be sad? How could she be fighting tears?

"My dear," David murmured, "let me take you to the vicarage."

Alice nodded, not trusting herself to speak. She held the hatbox containing her other new hat in one hand and the crumpled cloche in the other as she followed him out of the station to Goswell's lonely high street. David led her along the road with sheep pasture on either side, towards the church she could see in the distance, a square Norman tower with a clump of buildings behind, no more than shadowy hulks in the darkness. Everything felt very quiet and strangely empty, as if they were the only people left in the world. She could see a few raggedy humps in the darkness of the pasture, and when one bleated balefully she jumped and nearly stumbled in the heels she still wasn't used to wearing.

"The church is a little bit away from the main village," David explained. "It used to be a monastery, about a thousand years ago."

Alice did not reply. Strangely, when she had pictured the church and the village and the vicarage, they had all been together, not with the church set on its own desolate patch of ground, separated from everything else by a muddy sheep pasture. David must have explained it to her before, but in her mind it had been so very different. Cosier, perhaps, and the sun had always been shining, the wind David talked about warm and caressing, not icy and relentless.

They walked down a twisting lane, past the church shrouded in darkness, to the large square house beyond, dark against a darker sky.

David turned to her with a smile. "Here we are."

He led her up a set of stone steps to a large black door, bow windows on either side with the drapes drawn tightly across, shutting out all light. The Vicarage.

Alice had imagined this house many times, imagined herself in its large, gracious rooms, smiling and quietly elegant, yet now in the dark it looked both unfriendly and forbidding. The only sound was the relentless sweep of the wind and the rattle of bare branches against the glass panes above, like skeletal fingers tapping on a door, begging entrance. She hoped – quite desperately – that everything would improve with daylight.

David fit a large iron key in the lock and opened the door, pausing to return the key to his pocket before he turned to Alice. "Welcome home, Mrs James."

Alice let out a little gasp of surprise as he swept her into his arms and over the threshold. He set her down gently, his hands on her shoulders, and kissed her on the lips.

"Come inside," David said, and smiling shyly, Alice followed him into a soaring vestibule, tiled in dark red and green and yellow. The air inside the house was, if anything, colder than outside. "I'm afraid the fires have probably gone out," David apologized, "but I'll get the one in the parlour going and we'll be as cosy as two bugs in a rug."

Alice nodded, trying to hold onto her smile. Nothing about this huge, dark house felt cosy or even familiar, despite her many imaginings. Her heels clicked across the tiles, the sound echoing through the high-ceilinged rooms.

She stood in the front parlour trying not to shiver even though she wore her coat as David set about building up the fire. It hadn't gone out completely, so with a few scuttles of coal and a twist of paper he had it blazing again.

Alice gazed around the parlour – a large, ornate room with heavy, dark furniture that was twice the size of the unused sitting room back on Grange Road.

Grange Road… she could not keep a wave of homesickness from washing over her at the thought of that dear place. Was her father sitting alone in his study, poring over his dusty old books without anyone to remind him to go to bed? Mrs Chesney would have left before supper, leaving a plate on the hob for him, although Alice wondered if her father would even remember to eat it without anybody to tell him. What if it went cold, or burned from being too close to the stove? What if the whole house burned down because her father was so forgetful?

"Mrs Sutherland will have left us something in the kitchen," David said, and Alice blinked, forcing away such needless worries. Her father would be fine. It might take him a short while to learn to fend for himself, but he would do it, with Mrs Chesney's help.

"I'll go have a look," Alice said, and found her way to the back of the house and the large kitchen that was comforting in its surprising familiarity: a scrubbed pine table and a large blackened range that gave out a much-needed warmth. Here was a room you could sit and be warm in.

She poked her head in a larder and found only crockery, and then realized there was a second one for food. There on a slate shelf, covered by a dishcloth, was a plate of cold ham and boiled potatoes. It had been left there for several hours and with the fat congealing on the ham and the potatoes cold and stolid, it did not look like the most appetizing of meals, but Alice remembered how David had eaten Mrs Chesney's cold game pie when they'd first met and decided she could manage a bit of ham.

She found a loaf of bread and a dish of butter and managed to boil the huge brass kettle on the range and make a half-decent pot of tea. Anything more was beyond her, but she thought all in all it would make a meal, and she felt a little burst of pride that she had done this – she had made a meal for her new husband in her new kitchen.

And it did make a meal, a lovely meal, their first one in their home as husband and wife. Sitting in the parlour with her plate balanced on her lap and the fire going merrily, Alice felt her spirits lift. *This* was how it was meant to be, how it would always be.

"Mrs Sutherland would have six fits if she knew we were eating in here," David said, his eyes twinkling as merrily as the fire. "But I won't tell her if you won't."

"I won't," Alice promised, and they grinned conspiratorially at each other. In that moment Alice knew everything would be all right. The house might be cold and dark and the wind relentless, but she felt a pure and perfect joy that this new life of hers – of theirs – would be just as David told her in his letters. It would surely, *surely* be wonderful.

CHAPTER EIGHT

Jane

Jane gazed around the village hall with its peeling paint and plastic chairs, a makeshift bar visible in one corner, and almost turned around and left. But her arms were full of clothes for the swish party Ellen had convinced her to go to, and several women had already turned her way, so she had no choice but to step into the warm fug of the room, a silk blouse slipping from her armful.

"Five pounds gets you five pieces of clothing and a glass of wine," the woman at a formica table by the door informed her cheerfully. "Isn't this something," she added as she retrieved the blouse from the rather grimy tiled floor. "La-di-da."

Now Jane really wanted to leave. Somehow she managed to put the clothes she'd brought on a chair, and fish into her purse for the requisite five pounds. She could feel some of the women gathered in tight little knots glancing over at her, curious without seeming friendly.

"Just hang your things up there," the woman said, pointing to a rusted old coat rack. "And the wine's in the corner."

Jane murmured her thanks and made her way over to the rack, carefully hanging up the clothes she'd brought. The longer she spent doing this, the more she prolonged the awful moment when she'd turn around and face all those women, and feel completely alone and friendless. Although, come to think of it, she already felt that way.

Swallowing hard, a prickly heat breaking out all over her body, she reached for a black Armani skirt she used to wear for work, but figured she'd have no need for now. Why on earth had she brought her business clothes, her New York clothes? They stood out glaringly next to the inexpensive skirts and sparkly tops from Dorothy Perkins and Next, making her feel like even more of an outsider. An *other*.

Well, she knew why she'd brought these clothes. She didn't have any others. She hung up the last item, a lace slip dress from Escada, and with a deep breath squared her shoulders and turned around.

She stood there for a moment, willing someone to say something or at least smile, but everyone was chatting in their tight little groups, heads and shoulders angled away from her. Fine.

With another deep breath she headed for the little bar in the corner – self-service – and poured herself a large glass of cheap white wine. Plonk, Andrew would have called it, but Jane couldn't say those British-sounding words without feeling like an impostor.

She turned around and surveyed the room, sipping her wine. No one was even looking at her, yet she still felt painfully conspicuous, as if she were in a high school cafeteria, holding her tray at the head of the lunch line, looking for a friendly face or at least a place to sit.

"Jane!"

She turned and with a tidal wave of relief saw Ellen coming into the hall, her arms full of clothes – worn fleeces and a couple of pairs of jeans.

"They don't fit any more," she said, making a face, and Jane smiled in sympathy, although she'd been wearing the same size since Merrie was six months old. New Yorkers were relentless about their weight. Ellen dumped her clothes in a chair and fished for her five pounds just as Jane had, talking all the while. "Sorry I'm late. Sophie had a strop right before bedtime – she doesn't like me going out." She made another face before scooping up her clothes and turning towards the hall. "I'll hang these up."

"Let me help," Jane said. It would be better, she felt, to keep busy.

"This must be yours," Ellen said, admiring the slip dress Jane had felt so self-conscious about. "Where on earth did you wear it?"

"Oh, just a fundraiser," she mumbled, but she felt a sudden shaft of memory pierce her with its pain. She'd worn it to Women For Change's annual gala last year, and just the thought of being back in the ballroom of The Yale Club, holding a glass of champagne as she talked about the difference the charity – *her* charity – had made in the lives of so many women, offering education, housing, jobs... She swallowed hard and forced the memory away. Different life now. That one was gone, probably forever.

"Oh, and there's *wine!*" Ellen said in a voice that suggested this was an unimaginable treat, and Jane trailed her over to the bar. She'd teased Andrew before about how the British could be so satisfied with so little. A glass of wine and a few bowls of stale crisps in a shabby village hall was clearly a source of delight for Ellen. To Jane it felt like a rare kind of torture.

She'd seen Andrew react in the same way to a cup of instant coffee with UHT milk and a plain digestive. "Oh, *coffee!*" he'd say, rubbing his hands together, as if someone had just presented him with a freshly made cappuccino dusted with chocolate and in a porcelain cup. Even sixteen years hadn't diminished that delight in simple pleasures; Jane didn't think she'd ever found it.

"Sorry, have you been here on your own long?" Ellen asked as she sipped her wine and Jane shrugged.

"Just a few minutes—"

"Let me introduce you to some people."

Jane steeled herself. She did not want to meet a few people, didn't want to endure the awkward chitchat that would ensue, but she knew she had no choice. She'd allowed Ellen to convince her to come to this party; she had to see it through, even if she utterly wasn't in the mood.

Ellen made her way to one of the formica-topped tables and pulled up a couple of plastic chairs. The other women shifted so there was almost but not quite enough room for Jane to be part of the circle. She perched on the edge of her chair and sipped her wine as the other women barraged Ellen with the usual school mum greetings, or so she assumed, having very little knowledge of that world – or this.

"Sophie give you grief tonight, then, love?"

"How's Alyssa doing with those A-Levels? Matt's failing maths at the moment, but I'm hoping it'll turn round—"

"Were those new boots you had on yesterday?"

Jane smiled and sipped her wine. Ellen answered the questions with her usual cheerful good humour, and then she put her hand on Jane's arm and urged her forward, although there was little Jane could do except scoot even further to the edge of her chair. "Everyone, this is Jane Hatton, she's moved into the old vicarage. Her daughter Merrie's in Sophie's year… Jane, this is everyone." Ellen smiled round the group, and Jane forced her own lips into a smile. Or something that hopefully looked like a smile, because she felt horribly self-conscious and stiff, and the dutiful smiles and murmurs of greeting from round the group did little to put her at ease.

After a brief pause someone asked, "You're American, then?" and Jane nodded, forcing herself to add something to this statement.

"Yes... we moved from New York in late August."

A few people nodded, and Jane could tell this wasn't news to them, but no one said anything more and after a few seconds the conversation resumed, centring around a party Jane had obviously not gone to. She still didn't know anyone's names.

Ellen attempted to engage her in conversation, but at this point Jane didn't really want to talk to anyone. She excused herself to go to the toilet so Ellen wouldn't be trapped talking to her all evening, and as she made her way down the dark, narrow corridor that led to some toilet stalls in the back, she wondered if she could just sneak out and go home. She could explain to Ellen later if needed, say something about a headache or an upset stomach.

When she came out of the stall, however, Ellen was waiting there with an anxious look on her face. "I'm sorry, Jane. Are you having an awful time?"

"No, of course not," Jane lied, trying to smile.

"People aren't used to outsiders here. Offcomers, we call them. It's not that they're trying to be unfriendly..."

It just comes naturally? Jane filled in silently. "Don't worry, Ellen," she said, and patted her arm. "I understand."

And really, she couldn't blame the other women entirely for her dismal evening. Just as Dorothy had said, she needed to make an effort. If she'd turned to the woman next to her and engaged her with a bright smile and a bit of conversation, things might have turned out differently. She might be back in there laughing and chatting over a second glass of wine.

The trouble was, Jane knew, she didn't even *want* to be back in there. She didn't want to get to know any of those women, or anyone in Goswell, and where did that leave her?

"Come on," Ellen said. "We're going to start the clothes swap soon."

When Jane returned to the hall the other women had risen from their seats and were rifling through the clothing on the racks.

"This must be yours," a woman with short dark hair and a gap-toothed smile said, holding the Armani skirt. Jane flushed, wishing yet again, and just as futilely, that she'd brought more appropriate clothing to this wretched event.

"Yes," she acknowledged with as wry a smile as she could manage. "I'm afraid it is."

"Afraid?" The woman shook her head. "I only wish I had clothes like that, or a place to wear them to!"

"I don't, any more," Jane answered. "That's why I brought them here."

The woman gave her a frankly appraising look. "It must have been difficult," she said, "moving to a place like this. Did you love New York?"

Jane swallowed and rifled through a couple of jumpers. "Yes," she said quietly, "I did. Do. But my husband Andrew is British – he's from Keswick – and he wanted to move back."

"Still." The woman shook her head again. "To go from New York to little Goswell – I can't even imagine."

Jane swallowed a bubble of nearly hysterical laughter. *Neither can I.* Yet as she chose a few pieces of clothing at random to swap, she knew she appreciated the other woman's understanding of just how hard it was. At least someone was reaching out, even if she wasn't.

An interminable hour later she'd said her goodbyes, received a hug from Ellen and a few half-hearted smiles and waves from the rest of the group, and then headed out into the crisp night, clutching a purple fleece and a sparkly belt she thought Natalie might like.

The village was amazingly quiet for ten o'clock on a Saturday night. She heard a bout of laughter from the pub up the road, but as she headed in the opposite direction towards the church and vicarage, everything subsided into silence and stillness.

The church grounds were separated from the village by a sheep pasture, and Jane heard their mournful bleating as she walked by. It was such a lonely sound that she felt her heart twist inside her and thought with a sudden, icy panic, *I'm going to lose it. I might start crying right now, right here.*

She stopped and took a deep breath, then tipped her head back to stare at the sky. The clouds from earlier had cleared away, and the inky-black sky was spangled and glittering with stars, the moon gleaming so brightly it actually hurt her eyes to look right at it.

Gazing up at all that beauty, she knew she should feel reassured, or perhaps comforted in some way – but how? That the same moon that gleamed coldly over Goswell also shone on New York? Or that there was beauty here, if she could stop and look for it?

Jane lowered her head. She wasn't sure what the life lesson was meant to be, only that she was not ready to learn it. Resolutely she kept walking, down the long drive past the church now shrouded in darkness and then finally to the vicarage – her home – the house seeming to yawn emptily all around her even when she knew everyone she loved was inside.

"Did you have a nice evening?" Andrew asked as she came upstairs. He was already in bed, tucked up cosily, his reading glasses perched on his nose as he read some physics journal.

Jane smiled wearily. "It was OK."

"Meet some nice mums?" he pressed and something in her started to snap.

"*Women*, Andrew. We're just women."

"You know what I meant."

She nodded. "I know." She knew she couldn't begin to explain – and he wouldn't understand – the pressure she felt here, now that she wasn't working, now that there was nothing to do, to be just that: a mum. A better mother, more involved, more interested, and of course more fulfilled, than she'd ever felt before.

But I don't feel that way. At all.

She slipped into her pyjamas and brushed her teeth without speaking to Andrew, and when she came to bed the sheets on her side were cold. Andrew put his journal and glasses aside and switched off the bedside lamp.

He touched her shoulder, tentatively. They hadn't been very affectionate with each other lately, in bed or out of it. "OK?" he asked softly and Jane drew in a shuddering breath.

She started to nod, and then found she didn't have the energy to pretend any more. She slid her arms around his waist and felt him stiffen in surprise. "Hold me," she asked, and Andrew drew her against his chest.

"Always," he said, and Jane pressed her cheek against his shoulder and closed her eyes. Neither of them spoke.

CHAPTER NINE

Alice
Goswell, 1932

When Alice had agreed to become David's wife, she had not, she soon realized, understood just what that meant. Not only was she David's wife, but she was also the *vicar's* wife, which seemed a completely different thing altogether, a strange and foreign thing, with expectations and abilities she had not even begun to consider.

Alice's only experience of such a person was the indomitable Mrs Jessop, the wife of the vicar of St Mark's back in Newnham. Mrs Jessop was fifty if she were a day, with iron-grey hair done up in a tight French roll. She always spoke briskly, and eyed you up and down, as if inspecting you. At least Alice had felt inspected. And she rather thought she had not come quite up to scratch.

Mrs Jessop ran the Girl Guides, the Sunday school, and the Mother's Union, all with that same brisk efficiency. Alice and her father had been to the vicarage twice for dinner, along with at least ten other people. On both occasions they had been served a delicious three-course meal – four if you counted the cheese and biscuits after – and Mrs Jessop had sat at the head of the table with gracious if rather officious confidence, reminding her absent-minded husband to say grace, and seeming to manage everything with a slightly beady aplomb and assurance.

Alice could not imagine a person more unlike her in every respect and yet, just a few days into her new life in Goswell, she began to realize with an encroaching panic that this was the kind of person she was expected to be.

Of course no one came out and said it like that. Everyone was friendly, but it was a friendliness Alice wasn't certain she liked or trusted. Three days after she and David had stepped off that train Elizabeth Dunston, the wife of one of the churchwardens, came to visit, dressed far more smartly than Alice, who was wearing a rather creased dress – all her things had needed ironing after coming out of the trunk – and an old cardigan that still smelled, rather wonderfully, Alice thought, of her father's pipe.

"Oh, but you *are* young, aren't you?" Mrs Dunston exclaimed, making Alice feel as if she were wearing a pinafore and had her hair in plaits. She already felt a bit muddled, because she had not known which room to serve tea in, and had finally settled on the dining room, which was warmer and cosier than the sitting room, which felt to her a bit like a dark, gloomy cave.

However a fire had not been laid in the dining room, and before she could say it didn't matter and they'd go to the sitting room after all, Mrs Sutherland had set to making one, with many clucks and sighs while Mrs Dunston waited, still with her coat and handbag, all of it making Alice feel as if she were inconveniencing everyone quite a lot.

The conversation had not gone well. It hadn't gone badly, particularly, but it left Alice feeling both overwhelmed and uncertain. Mrs Dunston had talked about the Sunday school, and which class Alice would teach, and the Mother's Union, and if she would take part in a charity drive for orphans in Barrow. She had reeled off half a dozen people Alice had never heard of but seemed expected to know, and asked, delicately, if she intended on entertaining?

"It's such a lovely house for dinner parties," Mrs Dunston said, gazing around at the high, corniced ceiling and the beautifully tiled fireplace. "The vicar before David – Mr Sanderson – entertained quite a lot. His wife was lovely, always made people feel so welcome. She ran the Sunday school for over thirty years."

Alice had nothing to say to this; she had never taught a Sunday school class, and barely knew what the Mother's Union was. She was not quite twenty years old.

After Mrs Dunston left Alice wandered back to the kitchen where Mrs Sutherland was putting away the tea things. Although they had only a short acquaintance Alice had got the distinct feeling that Mrs Sutherland did not think particularly highly of her. She'd been polite, of course, but she tended to ignore her rather a lot. At least, Alice felt ignored.

Whenever Mrs Sutherland asked questions about when dinner should be served or if she should buy a roast for Sunday from the butcher's boy who called round to the vicarage every Thursday, she looked at David, clearly expecting him to answer although Alice felt surely that buying roasts and setting supper times was her domain.

Yet perhaps it wasn't. In truth she felt completely ill-equipped to have any domain at all, or to preside over the yawning vicarage like Mrs Jessop had back in Newnham. She had expected to be *David's* wife, not a nameless vicar's wife, this person of officious importance that seemed so far removed from who she really was.

Other people visited, wives mainly, but Alice forgot their names. She was so used to spending her days curled up with a book that she had forgotten how exhausting it was to be with people all the time, to answer politely and ask thoughtful questions and sit very straight with her ankles crossed and an expression of interest on her face.

"Poor love," David said one evening, when it was just the two of them by the fire. It was Alice's favourite time of day, the hour or two after supper when David was hers alone. Sooner or later he'd be called out to some meeting or crisis, it didn't matter which, and Alice would spend the rest of the evening alone.

Eventually she would go up to their bedroom, which was always freezing even if Mrs Sutherland remembered to stoke the fire before she left, and lie curled up and shivering until David slipped in much later, and drew her into his warm, welcoming arms. That was another favourite part of her day.

"I hope it's not too much for you," he said, drawing her onto his lap in front of the cheery fire. "Meeting all these people, and dealing with all of their fuss."

"I suppose it's quite important to them, you taking a wife," Alice said. "They all seem so very fond of you." They did not, she felt, seem very fond of her. They seemed surprised she was so young and rather dubious as to whether she would manage. She didn't say this to David, however; she knew it would only worry him. He wanted her to love it here as much as he did, and she *would*. Of course she would, because he was here, and she was married to him.

Still Alice could not keep from feeling a creeping sensation of disappointment; none of it – except, perhaps, for the few brief hours she spent with David – was what she had hoped for. When she wasn't with him she felt both lonely and overwhelmed, the house stretching all around her, her only companion Mrs Sutherland.

Only that morning the housekeeper had asked her if she would be seeing to the hiring of the housemaids.

"Housemaids?" Alice had repeated rather blankly. Back on Grange Road there had only been Mrs Chesney, as well as a woman who did the washing and heavy work, although Alice had barely known her name. Mrs Chesney had handled it all.

"There's room for at least four in the attics," Mrs Sutherland had said briskly. "And now Mr James is married, well, it's only fitting he has a staff, isn't it?"

A *staff*. It sounded awfully officious and important and, well – rather grown up. Alice had never thought of such things before.

"If you'd rather, I could see to it," Mrs Sutherland had offered, and Alice had turned to her with a kind of guilty relief.

"Oh, would you? That would be so helpful, Mrs Sutherland."

Mrs Sutherland had nodded, seeming, Alice thought, both pleased and disapproving. She supposed she should really see to the hiring of housemaids, since she was now the mistress of this house, yet she wouldn't know the first thing about any of it. The thought of asking questions and seeming severe was utterly beyond her. She would be intimidated by the housemaids, with their calm capability, rather than the other way round, and she had a feeling Mrs Sutherland knew it.

"I don't know the first thing about hiring housemaids," Alice said to David as they sat in front of the fire that evening. "I'm sure Mrs Sutherland shall make a better job of it than I ever could."

"As long as you're happy having her do it," David said. "That's the important thing."

"I'm happy," Alice assured him, but a twisting inside her made her feel that wasn't quite true. Later, when she was alone, she asked herself if she was truly happy. She examined her feelings as if they were dusty objects in need of a polish, and decided that she wasn't *un*happy. The moments alone with David were the most wonderful she'd ever known. Yet that's all they were: moments. Moments in an otherwise awkward and rather endless day.

She didn't want to burden David with the petty concerns that dogged her: the way Mrs Sutherland clucked whenever Alice didn't know how to do something, or how the ladies of the parish seemed to eye her up and down (similar to Mrs Jessop, really) and then dismiss her.

The first Sunday she'd been besieged by introductions; people seemed to assume she knew who they were when, of course, she didn't. She didn't know anyone at all. She smiled and shook hands and listened with what she hoped was an expression of cheerful attentiveness when, just as with Mrs Dunston, they asked her if she'd join the Mother's Union, take a Sunday school class, change the décor of the vicarage, or take a relative into service. "Our Nellie would sort you out. She's ever so good with the washing." By the time she tottered across to the vicarage she was exhausted, overwhelmed, and almost near tears. It was all so *strange*, and she knew David, despite how much he loved her, would not understand.

After those first few weeks Alice found herself alone again, and in some ways almost forgotten. Part of her was, of course, relieved, but another part felt hurt and lonelier than ever.

Still, she kept all these thoughts to herself; she knew David would only worry and fuss, and he couldn't do anything about it, not really. She told herself she'd only been in Goswell for a few weeks, and she was bound to feel more at home the longer she was there.

Yet as her first month drew to a close Alice did not feel more at home. The days were dark, wet, and windy, and even with three new housemaids seeing to all the fires, the vicarage was still draughty and icily cold. Christmas had passed quietly, with David busy with all the services. They'd exchanged presents alone in the huge parlour, and Alice had attempted to cook the roast Mrs Sutherland had bought specially, but it was burned on the outside and raw in the middle and she didn't know why.

"It's *awful*," she said as they sat like a king and queen at either end of the dining room table, and David just smiled.

"Never mind. Between the burned and the raw bits there's some that's just right. We're like the three little bears, Alice."

She laughed, and then quite suddenly, burst into tears. She put her hands up to her face but not before David had seen her, and she had seen him looking dumbfounded and appalled.

"I'm sorry," she managed after a moment when she'd given a loud and most inelegant sniff. "I'm sorry. I'm crying and it's Christmas—"

"But my love," David said as he came round the huge table to kneel by her side. "Why are you crying? Because I've missed something awfully important to have you this way and not even have known you were unhappy."

"I'm not unhappy," Alice insisted, as much to herself as to him. David drew her hands away from her wet and blotchy face and chafed them with his own.

"If you're not unhappy, then why are you crying?" he asked gently.

"It's just… everything is so strange, David. So different from what I've known, and even what I expected—" She stopped, not wanting to admit to David the extent of her disappointments. "And I'm so delighted to be your wife," she continued hurriedly, "but not – not—" She stopped, feeling a sob well up like a balloon in her throat, unwilling to explain just what she didn't want to – and couldn't – be.

David squeezed her hands, his face so endearingly concerned, everything about him familiar and wonderful and beloved – and yet, even as she gazed at him, blinking back tears, she was afraid it wasn't enough. She so wanted it to be enough, for him to be enough for her to be happy here, and she prayed that he would be. In time, perhaps, as she learned to adjust. To settle.

"Not what?" David asked.

"Oh, it doesn't matter—"

"It does, Alice. Anything that upsets or concerns you in the least matters to me."

She sniffed, the sound loud in the cavernous room. "You're too good to me."

"I am not. The Bible requires husbands to love their wives as they love their own bodies, Alice. So please tell me what it is that troubles you so." He bent forward and brushed a kiss against her forehead, and Alice closed her eyes.

"I didn't expect to be a – a *vicar's* wife," she confessed, her eyes still closed. "I know I should have considered such a thing, and what it meant to be your wife, the role I would have, but I – I didn't. I was so wrapped up in you." She opened her eyes and stared at him in desolation, yet with a grim resignation in her words. "I don't think I'll ever be a proper vicar's wife, David."

David gazed at her seriously for a moment, a crease between his brows, her hands still in his. "What," he finally asked, "is a proper vicar's wife, do you think?"

"Oh, you *know*. Someone who takes Sunday school classes and has twelve people to dinner at least once a week and arranges flowers and polishes silver and knows everyone's names and does all sorts of good works—"

"Slow down," David said with a chuckle, and squeezed her hands. "One person could certainly not do all that."

"You do," Alice objected, and he arched an eyebrow.

"I do not, I am quite sure, polish the silver. Nor do I arrange flowers and I don't know everyone's name. I've been here for over a year and I still forget people's names at the door. It's most inconvenient and, unfortunately, rather obvious."

"Oh, David." Alice shook her head, smiling through her tears. "That might be so, but everyone loves and admires you still."

"Is that what you wish for? Everyone's admiration?"

"No," Alice said slowly, "I'm not quite as shallow as that."

"I never thought you were, my love. I'm only trying to understand what seems to be the problem, and how I can fix it."

Alice didn't answer, for she knew it was not – and never would be – that simple. Why couldn't David see it? Why couldn't he understand that she, at nineteen years old and utterly inexperienced in life, was not and never could be a suitable vicar's wife? That she'd never be the kind of woman he needed by his side, that everyone *expected* by his side?

"Darling Alice," David said, and pressed his hand against her still-damp cheek, "I love you so very, very much and if you love me back half that amount, that is all the requirement I need from a wife. I have no great regard for polished silver, and flowers are lovely but we've plenty in the garden in spring and you can stick them in a vase any old way and I wouldn't care. As for the rest – if you wish to take a Sunday school class, then by all means do. And if you don't, then don't. The diocese appointed me, not you, and all I require is that you love me and let me love you back." He smiled at her, and with his thumbs gently wiped away the traces of her tears.

"I love you more than half back," Alice answered shakily. "I love you more than anything – except God, of course."

David drew her to him, smiling as he kissed her gently. "Now did you say that because I'm a vicar, and that's the sort of thing a wretched vicar's wife must say?"

"No," Alice said, putting her arms around him. "I meant it. I do love God for bringing you to me, for allowing me to be your wife. And I love you." She kissed him back and rested her head against his shoulder. Some of the awful misery she'd been holding inside her like a stone in her stomach had eased, but even in the comfort of David's arms, in the warmth of knowing how much he loved her, she still felt a heaviness inside, a weight or even a dread she could not explain to David now, or perhaps ever.

She was thankful God had brought David to her, she knew, but she did not think she was very grateful He'd brought her here, to Goswell.

January and February passed slowly, endless and empty. David was busy with the parish, and had left Alice to her own devices, which weren't, unfortunately, very many. She did try to assert herself in a few small ways; she baked a cake under Mrs Sutherland's beady eye, but she had never used a range like this one before and it fell flat. She offered to take a Sunday school class, but despite Mrs Dunston's earlier expectations, she was assured they were not in need of teachers. She asked David if they should have someone over for supper, but he told her they needn't think about that until they'd had their honeymoon – a month of just the two of them – except he wasn't there very often and it had been more than a month.

At the end of her alleged honeymoon Alice asked herself again if she were happy, and this time, with the wind howling outside and making the windowpanes rattle, her bedroom so cold she'd developed chilblains, and David out for yet another interminable evening, she finally admitted to herself that she was not.

She was miserable.

CHAPTER NINE

Jane

Rain lashed against the windows as Jane reached for her scarf and gloves. October, and she was already dressing for winter. Sighing, making a decidedly half-hearted attempt to banish such negative thoughts, she turned to Andrew.

"Ready?"

He nodded and slipped on his own coat. They were both attending Copeland Academy's Parents' Evening, and Jane was dreading it. In the month since school had started, Natalie had not seemed to warm to life in Goswell at all. She went to school in silence, came home in a sulk, and barely spoke to anyone. When Jane had mentioned her concerns to Andrew, he'd just shrugged.

"Give her time. She's a teenager, and it's been a big change. It's not all going to happen at once."

No, it wasn't, but Jane already knew that. She also knew she couldn't put a dent in Andrew's unflagging optimism, and wasn't sure she wanted to. Ever since the night when she'd come home from the swish party feeling lonely and miserable and he'd held her, they'd reached a kind of wary and mostly amicable truce.

They didn't talk about a lot of things, which was probably better for both of them, but that left Jane feeling as if every conversation was a negotiation, navigating around the things she couldn't say, the things that were piling up inside her, leaving little room for anything else.

Occasionally she felt Natalie might be making some progress at school; once Jane had come upstairs with a pile of folded uniform – she was becoming so domestic – to find Natalie on the phone, laughing at something someone had said. She waited until her daughter had ended the call and then said as lightly as she could, "Who was that?"

Natalie had just shrugged, her sulky gaze sliding away from Jane's. "Nobody."

"It had to have been someone, Nat—"

"Why do you care?" Natalie turned on Jane, suddenly angry and defiant. Surprised, Jane took a step back and dropped one of Ben's school jumpers.

"I'm just interested," she answered. "In your life, your friends—"

Natalie sighed and sloped off towards her room. "It was just someone from school, asking about homework." The door closed with something between a click and a slam.

At least she wasn't skipping school any more, Jane told herself as she headed out to the car. Natalie had, albeit sulkily, agreed to babysit her younger siblings so both her parents could go to the Parents' Evening.

The night was endlessly dark, the rain relentless against the car windows as Andrew drove down the narrow stretch of road to Endsleigh. Jane stared out the window, made out the ragged humps of a few sheep in the night-shrouded fields.

"Half-term is in a few weeks' time," he mused aloud. "My mother wants us to stop for a few days with her in Keswick."

"Does she?" Jane kept her gaze fixed on the window and its lack of view. The prospect of a few days with Dorothy, despite the older woman's recent attempt at some sort of reconciliation – if that's what it had indeed been – did not enthuse her at all. In any case, over the last few weeks she'd started thinking about her own plans for half-term.

She cleared her throat, the noise loud in the small space of the car. "I was actually thinking about taking the kids to New York for half-term."

Silence fell like a thunder-clap. She sneaked a look at Andrew, saw his hands had tightened on the steering wheel. "Do you really think that's a good idea?" he asked after a long, taut moment.

She thought it was a great idea, Jane thought irritably, otherwise she wouldn't have suggested it. It had come to her a week or so ago when she'd got a newsy email from Claudia, her former PA at Women For Change. Just the throwaway details about life in the city had made a lump rise in Jane's throat. She missed it so much. She missed who she'd been there: a woman with a full, busy life, a worthwhile career, useful and full of purpose. Maybe she'd been too busy, too stressed, too preoccupied, but she wanted just a taste of that life again. That Jane. After over a month of lonely isolation she craved the reminder of who she'd once been.

"Natalie really misses her friends," she told Andrew, and his jaw bunched.

"You actually want her to reconnect with those friends, Jane? The ones who had parties when their parents were out, and got up to who knows what kind of trouble? Who helped her to get suspended for underage drinking, for heaven's sake?"

Jane closed her eyes. She should have known this would start an argument. "Of course I don't want her to be negatively influenced," she said evenly. "But they were her *friends*, Andrew, and we've completely uprooted her—"

"You mean we've completely uprooted you."

Shock iced through her at his coldly matter-of-fact tone. She didn't want this to be about her, even though she knew it was. "Well, yes. I feel uprooted too. And I'd like to see my friends. Surely that's reasonable." She didn't make it a question.

Andrew sighed. He'd pulled into the school car park, and parents were heading towards the front doors in a steady stream, their shoulders bowed against the wind and rain. "Yes, I suppose it is. But we've only been here a month, Jane. I told you before that we only needed time, but how can you or any of us give it a chance if we're always looking back? Never letting go?"

She thought of what Dorothy had said to her a few weeks ago, about making an effort. Didn't anyone realize how much of an effort it was just to *be* here? To have given up her job, her life, for the sake of her husband and family? She swallowed it all down. "I'm trying, Andrew," she said quietly. "As much as I can. Honestly."

He stared at her, and Jane braced herself for more recriminations. Then he smiled tiredly and touched her cheek. "I know you are," he said, but the way he said it made Jane think he thought it wasn't enough. And maybe, she thought wearily, it wasn't. She just didn't know how much more she had to give.

Inside the school she blinked under the unforgiving fluorescent lights and went to find Ben's classroom, Andrew strolling next to her, obviously interested in the noticeboards and glass cases with art displays. Jane barely registered any of it. She was conscious of a constant, low-level anxiety about the meetings tonight; not so much with Ben's teacher, but with Natalie's. Considering Natalie's attitude at home, she doubted her teachers would have anything good to say. At least Ben was easy. He'd made friends, did sport, seemed as well-adjusted as Merrie.

"Good evening, Mr and Mrs Hatton." A round-faced young woman smiled at them from behind a desk and shuffled a few papers. "Ben is such a delightful and high-energy boy."

"Yes, he is that," Jane agreed wryly. "Manic" was more like it.

"He's adjusted well, socially speaking," the teacher, Mrs Stanfield, continued. "He makes friends easily."

"He always did," Andrew chipped in. "Even as a baby he was always social, charming everyone."

Mrs Stanfield nodded in smiling agreement. Then she turned serious, her hands stilling on the pile of papers, and asked, "Has Ben ever been tested for possible learning disabilities?"

Jane stared at her blankly, the words not seeming to make sense. Even Andrew had nothing to say; he looked as blank as Jane felt.

"Learning disabilities?" she finally repeated, scrambling to order her thoughts. "No, no, he hasn't. He's never been flagged as... as having any trouble." Her mind was racing, trying to remember any issues Ben might have had. He'd been a bit slow learning to read, but surely only by New York City standards, where it was de rigueur to have your child reading several years above their age level. He'd scored average grades at his primary school, but average didn't mean learning disabled. He'd gone to a very good – and very expensive – private school in one of the world's most academically competitive environments. Just what kind of learning disability was his teacher talking about?

"I see I've surprised you," Mrs Stanfield said. "I'm sorry. I only ask because I've noticed that Ben has trouble reading fluently, and also fully grasping the concepts he's just read about." Jane swallowed, and smiling, Mrs Stanfield continued, "I'm not saying I think it's terribly serious, but it's certainly something we should address so Ben has as successful an experience here as possible."

"Of course," Andrew said, filling in the silence.

Jane felt this was somehow her responsibility. She was Ben's mother; she should have known this. She should have seen it herself, when she read to him before bed, or looked over his homework, or met with his teachers. The problem was, she hadn't done any of those things, not regularly. She couldn't remember the last time she'd read to Ben or even talked about a book with him. As for his homework… the only work of his she'd seen this year was the 35 on the literacy test. She'd meant to talk to Andrew about it, and check Ben's work, but lost in her own misery, she'd forgotten.

She felt a hot, prickly flush of shame crawl over her body at the realization that she'd had no idea about any of this. She'd been smugly complacent, thinking Ben was *fine*, he was sorted, as if his ease at making friendships and his general happiness were somehow her doing.

"Jane?" Andrew was looking at her, eyes narrowed in concern, and mechanically she nodded.

"Of course. Yes." Some distant part of her brain had registered that the teacher had talked about testing options, and learning support, and reassessing Ben's needs at the next conference. "Yes," she said again. "Thank you."

And then Andrew had his hand on her elbow and was guiding her from the classroom and out into the fluorescent-lit hallway with the laborious essays pinned to noticeboards and the vague scent of gym socks and unwashed teenagers hanging in the air.

"You're surprised," he said quietly as they both fell into step to walk to the block of classrooms where Natalie's teachers waited.

"Shocked, actually."

"I guess that fancy prep school in New York didn't catch it."

Jane turned to him, even more shocked, for she knew he was attempting to turn this into a see-how-much-better-life-here-is lesson. "St Mark's was very good," she said shortly. "If they didn't pick up on something, it's not because they did something wrong." She didn't blame St Mark's for somehow failing Ben; she blamed herself. "Anyway, he might not have a learning disability," she said. "He still needs to be tested. Maybe he's just having trouble with the British spellings or something."

Andrew said nothing, which was enough of an answer, and they walked in silence to Natalie's classroom.

Natalie's conference was as much a shock as Ben's had been, for the opposite reason.

"She always hands her homework in," her maths teacher supplied helpfully. "A bit quiet in class, but really, a model student."

"And what about socially?" Jane asked, her voice strained with nerves.

"She's always in a big group of girls," her home-room teacher said. "Sits with them at lunch. It takes a while to make friends of course, but I have no real concerns about her adjustment here."

Jane was stunned. If Natalie was adjusting so well, why did she seem so miserable at home, slamming into the house and enduring family dinners in sulky silence? Why had she skipped school, said she hated it?

Sitting in that over-bright classroom, sifting through

samples of Natalie's exemplary work, Jane had the awful, creeping feeling that this somehow was her fault too. Had her own unhappiness rubbed off on Natalie? If she were happier, would her daughter be happier as well?

And how could she not know her children at all?

"Well, that's a relief, anyway," Andrew said as they headed out into the car park. "I knew you were concerned about Natalie." The rain and wind had both stopped, and the night was quiet and still. Jane didn't answer, for her mind was still spinning from the night's revelations. Despite the good news about Natalie, she didn't feel relieved. She felt more anxious and uncertain than ever.

Andrew took hold of her arm, and she turned to him in surprise. "Look."

"What?"

In answer he put one finger under her chin and tilted her head upwards. Still surprised and now a little bit annoyed, Jane blinked. The sky stretched inky-black above them.

"Don't you see them?" Andrew said softly, and then she did. Stars. Hundreds of thousands of stars, like diamonds spangled across an expanse of black velvet, just as she'd seen by herself that night walking home, although tonight was even clearer, even better.

She'd never seen so many before; she'd never lived in a place where so many could be seen. In New York the city lights had turned the sky a dull red and starless.

Andrew let out a happy little sigh, and Jane felt something in her start to thaw, just a little. She hadn't wanted to see the beauty of the stars before, and she still wasn't sure she did now, but she still felt a softening inside, a relenting. "They're beautiful," she said quietly, meaning it, and he squeezed her hand.

In the car on the way back to Goswell, Andrew spoke into the silence, staring straight ahead. "I'm sorry things have been so difficult for you here, Jane. I know I was asking a lot of you, to give up everything and move all this way. I'm sorry for not seeming understanding earlier."

This little speech sounded stiltedly rehearsed, and yet utterly heartfelt. Jane swallowed past the sudden tightness in her throat.

"Thank you for saying that. I'm sorry it hasn't seemed like I've been trying." She turned to gaze out the window. "I know I – I need to try harder."

He didn't speak for a moment, and then finally said, "If you want to go to New York for half-term, I won't mind. It would be good for you to see your friends and family, and good for the children too. I could catch up on some work and DIY here." He flexed his fingers on the steering wheel. "I can look into airfares, if you like."

Jane blinked hard. "Thank you," she whispered.

CHAPTER TEN

Alice
Goswell, 1932

Alice sat alone in the front pew of the church as she always did. The church was cold even though it was April and daffodils bloomed outside. Spring had come to Goswell, and the sight of the crocuses and snowdrops poking their heads through the frost-tipped grass had lightened Alice's heart – even if the interior of the church still felt as cold as a tomb.

She shifted in the hard pew, conscious of the stares boring into her back. Not that anyone was actually staring at her. She was undoubtedly being oversensitive and in all likelihood most people weren't paying any attention to her at all. They generally didn't.

In the nearly four months since she'd been living in Goswell she had not made many friends. She had, she supposed, received a certain level of acceptance, and most of the parishioners smiled and said hello to her after the service, or in the village. Yet she still didn't feel as if she had a *role*. Or as if Goswell, despite all her hopes, was her home.

She'd so wanted to love it all. She'd wanted, quite desperately, to fall in love with the sweeping fells, the wild sea, the narrow, twisting high street and the rambling old vicarage. She'd arrived in Goswell fully believing she would, that it was only a matter of time, and even after enduring several months of Mrs Sutherland's sniffs and clucks, and

Mrs Dunston's pitying shakes of her head, and all the other villagers who didn't seem as if they quite knew what to *do* with a nineteen- (well, twenty- now) year-old vicar's wife, she'd believed she could love it here if she just gave it enough time. If she just tried a little more.

And she had tried, in her small, tentative ways. She'd joined the Mothers' Union, only to discover their current project was knitting mittens for orphans and she didn't know how to knit. She'd gone to Mrs Dunston's for coffee with several other women, and sat with her cup perched awkwardly on her lap as the talk swirled around her like autumn leaves, and she could not snatch at even one.

Most of the women had daughters her age, and their daughters, Alice realized, were far more useful and accomplished than she was. Every time she admitted some failing – she didn't sew, had never gardened, didn't play an instrument – she was met with a kind of appalled silence before the conversation moved on and Alice stared down at her lap, feeling wretched and more useless than ever.

It was only now, ironically when spring had finally come to this forsaken place and the world began to look beautiful again, that Alice started to think that she wouldn't ever find her place here. That she might, in fact, spend the rest of her life in a place that made her cold and miserable with people who neither understood nor even liked her.

Tears pricked her eyes at the thought, and Alice stared blindly down at her prayer book. Why on earth was she indulging in such self-pitying thoughts now, in church, when her mind should be fixed on nobler things above? Yet she felt as if her soul were mired in doubt and hopelessness, as if she could not even begin to glimpse anything above at all.

The organ started with its sonorous creakings, and Alice rose with the rest of the congregation. For a few seconds spots swam before her eyes, and she blinked rapidly to clear them. It would not do to faint in the front pew, during the first hymn.

Yet as the choir processed down the aisle, followed by David in his clerical robes, giving her a rakish wink as he always did, making Alice's spirits lift just a little, the spots did not go away. By the time they were meant to kneel for confession, she felt so light-headed that she sank back onto her heels, causing a sudden intake of disapproving breath from behind her as the world continued to spin.

Distantly Alice realized everyone had risen, and she had not. She felt as if she couldn't move, as if every bone and muscle and nerve was focused on simply keeping herself conscious. How absurd to feel so dizzy, so suddenly.

Then, quite suddenly, she felt a firm hand on her elbow, and a warm voice in her ear.

"There you are, dearie. Come with me now, for you're sure to keel right over if you stay a minute longer."

With the hand firmly clamped on her elbow, Alice was able to rise and be escorted from the church. She wondered what David would think, what everyone else would think. The vicar's wife taking ill in the middle of the service! It would surely set people to whispering.

Outside in the fresh air, Alice drew a deep, shaking breath and leaned against the side of the church. The dizziness began to recede and she opened her eyes to look at her rescuer. To her surprise the woman who stood in front of her looked not much older than she was, with curly ginger hair and a friendly, freckled face.

"Better now?" she asked kindly, and Alice managed a shaky smile.

"I think so. Thank you so much. I don't know what came over me."

"The dizziness came on suddenly, did it?" the woman asked and Alice nodded.

"I – I'm afraid I don't know your name. I'm sorry." She felt, by this time, she should be acquainted with everyone who came through the church doors, but she woefully wasn't.

The woman let out a surprisingly throaty laugh. "And I don't know why you should. According to most of the ladies of this parish, I'm no better than I should be. But my name is Flora, Mrs James. Flora Welton."

"Pleased to meet you," Alice said, meaning it, but before she could offer her hand to Flora the doors to the church opened and Mrs Sutherland hurried out. She cast one dark look towards Flora before taking Alice by the arm.

"Goodness me, you gave the whole congregation a fright. I thought you were going to keel right over."

Alice felt as if she ought to apologize for feeling so poorly, but before she could frame a suitable answer Mrs Sutherland was already hurrying her down the church path, away from Flora Welton and towards the vicarage.

She brought a bemused Alice straight to the kitchen; the house was empty since everyone was at church and Alice found she actually liked the silence. So much of her day felt taken up with apologizing for her presence: to the housemaids when she interrupted them stoking a fire, or was in the way of their tasks; to the visitors who stopped by, it seemed, only to talk to David and got her instead; even to Mrs Sutherland, who arched an eyebrow in silent and rather impatient expectation whenever she ventured into the kitchen.

Just as she was doing now, having banged the kettle onto the range.

136

"I'm sorry," Alice said, because Mrs Sutherland was looking at her as if she expected an apology. She wished she didn't feel so chastened by her housekeeper – her own servant, for heaven's sake! – but the truth was, she did. Quite awfully.

"Sorry?" Mrs Sutherland's eyebrow arched higher. "And what on earth are you sorry about?"

"For… for coming over so queer, I suppose," Alice said, flushing. Clearly an apology was not what Mrs Sutherland had been looking for.

"Well, it's no more than I'd expect, considering," Mrs Sutherland said and Alice stared down at her lap, her gloved hands clenched into helpless fists. No more than her housekeeper would expect from such a pathetic, useless creature as herself, clearly. It seemed to be what everyone else in Goswell thought.

"Even so," she whispered, still staring at her lap, "I should have acted with more – with more decorum, I suppose."

Mrs Sutherland let out a most inelegant snort. "There isn't much decorum to be had in your situation, I'm afraid."

Alice looked up, startled by the housekeeper's matter-of-fact tone. She knew Mrs Sutherland had little patience for her, but surely this breached even her bounds of appropriate conversation between a mistress and her servant. "I'm not sure—"

"Goodness gracious, child," Mrs Sutherland said, looking at her rather oddly. "You don't know what you're about, do you?"

Alice bit her lip. "Really, Mrs Sutherland, I think—"

The kettle began to whistle shrilly, but Alice could still hear Mrs Sutherland's next words. "My dear, if I'm not much mistaken, you're going to have a baby."

Alice stared at her, her mind blank, spinning. "A baby," she repeated, and then blushed furiously, for it was ridiculous that she had never once even considered such a possibility. She knew the lovely things she and David did in their marriage bed could result in a baby. She wasn't quite that naïve or stupid. And yet... a *baby*. She didn't feel old or capable enough to bring up a child. The thought of it terrified her.

"Don't look so shocked," Mrs Sutherland said, "or you might keel over yet again."

"I'm just surprised," Alice managed. "I didn't expect..."

"Well, you're expecting now," Mrs Sutherland said, and Alice saw the housekeeper was smiling at her, which was a rare occurrence indeed. She smiled back, and some of her terror receded at the sudden and incredible thought that she would be a mother. David would be a father. They would, in fact, be that wondrous thing Alice barely remembered since her own mother had died when she was three: a *family*.

And just like before, when David had proposed, she felt a wonderful certainty flood through her that this, again, was what she'd been waiting for. Who she was meant to be. David's wife, and the mother of his children.

She smiled up at Mrs Sutherland. "I can't wait to tell David."

"He'll be pleased," Mrs Sutherland agreed with a brisk nod and another smile. "Pleased as punch, I imagine."

Alice stood up. "I should get back to church. Everyone will wonder what has happened to me."

"Oh, I think they've guessed aright," the housekeeper answered, and Alice stilled.

"Do you mean – do you mean, Mrs Sutherland, that everyone already knows I'm... I'm expecting? Even when I didn't?"

Mrs Sutherland eyed her with something close to pity. "It's likely enough that they would, Mrs James. We're country folk, after all, and the Reverend's had his pretty young wife with him for nearly half a year now. Something's bound to happen, don't you think?"

Alice had absolutely nothing to say to this. She blushed, and felt herself come over dizzy once more.

"Now, now," Mrs Sutherland said soothingly, "we'd best get you up to bed."

"I'm perfectly well—"

"The Reverend wouldn't thank me for bringing you back to church when you've had a fainting spell. It's up to bed with you for the rest of the day, and that's that."

Obediently Alice let Mrs Sutherland bundle her up to bed, and she stoked the fire herself, since the housemaids were all over at the church, undoubtedly giggling in the back pew as they usually did. Yet when Mrs Sutherland had left in the hopes that there was still time to take communion, Alice lay in bed with the covers up to her chin as if she were a sickly child and felt humiliation sweep over her at the thought that everyone in Goswell had been looking at her and thinking she was going to have a baby when she hadn't even known herself.

She closed her eyes, fighting against that tide of shame, for she wanted only to feel happiness now. She had never even thought of having a baby – why she hadn't, she couldn't even say – and yet now the knowledge was like a pearl hidden inside her, treasured and so very valuable. A pearl of great price, this child, for she wanted it so very much. She placed one slender hand against her still-flat stomach. Could there actually be a tiny bud of a baby nestled in there, growing quietly into life? It truly was a miracle.

She must have drifted off to sleep, for it was some time later that she stirred to wakefulness at the sound of David's quick step on the stairs, and then the door to their bedroom opened and he peeked his head around the frame.

"Alice! Did I wake you, my darling?"

"It's all right."

"Is it true, then? You're going to have a baby?"

Alice felt a twinge of disappointment, like pricking yourself with a needle. "Did Mrs Sutherland tell you?"

"Yes, she did. I was so concerned when I saw you being taken out of the church. I thought you were ill."

"Just a bit dizzy," Alice assured him. She tried to suppress the resentment she felt that Mrs Sutherland had told David her news. She might not have known it herself, but wasn't it her news to share?

Apparently not.

"You are pleased?" she asked, for David hadn't said anything more.

"Pleased?" he repeated, and sank onto the edge of the bed, taking her hands in his. "Darling, I'm over the moon. I'm speechless, because it never even occurred to me—"

"Nor me," Alice confessed, glad to have shared this ridiculous ignorance. "Mrs Sutherland had to tell me – I didn't even know!"

He laughed and squeezed her hands. "We're quite a pair, aren't we? She said you'd been off your food for a while, not having much for breakfast, and I confess I didn't even notice."

Nor had she, Alice realized. She had been feeling a bit queasy in the mornings, but she had dismissed it as merely being tired of Mrs Sutherland's stodgy porridge.

"I never even thought of a baby," David said quietly, "even though I've always known I wanted children. I was just so caught up in being with *you*…"

And Alice knew she had been the same. Despite the challenges and miseries of her life in Goswell, she had never once questioned her happiness with David. Every moment with him had been a joy.

"Well, now you can be caught up in someone else," Alice said with a self-conscious pat of her middle. "Whoever she or he is."

"May I?" David asked, and placed his own hand over hers, spreading his fingers across her abdomen with a smile.

"You can't feel anything yet," Alice said with a laugh. "It must be tiny, David, like a little bug."

"A little bug in a rug," he said, and kissed her. "But I love him or her already."

Alice smiled, feeling lighter and happier than she had since the night she'd arrived in Goswell. It had been hard here, yes, and lonely, yet for once the future looked wonderfully bright. The best, the sweetest, was still to come.

CHAPTER ELEVEN

Jane

As soon as Jane stepped out of the cab onto Fifty-Seventh Street, the fumes from the relentless stream of cars and taxi cabs stinging her eyes and the jackhammering from a nearby construction site ringing in her ears, she felt a smile bloom across her face.

She was home.

Next to her Merrie was covering her ears, Ben was looking at the pedestrian-clogged streets with something like scepticism, and Natalie looked, as usual, bored. They'd all been a bit nonplussed about their trip back to New York; Jane had expected a little enthusiasm, if not squeals of joy, when she'd told them how they were spending their half-term. Instead she'd been met with wary questions and even disappointment.

"Dad's not coming?" Ben said and Jane shook her head.

"He has to work—"

"Sophie's staying here for half-term," Merrie had said in a tragic voice. "We were going to go to the free swim at the pool in Whitehaven. Her mum said she'd take us."

"You can do that another time, sweetheart—"

"I have exams next week," Natalie had volunteered sullenly. "I need to study—"

"You can bring your books on the plane—"

"They're *heavy*—"

"Oh, for heaven's sake," Jane had snapped then. "I

thought you'd be happy to go back home and see your friends. This was meant to be a treat."

Three pairs of eyes had stared at her in silent, accusing acceptance. Then Merrie had whispered, "But this is home now, Mummy."

Jane had not broached the subject again. They were going, the tickets were booked, it was that simple. And really, shouldn't she be a bit glad or at least relieved that they were so settled in Goswell? Instead she felt disgruntled and a little bit ashamed, like she'd let everyone down by not being as well adjusted as they were.

Things had improved when they'd arrived in the States and gone directly to her parents' house in Connecticut. The weather, thankfully, was beautiful, clear blue skies and lemony sunshine and crisp breezes. A perfect New England autumn. And her parents had been thrilled to see the children, had taken them to the local farm to pick apples and drink cider and eat hot, sugary donuts. They'd gone to a corn maze and had a hay ride and done all the autumnal things they did when visiting her parents, except now everything felt special, because none of it, Jane knew, was available back in cold, windy Cumbria.

"Do you know we have fireworks in England in the fall?" Merrie told Jane's mother Karen one afternoon when they were all out on the front porch, the sun mellow, crimson and gold leaves blowing across the yard.

"Do you? And not in July, I suppose?" Karen answered. "No celebrating Independence Day in England!"

"It's called Guy Fawkes Day," Merrie explained. "My best friend Sophie told me about it. Sometimes you even make a straw man and burn him!"

"Goodness." Karen met Jane's eyes over Merrie's dark head. "That sounds rather alarming. And exciting, I suppose."

When Merrie had scampered off to play on the rope swing with Ben, Karen raised her eyebrows. "I've heard all about the children, and especially Merrie. Her school dinners are something else, apparently. But what about you, Jane? You've barely phoned or emailed since you got over there. How are you coping?"

Jane gave her mother a rather twisted smile. "Coping," she said, "is probably the right word."

Karen nodded in sympathy. "It's bound to be hard, at first."

"Yes." Jane knew she didn't want to spill all her unhappiness to her mother. It felt unfair to Andrew and, she had an awful feeling, would make her look petty and selfish. She *felt* petty and selfish, yet how could you force happiness?

Karen patted her arm. "It will come in time," she said. "Just give it time."

The same advice everyone else seemed to be giving her, and Jane accepted it with a tired smile. She didn't feel like explaining that she didn't think time would be enough, and in any case, she didn't want any more time. If she could move back to Manhattan tomorrow, she would.

And now she was here, breathing in the car fumes and the smell of greasy food from the street vendors, people pushing past her in indifference or impatience, and she felt her heart sing. She was home, no matter what her children had said, and she wasn't going to think about Goswell once while she was here.

She'd arranged for all the children to spend the afternoon at their old schools, to which they'd all objected, not wanting to go to school on a holiday, but Jane remained determinedly upbeat.

"But you'll see your friends all at once," she cajoled. "No one will miss out."

Eventually she'd mostly convinced them of the benefits of this plan, and now she was going to drop them off before heading over to her former office and visiting with her own colleagues and friends.

Jane felt fired up with adrenalin and exhilaration as she walked through midtown after dropping the kids off at their schools. It was a beautiful day, and she'd chosen to walk rather than take a cab or bus. She wanted to soak up every aspect of the city: the tall buildings with the sunlight glinting in their windows, the endless, artful display in shop windows, the bustle and buzz she loved so much.

Not, she acknowledged fairly, that it was all perfect. She'd forgotten just how loud and dirty and crowded everything was. Yet despite the people pushing past her and the endless noise, she felt more alive and excited walking across Fifty-Seventh Street than she had at any moment in Goswell. The thought scared her.

This wasn't her real life; Goswell was. And that thought scared her even more. She wasn't going to think about Goswell today, she reminded herself. She wasn't going to think about it at all. And for a while, as she was swept into the buzz of her old office, that was easy.

"We have missed you *so* much," her former PA, Claudia, squealed as she entered the office of Women For Change. Jane stood in the shabby little reception room with its second-hand sofa and sputtering coffee machine and felt a wave of love for all that she'd once known and now missed. The four women who worked for the charity that helped disadvantaged women take positive steps to regain control of their lives clamoured around her with hugs and exclamations.

Fifteen minutes later Jane sat in her old office cradling a mug of coffee while Claudia shut the door.

"So, are you loving country life?" she asked as she sat down and sipped her own coffee.

Jane hadn't yet decided how honest she wanted to be. "Getting used to it," she finally said, and Claudia nodded knowingly.

"It must be so different." Jane just nodded, and Claudia leaned forward, her expression softening into sympathy. "Do you hate it?"

Jane stared at her, too shocked by her friend's candour to dissemble. She felt her face start to crumple and she looked down, blinking hard. "Sorry…" she mumbled, and Claudia clucked and handed her several tissues.

"What was Andrew thinking, hauling you out there? You're a born-and-bred New Yorker."

Jane dabbed her eyes. "I agreed, though."

"Only because you're a saint."

"I'm not a saint." She drew a shuddering breath. It had felt good to break down a little, like releasing the pressure on a valve. Yet she wasn't about to break down completely. She wasn't sure she could recover from that. "In fact, I'm behaving pretty awfully. I haven't really tried to settle in or meet people."

Claudia shrugged. "You've been there for less than two months."

Had it been less than two months? It felt like forever. Jane blew her nose. "The trouble is, I can't seem to want to make an effort. I don't want to feel like it's home there, even if that's best for the children. Maybe even best for me."

"I'm not sure how it's best for you," Claudia answered rather tartly, and Jane just sighed. Confiding in her fiercely single and independent friend was probably not one of her best ideas. Claudia would never understand the compromise and self-sacrifice needed to make a marriage, a family work.

And yet even though she understood it – in theory – she was clearly having trouble putting it into practice. Sighing again, she shook her head. "I don't really want to talk about life in Goswell. Tell me what's going on here. What about you? And Women For Change? Have you found a new director?"

Claudia made a face. "It's not so easy to fill your shoes. You gave your heart and soul to this job."

"I know." And there hadn't been much left over for her family. Jane gazed unseeingly out the window. Did she miss those ten- and twelve-hour workdays, scrambling for childcare as she rushed to deal with one crisis or another, dialling for takeout as she fired another email at the same time? She'd lived her life in a distracted, fractured state, always dealing with several things at once. Yet now she felt as if she were dealing with nothing. Surely there had to be some happy medium… but how? *Where?*

"Actually," Claudia said reluctantly, "we're having a bit of a nightmare with the charity gala."

Jane snapped back to attention. "What do you mean?" The annual charity gala was a crucial way of raising financial support. Jane had always organized it herself, soliciting donations for the silent auction as well as courting several of their bigger supporters.

"I don't have the knack for chatting people up the way you do," Claudia explained with a resigned shrug.

"Most people just want someone to listen."

"Agatha Canter has withdrawn her support."

"Oh no!" Jane was appalled. Agatha was a lovely eighty-nine-year-old widow who lived in a huge apartment on Fifth Avenue and gave very generously to the charity. The idea that she would have withdrawn her support was unthinkable. "Did you visit her?"

"I tried, but she sent me away." Claudia sighed. "She wanted you."

"She doesn't like change."

"And yet she donates – or did – a huge sum of money to Women For Change."

"I know, I know." Jane smiled just to think of the feisty octogenarian. She'd always liked visiting Agatha. "But maybe if you write her…"

"I've tried." Claudia just shrugged. "Anyway, here I am, complaining to you, when that's the last thing I should be doing. We'll survive somehow without Agatha's support. You don't need to worry."

Jane said nothing, for she knew well enough just how much Women For Change relied on donations like Agatha Canter's. And she knew she would worry, because even an ocean away, Women For Change still felt like her responsibility, her baby. Sitting in her old office, her fingers itched to pick up the phone and make a few calls to donors. She wanted to read the briefs on the charity's initiatives, from offering classes in computers and typing to repairs to the shelter they ran down in the Bowery. She wanted to feel alive again, and vital, doing something nobody, not even Claudia, could do. It was, she saw suddenly, a selfish impulse. It was about her, and how she felt, rather than any good she might do for the cause she'd kept close to her heart for so many years.

"What about the charity gala? You said you were having trouble with it?"

"Just little things. Most of our sponsors are used to dealing with you—"

"I wasn't that important," Jane protested, and Claudia shook her head.

"Jane, you practically *were* this charity. Maybe if there had been some warning, but your move came together so suddenly, and everyone has been shocked that you're not there."

Jane bit her lip, knowing that was her fault. She hadn't told anyone about Andrew's interview and the possibility of moving until near the end, when the reality had been staring her starkly in the face. She hadn't wanted it to be real, and in the end her avoidance tactics had hurt the charity.

"I'm sorry," she said quietly.

Claudia shook her head. "I'm the one who is sorry. I shouldn't be burdening you with this."

"I don't mind. Tell me what's going on."

Claudia hesitated, taking a sip of coffee, and then finally capitulated with a shrug. "The Yale Club has raised its rates—"

"How much?"

"Twenty per cent—"

"That's outrageous!"

Claudia shrugged again. "They said they were giving us a cut rate before, and now—"

"They gave us a cut rate for the charity's sake, not mine," Jane huffed, outraged on Claudia's behalf. "They shouldn't raise it just because I'm gone."

"That's how things work in this business. Everyone's looking out for number one."

"I'm sorry, Claudia. I wish there'd been more time to arrange things. I should have told you and the board of directors about the possibility of moving earlier. I just didn't want to admit it, even to myself."

"I understand." They both lapsed into a rather morose silence, consumed by the concerns of the charity.

"What would really be great," Claudia said finally, only half-joking, "is if you came back and managed the gala this year, eased all our sponsors and donors into working with me.

How long did you say you were here for?"

"Only three more days."

"Oh, well. I don't suppose you want to come back for a few weeks next month? You could stay with me, see the gala through and be home well before Christmas."

Jane stared at Claudia in surprise, for despite her light tone Jane sensed a sincere – and desperate – offer. "Are you actually serious?"

"Well, since you asked, yes, I am. It would make a big difference to us, Jane. And you're not working in England, are you? There's no reason why you couldn't come back to the city for a month or so. It could be really fun." She smiled, her meticulously plucked eyebrows arching. "Intense, crazy, and really fun."

"I can't…" Jane heard the doubt in her own voice. Already her mind was spinning through scenarios, wondering how she could make it work.

"Give me three good reasons why you can't," Claudia said, leaning forward, her eyes bright. Clearly she was starting to really get into this idea.

"I can give you exactly three," Jane answered flatly. "Natalie, Ben, and Merrie."

Claudia blinked, and Jane realized it was taking her a second to make the connection. Had Claudia not even remembered the names of her children? They'd worked together for seven years. And yet, despite a few visits to the shelter with Natalie, she'd never brought the children to the office or any charity-related event. She'd had a couple of school photos pinned to her bulletin board, that was all.

"They're old enough to look after themselves for a bit, aren't they?" Claudia said after a moment. "Anyway, what are nannies for?"

"I can't…" She could just imagine Andrew's appalled reaction if she suggested hiring a nanny in Goswell. She didn't know if they even *had* nannies there. If people needed childcare they looked to their parents; Jane had seen the grandparents at the school pickup, looking stoic and a bit resigned as they fetched their offspring's offspring. Most people in Goswell, she knew, were born-and-bred Cumbrian. Not like an outsider, an offcomer.

In any case, they'd moved to a place like Goswell, she knew, to get away from the urban lifestyle: the frenetic pace, the constant stress, the fact that other people had been raising their children.

But I didn't know it would be like this, she told herself rather urgently. *Feel like this.*

"You can," Claudia said firmly and Jane stared at her helplessly.

I can, she thought. *I could. Why should Andrew stop me? Why shouldn't I have this one month of my old life, my old self?*

"I'll think about it," she finally said, and Claudia let out a crowing laugh of triumphant glee. "I'm not promising anything," she warned, and her former assistant just smiled.

Yet sitting there watching the sun start to set, gilding the skyscrapers to gold, Jane knew she had already made up her mind. She would do it.

CHAPTER ELEVEN

Alice
Goswell, 1932

For the first trimester of her pregnancy, Alice felt mostly sleepy and satisfyingly content. An entire afternoon could pass with her not moving from the armchair by the fire in the sitting room, daydreams drifting through her mind like boats bobbing on a placid sea. She pictured herself rocking a baby, David looking on with a loving smile. It was all pleasantly hazy, yet still so real.

Sometimes David would come in after his pastoral visits and find her there, half-dozing. "Poor darling," he'd say, "are you so very tired?" And he'd kiss her and draw her onto his lap, and Alice would smile and rest her head against his shoulder. She did feel tired, yet it was not unpleasant. All the little slights and sorrows that had worried her from the moment she'd come to Goswell seemed to fade in importance and even reality, and never more so than when she was in David's arms.

When she began to show, sometime around her fourth month of pregnancy, she had a sudden burst of energy and began to go walking. The weather had turned fine and the entire countryside seemed transformed. Banks of orange lilies blazed along the lonely stretch of road to the sea, and the churchyard held glorious pockets of tulips and bluebells. This rugged land that had felt so hostile and untamed seemed gentle and friendly with its new mantle of flowers, and Alice began to explore it with vigour.

She walked down to the beach and along the windswept coastal path; on a clear day she could see the blurred, violet shape of the Isle of Man. She explored the steep forests that bordered the village to the north, walking through the silvery, dew-tipped grass to the top of the hill, where the village spread out amid the vibrant green of the sheep pastures, a friendly jumble of farmhouses, barns, and terraced cottages.

It *felt* friendly now, for as Alice's state became known throughout the village (which didn't take long, thanks to Mrs Sutherland), she noticed how people smiled and greeted her in the street; they'd done so before, but now they stopped to chat and she felt the warmth of their approval. At church someone was always quick to help her to stand during the hymns, or hand her a prayer book or church bulletin. She'd finally found her role, and with it came acceptance and a sense of peaceful contentment. No longer did she suggest they have dinner parties or she take a Sunday school class; such things would hardly be expected from a woman in her condition, and for that Alice was glad. All she needed to do was nurture the child inside her, and give it the love she longed to when it was born.

She was walking along the main street one afternoon, having come out of Taylor's Gifts and Sweets with a postcard to send to her father, when she recognized the ginger hair and freckles of Flora Welton. She started forward impulsively.

"Miss Welton!"

Flora Welton turned at the sound of her name, but when she saw it was Alice she tensed, her expression turning strangely hooded. Alice felt a flash of disappointment; she had expected Flora to be pleased to see her.

"It's good to see you," she ventured uncertainly, for Flora was clutching her handbag to her and looking down the street as if she longed to escape.

"You're looking well, Mrs James."

"Thank you. I'm expecting, as you can see." She patted her small round bump with an awkward and self-conscious pride. She'd only recently started having to wear the smocked dresses required by her pregnancy. "That's why I came over so funny in church, when you took me out for some fresh air a few months ago. I never did get to thank you properly—"

"It's no trouble, Mrs James," Flora said, but Alice heard little warmth in her words and Flora was still glancing down the street, as if she would rather be anywhere else.

Disappointment sharpened into hurt. "Flora, you were so kind to me—" she began, only to have the young woman give a quick and decisive shake of her head.

"It really was no trouble. But I'm afraid I must be off. I'm catching the train to Barrow." And without a proper farewell, she hurried down the main street.

Alice watched her go with something like sorrow. She had been looking forward to seeing Flora Welton again, had even imagined that they might become friends. Yet for some reason – and none that Alice could fathom – Flora Welton had no interest in furthering their acquaintance.

The next day as she was eating lunch, Alice decided to ask Mrs Sutherland about her exchange with Flora. Alice had taken to eating her lunch in the kitchen, to keep the maids from having to lay a fire in the dining room, and also because she preferred Mrs Sutherland's company to none at all.

"Mrs Sutherland," she asked, spearing a piece of boiled ham, "do you know Flora Welton?"

Mrs Sutherland sniffed rather disparagingly as she briskly

cracked eggs into a bowl. "I should do. I've lived in this village all my life."

"Of course," Alice murmured. In the seven months since she'd lived in Goswell, she'd become used to the way Mrs Sutherland spoke, seeming to take affront at everything. "Has she lived in the village all her life, as well?"

Mrs Sutherland glanced over at her, elbow-deep in flour, her eyes narrowed. "Why are you asking about Flora Welton?"

"She was kind to me in church—"

"That girl has been too kind in her time," Mrs Sutherland said darkly, and Alice frowned.

"How can anyone be too kind?"

"Never you mind." She began to stir the cake batter she was making with repressively brisk movements.

"I'm not a child, Mrs Sutherland." Even if she were eating in the kitchen under Mrs Sutherland's beady eye, as if the woman were her nursemaid, Alice felt an uncomfortable, prickling awareness that if Mrs Sutherland treated her like a child, it was at least in part because she allowed it, and had done so ever since she'd arrived. It had seemed simpler somehow, and despite the older woman's briskness Alice realized she had liked feeling almost mothered. Yet now that she was going to be a mother herself, perhaps that should stop. She'd start taking her luncheon in the dining room too, the way most wives did – or at least she thought they did. Despite her happiness with David, she wasn't quite sure she felt like a proper, grown-up wife.

"I'd like to know about Flora Welton," she said firmly, her voice seeming to ring in the big, high-ceilinged room.

Mrs Sutherland continued stirring. "There's nothing to know," she said flatly, exactly the way a mother would to a child, and despite her earlier bravado Alice didn't ask anything more.

That August David took three glorious weeks off from work, and they went first to Keswick, to visit his parents, whom Alice had only met twice but found kind if rather dour, and then to Cambridge to stay with her father.

When Alice stepped into the tall, narrow house on Grange Road she felt tears sting her eyes and she blinked them back hurriedly, not wanting David to see her cry, yet overwhelmed at finally being in the only place she still thought of as home. She had missed everything: the sitting room with its heavy, dark furniture; the gloomy kitchen with the windows covered by ivy so the only light that filtered in was greenish and cloudy; Mrs Chesney and her awful cooking and, of course, her dear, absent-minded father, who, in the eight months since she'd last seen him, had become just a bit more owlish and forgetful. When she hugged him he kept patting her on her back, as if he were soothing her, even though she was smiling.

"Dear Alice," he said. "Dear, dear Alice." And leaning back a little to look at him, Alice realized he wasn't soothing her; he was soothing himself, blinking back tears.

Even the things she'd disliked before felt dear now, because they were familiar and so beloved. She gobbled up Mrs Chesney's greasy game pie, exchanging knowing looks with David as they remembered their first meal taken together. When her father pottered around the downstairs looking for his spectacles, Alice lovingly plucked them from where he'd left them on the mantel. Nothing annoyed or exasperated her; everything felt only dear and precious.

They spent a fortnight in Cambridge, doing all the things they'd done in those few lovely weeks of courtship before they were married: punting on the Cam, strolling through the college Backs, taking tea in quaint little shops on King Street. Every moment was a balm to Alice's soul, filling her up with happiness like she'd been a dry and empty well, now near to overflowing. She did not let herself think about when it would end, the arduous and dirty journey by rail back up to Goswell, or the bleakness that would greet her on return.

One afternoon they took a picnic across the meadows to Grantchester and lay on a blanket in the Orchard Tea Garden, bees bumbling lazily through the air, the remnants of their cream tea scattered on the blanket around them. Alice lay on her back and stared up at a hazy blue sky with fleecy white clouds scudding across it, exactly like cotton wool, David's hand loosely linked with hers. She felt, she thought then, perfectly content.

"I wish," she said impulsively, turning her head to look at David who was also gazing up at the sky, "we could stay like this forever."

He let out a dry chuckle. "I imagine it would grow a bit dull, but I know what you mean." He laced her fingers with his own, drawing her hand towards him. "But you are looking forward to being back in Goswell, aren't you, my love? It's home now."

Alice gazed at him and saw a hint of anxiety clouding those hazel eyes she loved. David so rarely looked worried or anxious about anything, it took her a moment to realize that's what it was. He was afraid she wasn't happy in Goswell, she realized with a pang, and she knew that he was, at least in part, right. She squeezed his hand. "Of course I am," she said.

Yet she refused to think of the ever-approaching reality of their return, wanting only to cherish these golden days in Cambridge. The night before they left Alice lay in bed with her head on David's shoulder – they slept in the guest bedroom now, which had all through her childhood been reserved for Important People – and his hand resting lightly on her swelling bump.

A tiny foot or elbow impatiently kicked his hand off, and David laughed softly.

"He's a strong-willed little fellow, isn't he? Wants his mummy all to himself."

"It might be a girl, you know," Alice said. "Would you mind?"

"Mind? Why on earth should I mind?" He gathered her more closely to him, his hand sliding up and down her bare arm. "As long as she doesn't have the James nose. It's a bit much on a female face, I've always thought. Well, you know, you've met my Aunt Doris."

"*David!*" Alice covered her mouth to stifle her laughter. From the bedroom down the hall she could hear her father's sonorous snores.

He pressed a kiss on the top of her head. "I'm so glad we're going home tomorrow. I confess I've missed Goswell and our life there."

Alice snuggled closer and didn't answer, because she wanted neither to lie nor to admit the truth: she wasn't looking forward to returning to Goswell, not really. Not even at all. If she and David could stay in Cambridge, even in her father's house on Grange Road, she would, she thought with a little remorseful pang, be quite completely happy.

The day they arrived back in Goswell in late August it was windy and wet, and as cold as any day in December. Alice stepped off the train, her hand held firmly in David's, for she was ungainly now, with only a little over two months left in her pregnancy, and she felt quite exhausted from spending all day on various trains, every muscle aching.

She gave him what she hoped was a cheerful smile as they walked from the station down the lonely stretch of road to the church and vicarage, the wind sweeping relentlessly across the sheep pasture, straight from the slate-grey sea. Nothing had changed in Goswell, she thought, and she hadn't changed towards it. Part of her had hoped, she saw now, that she might have felt differently about things once she'd returned, but the village seemed as cold and windy and unfriendly as ever, the vicarage draughty and empty-feeling.

Mrs Sutherland met them at the door, bustling around them as she chattered on about what had happened in the village since they'd been gone – three babies had been born, two saints called heavenward, and an accident with a horse and cart on the beach road that fortunately hadn't left anyone seriously injured but had lamed the horse, poor creature.

Alice, tired and still aching from the journey, let it all wash over her as Mrs Sutherland settled her and David in the dining room, a fire blazing merrily in the grate, and brought them the supper she'd been keeping warm on the range.

When Mrs Sutherland had retired, promising that the three maids who saw to the general washing and cleaning and hauling of coal would be reporting bright and early tomorrow, Alice asked rather suddenly,

"David, do you know Flora Welton?"

David looked up from his steak and kidney pie, bemused. "I do. Why do you ask?"

"Because she was so kind to me when I took a turn in church, and then when I met her in the street she acted almost as if she didn't wish to see me. And Mrs Sutherland didn't seem to have much to say of her – not that she'd tell to me, at any rate."

"No, I don't suppose she would."

Annoyance flashed through Alice, surprising her, for she never felt angry at David. "I'm not a child, even if Mrs Sutherland treats me like one."

"I should say not! But Mrs Sutherland treats everyone like a child," he teased her with a smile. "She's always after me to button up my overcoat before I go out."

Alice did not reply, for she felt there was a marked difference between Mrs Sutherland's smiling indulgence of David and her rather school-teacherish sternness with her.

"In any case," David continued, "I shall tell you. Flora Welton has a young child – he must be two or three now."

"You mean out of wedlock?" Despite her best attempt to seem worldly, Alice felt quite shocked.

"Indeed. And no one knows who the father is, and she refuses to name him, so of course everyone thinks the worst." He shook his head sadly. "Poor soul. She hasn't had an easy time of it, whatever her sins."

Alice nodded, her mind spinning with this new information. She leaned her head against the back of her chair, and David laid his hand against her cheek.

"My poor love. You look completely worn out. The train journey took ages, didn't it?"

"I don't feel very well," Alice confessed. She was dreadfully tired and she still ached all over, especially in her lower back which throbbed with regular flashes of pain.

"Do you want to finish your supper?"

She shook her head. "No… no, I shall just go to bed. Finish your own supper, David, and don't fuss over me."

But David did fuss, seeing her upstairs and to their bedroom, which was as cold and draughty as the rest of the house.

"Why does Mrs Sutherland never remember to light the fire in our bedroom?" Alice complained, knowing she sounded petulant but unable to keep herself from it. She sank onto the bed and pressed her hands against her bump, conscious now that the vague ache of before had solidified and sharpened into something real and far more painful, her belly tightening insistently every few minutes. She closed her eyes and listened to David moving about the bedroom, laying a fire and then fetching her night things.

"Darling?" he asked, and his voice was sharp with concern. Alice realized she was still sitting there, her hands on her bump, her eyes closed. She felt as if someone had laced an iron band around her middle and was, every few minutes, squeezing it quite viciously. She felt David sit next to her, and take her hands in his cold ones. "Alice, my love, say something, please."

She opened her eyes, felt another sharp pain stab her in the belly. She might not have known she was going to have a baby, but she didn't need Mrs Sutherland to tell her what was going on now. She focused on David's dear face even as she felt tears start in her eyes.

"Alice—" he said, and he sounded scared.

She clung to his hands and tried not to cry. "David, I think the baby's coming early."

"Early?" He gaped at her, dumbfounded. "You mean—"

"Now," she gasped. "David, the baby is coming now."

CHAPTER TWELVE

Jane

The day Jane arrived back in England was clear, sunny, and surprisingly warm; Andrew picked them all up in Manchester, cheerful as ever. Even in her fuzzy, jet-lagged state she felt something in her stir as she gazed out at the dramatic sweep of Grange Fell down to the tranquil, glittering expanse of Derwentwater. Really, on a day like this, she had to admit she lived in one of the most beautiful places on earth.

Seeing their tiredness, Andrew didn't ask any questions about the trip beyond the basics, and Jane was glad. Somehow what had seemed reasonable back in New York – returning for three weeks to help Claudia with the fundraiser – now felt outrageous and impossible. She did not want to think what Andrew's reaction to such an idea might be.

Back in Goswell, the children all flopped straight into bed but Jane felt too wired to sleep, and so she walked around the house, feeling the stillness of the place go straight through her. After the hustle of the city, the quietness felt almost unnatural.

"You all seem to have had a good time," Andrew ventured when he found her standing in front of the fireplace in their bedroom. They hadn't used it yet, which seemed a shame. Staring at it now, Jane realized she'd never noticed the intricate blue and yellow tile surround. It was a beautiful piece of work.

"We did." She turned to face him, smiling through her tiredness. "I think everyone was glad to see their friends."

"And were they glad to come back, do you think?"

Jane saw a shadow of vulnerability in Andrew's eyes that tore at her heart. For a moment all her frustration and homesickness fell away, and instead she felt a strange mix of sorrow and hope. Andrew so wanted them all to love it here. He wanted this to work, and she knew she wasn't letting it.

"I think so," she said after a moment. "No one complained, at any rate." The children had been, somewhat surprisingly, rather silent about their return to England. Perhaps the whirlwind trip, switching so speedily from one life to another, had been too much to process.

"That's something, at least."

"It is." Jane crossed to him, held out her hands to take his in hers. "Andrew—" She stopped, her heart thudding, as he looked at her in a kind of concerned alarm.

"What is it?"

Words crowded in her throat, words she knew she could not say just now. She couldn't tell him about her plan to return, not yet anyway. But when? Claudia wanted her back as soon as possible. She forced herself to give him a wobbly kind of smile. "I'm just… glad to see you again."

Andrew's grin nearly split his face. He squeezed her hands. "I'm glad too," he said, and Jane's heart twisted inside her. "I meant to tell you," he added, his hands still in hers, "my mother phoned. She'd going to visit her cousin this week, the one who was a housekeeper here ages ago. She said you could come along, if you liked."

"Oh…" Jane blinked as thoughts seemed to tumble and arrange themselves in her mind. Before she'd left, she'd been rather fascinated by the history of the house, the elusive Alice James who had written that shopping list. *Beef roast for Weltons, potatoes, tea, mint humbugs for David.* Yet she hadn't thought of the list or Alice the entire time she'd been in New York. Now she slid her hands from Andrew's and walked back to the fireplace, stared down into the empty, swept grate. "Isn't it strange," she said, almost to herself, "to think about who once lived here? The house would have so many stories to tell, if it could speak."

"You could still find them out," Andrew answered. "The housekeeper might remember all sorts of interesting things."

Jane nodded slowly, but she knew Dorothy's cousin wouldn't remember Alice James or her husband David. She looked up to gaze at the stark, leafless trees outside, the sheep pasture a muddy mess beyond. She imagined Alice gazing out at the same view, imagined her bustling around her bedroom, the house full of her children and servants, everyone useful and happy.

Had Alice been happy? Why, Jane wondered, did she feel as if she hadn't been, as if this unknown Alice shared some of her own homesickness and sorrow? It didn't make sense. She was projecting her own feelings onto a stranger, and to no purpose.

The next day the children went back to school, all willingly enough, and Jane found herself alone in the house once more. She made herself a cup of coffee and took out the yellowed scrap of paper that Alice James had written her list on, questions tumbling through her mind. How old had Alice been when she'd written it? What had been going on in her life? Who were the Weltons? It occurred to her that the Weltons, or at least their descendants, might still live in the village. Ellen had told her that there were plenty of families who had lived in the village for generations, sometimes even hundreds of years.

It also occurred to her that this was nothing but a shopping list, forgotten, unimportant, completely trivial.

Why did it fascinate her so much? Alice James, whatever her life had been like, was most certainly dead. Would finding out some small detail about who she was make any difference, or was it just that her own life felt so empty of purpose? She pushed her cup of coffee away. Tonight she would talk to Andrew about returning to New York.

Yet when the children were settled upstairs and Andrew was, as had become his habit, making a fire in the sitting room after dinner, Jane found the words wouldn't come. She stood by the door watching him carefully lay the kindling and newspaper in the fireplace, clearly enjoying every minute step of the process, and couldn't speak.

Andrew glanced back at her. "Did you ring my mother?"

"What? Oh... no, I forgot. I'll do it tomorrow." She didn't relish a conversation with Dorothy, even if she was curious about the housekeeper cousin and her memories.

"There we are." Andrew stood up, watching the flickering flames with an obvious sense of achievement. It had turned wet and windy again, and the windowpanes rattled, the drawn curtains muffling the plaintive sound.

"Andrew..." Jane took a step forward, and Andrew turned to her.

"You look awfully serious."

"I wanted to talk to you about something." She saw him tense, felt it, and her heart started thudding. Why did it have to be so hard? Why couldn't they have a reasonable conversation about this? Why did she feel like she was asking for something absurd, or even offensive? Annoyance pricked her, hardening into anger. This wasn't *fair*.

"All right, then," Andrew said, and settled himself in the chair by the fire. He gestured to the other one and Jane perched on its edge. "What's going on?"

Jane took a deep breath and plunged. "When I was in New York, Claudia – my former PA – asked if I could help out with Women For Change, just for a bit."

Andrew's expression didn't change. "I know who Claudia is, Jane. And how would you help from over here?"

"Well…" Another deep breath, and she forced herself to go on. "The fundraiser, as you might remember, is right before Christmas—"

"I remember."

She didn't like the way he said that, although she was honest enough to admit that the fundraiser had always taken over their family life from Thanksgiving to Christmas. Not the best time to be working twelve-hour days, yet it had been too successful for Jane to ever risk a change. With a pang of guilt she remembered the rushed shopping she'd done on Christmas Eve, the ready-made Christmas dinner she'd ordered from Fresh Direct. She pushed the thought away; she was never going to become some kind of June Cleaver, a Stepford wife who bottled her own jam and ironed all the bed sheets.

"Anyway," she continued, each word painful, "Claudia has asked me to go back to New York – just for a few weeks – to help run it. Just for this one year." She was talking faster now, her words running together. "Just to help with the transition, because there wasn't really time before I left, and she's finding it quite difficult."

Andrew didn't say anything for a moment. He glanced at the fire, and then stood up and shook a few coals from the scuttle onto the struggling flames. "Amazing," he said, half to himself, "how difficult it can be to keep a fire going. The draw from the chimney is incredible."

"Well, it is rather windy out," Jane managed. The

windowpanes rattled again. "Andrew, say something. About – about what I just said. What do you think?"

"What do I think?" He turned to face her, and he looked so weary that Jane felt tears thicken in her throat. This was ridiculous. All she was talking about was a couple of weeks. She forced herself to smile.

"Yes, what do you think?"

"I think," Andrew said slowly, "that you've already decided. So it doesn't really matter what I think." He said this without rancour or bitterness, just a sad statement of fact. Jane blinked hard, hating the awful mixture of emotions she felt. Guilt and sorrow, anger and frustration.

"It would be so helpful for the work," she said quietly. "Claudia's having a hard time of it."

Andrew sighed and sat down. "I know it would be, Jane. I'm not arguing that. I'm not arguing anything."

Frustration bit at her. "You don't seem happy, though—"

He let out a dry, humourless laugh. "I think that's asking a bit much, don't you?'

Anger spiked through her. "Why," she asked, her voice shaking, "do I have to give up everything and you don't?"

He stared at her in surprise. "Is that how you actually feel?"

Jane glanced away, her anger coming and going like the tide. "Sometimes."

"I didn't – don't – want you to give up anything, Jane. This move wasn't meant to turn you into a martyr."

"I don't mean to sound like a martyr, but it's *hard*, Andrew—"

"I know that." He hesitated then said, "I do understand a bit what you're going through, you know. I moved to another country for sixteen years."

"I know that," she answered back, biting down on what she really wanted to say, how that move had been his choice, how he'd had a job he loved, and he'd lived in a bustling, vibrant city with lots of ex-pats, not on the edge of the earth with no other Americans in a hundred-miles radius at least, not to mention a Starbucks or a Target or a Harvey Nichols. She missed so much of her old life, she couldn't even begin to explain it to him.

"I'm just not sure," Andrew said carefully, his gaze on the crackling fire, "that going back to New York will be… helpful in your adjustment to life here. We can't go back, Jane, and I'm afraid that having it in half-measures will only make it worse for you here."

We can't go back. He sounded so final, so certain, and yet she didn't feel sure at all. "This is about the charity," she said at last and he raised his eyebrows.

"Are you sure about that?"

"I want to help," she insisted stubbornly. "And all right, yes, I want to feel like my old self again."

"And you don't think you can feel that here?" he asked quietly.

"Not at the moment."

They stared at each other, clearly at an impasse. After a moment he shrugged. "If you want to go, go. I'm sure we'll manage somehow with the childcare and things." He glanced back at the fire, and for a moment his profile seemed hard and remote, so unlike the man she knew and loved, depended on to be cheerful and upbeat when she couldn't manage it. "Don't worry about us."

CHAPTER THIRTEEN

Alice
Goswell, 1939

Alice sat at the kitchen table and stared down at the blank piece of paper in front of her. Firmly, in her neatest script, she wrote *Beef roast for Weltons*. She was determined to invite Flora Welton and her family to Sunday lunch next week. She hadn't mentioned it to David yet, who she thought she could win round, or Mrs Sutherland, who would be undoubtedly disapproving. Yet in the eight years since she'd first come to Goswell, Flora Welton had been, in many ways, her closest friend.

Sighing, Alice rose from the table and gazed out at the church, visible from the kitchen window, its sandstone exterior now glinting almost gold under a summer sun. It was a beautiful, warm day, and David had promised they'd walk to the beach and have a proper cream tea at the little café that had opened there recently. It was Mrs Sutherland's day off, so the kitchen, for once, felt peaceful and quiet, her own domain. She found she liked Mrs Sutherland's days off, for she could make David's dinner herself, including dessert. She had, after much trying, mastered the art of baking on the contrary range and could turn out a very nice cake. Mrs Dunston had remarked upon her Victoria sponge at the summer fete last month.

The last eight years, Alice had to acknowledge, had not been easy, although to be fair, neither had they been as hard as those first few months. The darkest moment had been and always would be, the loss of her baby.

Her little girl had been, quite simply, born too early. She'd been lovely, with a mouth like a rosebud and her hands curled up into tiny, perfect fists, but so thin and white and still, as if her little body were carved of marble. Alice had held her, only briefly before the nurse had whisked her away, while David stood by her bed, his face stony in grief.

That, in some ways, had been the hardest part of the ordeal. Instead of turning towards him, Alice had felt herself withdraw from David and felt helpless to stop herself. He'd done the same, so they'd been cloaked in their separate grief and silence, and Alice had, for a few weeks, simply drifted through the days, a ghost in her own life. She barely remembered the hours passing, and ate nearly nothing at all. Part of her, even if she could not form the thought in her own mind, wished to die. To simply fade away into numb nothingness.

Then Mrs Sutherland had given her a talking to, telling her she needed to dress properly and get out for some air, and what about the poor vicar needing a proper wife again? Alice had stared at her beady eyes and thin mouth and thought, briefly, that she hated her. Mrs Sutherland had not lost a child. Mrs Sutherland had not been told by a doctor (who looked at his pocket watch in the middle of speaking to her) that due to "the trauma to her parts" – whatever that meant – it was unlikely there would be any more babies. Alice had not needed to be told. Holding her daughter in her arms, touching her cold cheek, she'd known in her heart she would not have any more children, and she grieved their loss too.

After Mrs Sutherland's pep talk Alice had told David that she wanted to go home. He'd looked stricken, but she'd been too weary to apologize for calling Grange Road rather than Goswell home. "Just for a few weeks," she said. "I need to… I need to see Father again." She looked away from him then, her voice hardening. "I need to be away from here."

It wasn't just her father she wanted. She wanted her own house, the familiar surroundings, Mrs Chesney's bustling warmth, even her own bed. And she wanted to be away from everything Goswell had become: the draughty, unfriendly house, Mrs Sutherland's beady censure, the endless parade of parishioners who would surely only like her less now because of her "failure". And David, too, she knew. She wanted to be away from him, and the realization tore at her heart.

David had agreed, and even took her on the train since he felt she was still too weak to travel on her own.

He'd stayed the night in Cambridge before returning north, and Alice had felt horribly relieved when he'd gone. The thought that she didn't want to see him was too awful to bear, and she'd wept into her pillow after he'd left, because at the time when she wanted to be closest to him he felt impossibly far away and she didn't know whose fault it was.

Those weeks in Cambridge had been healing in their own way. Mrs Chesney and her father had pampered her with cups of tea and plates of cake in bed and games of chess and draughts, and then when she was feeling stronger, walks along the Cam or to tea in Grantchester. It was early autumn, and the rolling meadows were golden under a mellow sun, so different from the wind and wet of Goswell. Alone in her bed in the dark, she felt she did not ever want to go back. She didn't even miss David, which was the worst thing of all; he felt like a stranger, like someone she'd once known but had lost touch with long ago. He didn't understand this new person she'd become, this woman with emptiness inside her and an ache that would never go away. He didn't understand her, and she didn't understand him.

He'd been kind after the birth, of course; David was always kind. He'd let her hold the tiny daughter she'd birthed, had agreed to name her Rose, after Alice's mother. Alice had asked him, beseechingly, if he wanted to hold her, but he'd just shaken his head. She'd felt angry at him then, terribly, deeply angry, but she hadn't said anything and the nurse had taken Rose away with a blanket over her face.

Alice had wanted to protest, to tell her not to put the blanket like that, as if she were dead, even though she knew she was. She hadn't said anything, and she'd never seen Rose again.

After an interminable week in the hospital where other mothers held their babies and pushed them round in big silver-wheeled prams, Alice was finally allowed home to the cold emptiness of the vicarage.

Things with David had not improved once she was home – if this draughty vicarage could ever be home. Alice spent hours on her own, staring at the pages of a book or out the window at the trees framing the sheep pasture, their leaves already stripped by the wind even though it was only late September. She kept her mind purposefully blank, for when she allowed thoughts to crystallize they were too awful to consider.

I hate it here was the thought that came the most, stabbing her inside like a knife that plunged again and again. *I hate it here. I've always hated it here, and I always will. Nothing will ever get better. It will only get worse.*

At night she and David had lain side by side, unspeaking, not touching. Beyond her asking to go back to Cambridge she didn't feel like they spoke to each other much at all.

A month after she'd arrived in Grange Road, David

returned unexpectedly. They'd been writing to each other, of course – newsy little notes that were the sort of thing you might write to a distant aunt or an old acquaintance. She'd written a paragraph in her very neatest cursive about the walk to Grantchester, commenting on the coppery leaves and the light scones and saying nothing of the darkness in her heart, the despair that swamped her until she felt as if she were suffocating under it, as if she were drowning in a sea of sorrow. She'd told him in her last letter that she would stay through at least till the end of November, which was still several weeks away, and he had not yet replied.

Then one afternoon when she was sitting in the chair by the window of her old bedroom – she was sleeping in her girl's bedroom rather than the spare room they'd once shared – he appeared in the doorway. She felt a leap inside of both alarm and joy, for she had missed him so much. Yet she'd missed the man he'd been before they'd lost Rose, before she'd lost who she was, who she'd wanted to be. She didn't know if that person – the person he was, and the person she was – would ever return. Perhaps they were too different now to find their way to each other again. Perhaps everything had changed too much, too terribly.

He held his hat in his hands, looking too large and mannish in the frilly confines of her room.

"Alice…"

"Hello, David." She smiled, stiffly, hating that they were awkward with each other. "I didn't expect you."

"I barely expected myself." He gave her the ghost of one of his old smiles. "I just came. Packed a case and got on a train without telling anyone."

"Not even Mrs Sutherland?" She raised her eyebrows, her smile cold.

"Not a soul. I expect I've put the entire household into disarray."

"We don't have a household." Her voice choked, and she turned to the window. "There was just me and you and Mrs Sutherland. Hardly a household."

David took an uncertain step into the room. "Was, Alice? Aren't we still a home – a family?"

Alice kept her face to the window. "Not a family," she said in a low voice. "Never that."

"Oh, Alice." David came to her side then and knelt in front of her, taking her hands in his, his head bowed. Alice turned to him in surprise, and saw that his shoulders shook silently with sobs. Instinctively she leaned forward as if to comfort him, to cradle him like the child she'd never had.

"I'm so sorry, Alice," he said, his voice a ragged, choked whisper. "I know I've failed you terribly. I didn't know what to say, what to do, and so I didn't do anything. I'm so sorry."

"Oh, David," she said softly, and threaded her hands through his hair, lifting his head so she could see his face, the tears trickling down his cheeks. She felt tears start in her own eyes.

"I think of her every day, you know," David whispered. "Our daughter. Our Rose. I think of her, and I wish I'd had the courage to hold her. I never felt her. I never felt how small and perfect she was."

Alice couldn't answer. She just held him, his head drawn against her breast as tears trickled down her own cheeks and dampened his hair.

"Please come home, Alice," he said in a broken whisper. "I've missed you so. Please come back to me. I'll try to be better, and give you what you need. Because I need you, darling. I need you so very much."

Alice lifted his head so he was gazing at her. She'd never seen him cry before, yet tears ran down both their faces as she kissed his lips, felt the hardness in her own heart give way even as a weary, gentle resignation took its place. Of course she would return to Goswell. To David.

"I'll come back," she promised softly. "I'll come back home."

And so a week later she'd returned to Goswell, to the wind and the rain and the fells she'd once thought beautiful, but now they seemed only stark and bleak. Parishioners came forward cautiously, offering condolences and cakes and casseroles, as if food could somehow ease the grief she knew she would always carry with her. You couldn't forget a thing like that, you could only learn to live with it, the way you would a limp or a missing limb.

David had to learn as well, to adjust to the bedrooms that would remain empty, the silence of a house lived in by too few people. The hopes they'd both had that had died before they'd ever truly been given life.

Alice forced herself to acknowledge a deeper grief than the loss of her daughter: the loss of the life she'd hoped and dreamed to have. She saw her days stretching out in front of her, living in a place she still did not like, with people who would never understand her. She no longer had the hope of motherhood and children gathered around her to soften these disappointments, and she faced them now stoically, knowing that this was the life she had chosen and would always have, with David.

Still, there had been happy moments, even ones of joy. They'd survived a tragedy and it had, Alice believed, made their marriage stronger. With time she began to make a place for herself, of sorts, in Goswell. She would never be a vicar's wife like the indomitable Mrs Jessop, but she was determined not to live on the periphery, like a lost child, any more. She had grown up, whether she'd wanted to or not.

She began inviting people to Sunday lunch, and even making the puddings herself. Mrs Sutherland stood by in tight-lipped silence as Alice measured out flour and cracked eggs. She learned the housemaids' names and engaged them in conversation when they came in to lay the fires or dust the old, dark furniture David had inherited from the farm in Keswick.

She didn't join the Mother's Union or take a Sunday school class, because they were too painful for her, but she visited the elderly who were homebound and brought them bottled fruit she'd made herself. She learned to be happy with these little kindnesses, with the simple smallness of a life she had once thought would be so much bigger.

And next Sunday, Alice told herself now, she would invite the Weltons to lunch. Over the years she'd made a point of always saying hello to Flora, and after several months of nervously bobbing her head back Flora had finally started talking to her. Just a few moments' chat in the street, and once, when Alice had awkwardly asked her to the vicarage for tea, Flora had looked scandalized.

"Oh, I couldn't, Mrs James. It wouldn't be proper." She'd flushed a deep red and bobbed a strange little curtsey. "But thank you for asking me. Thank you very much indeed."

Even so, Alice had always liked their little hurried conversations; she sensed in Flora a warmth and honesty she hadn't found in many people here. She hoped she would agree to come to lunch. Things were changing, after all, even in a place like Goswell.

"Hello, darling."

Alice turned from the window to see David standing in the doorway of the kitchen, looking both cheerful and tired.

The sunlight caught the glint of grey threads at his temples, and Alice felt a twisting inside her. He was thirty-five this year.

"Hello. What have you been up to?"

"I was listening to the wireless. It's not looking good, I'm afraid."

Alice nodded, for they'd taken to listening to the grim news of Europe every evening after supper. She didn't fully understand the significance of every speech or alliance, yet she felt the tension in the air, could almost see the storm clouds on the horizon. War, it seemed, was inevitable.

"It's never good news, is it?" she said, shaking her head.

"No. If it comes to actual war…" David paused, and Alice glanced at him, feeling he was going to say something both momentous and dreadful. Then he smiled and said instead, lightly, "and what have you been up to?"

"I was just making a shopping list for Sunday lunch." She glanced at the paper and wrote underneath the beef, *Potatoes, 5 lb, 6d.* She'd taken charge of the housekeeping several years back, much to Mrs Sutherland's chagrin, and tried to keep a stern account of money spent.

"Oh? And what shall we be dining on?"

"Beef, I think." She added tea to the list – a quarter of a pound should only cost four pence – and then looked up at him. "I'd like to invite the Weltons to lunch."

"The Weltons?"

"Flora Welton and her mother Edith and her little boy Jamie." Although Jamie wasn't so little any more; he was nearly eleven. Alice had seen him, with his shock of ginger hair just like Flora's, skipping to school.

David didn't say anything for a moment, and Alice knew he was considering the repercussions of inviting an unwed mother and her illegitimate son to lunch at the vicarage. Then he smiled at her, and her heart swelled with love. "What a splendid idea. I shall look forward to it."

Smiling, Alice impulsively added to her list, *Mint Humbugs for David, 1d.* She hadn't bought any for him for ages, and she wanted to give him a treat. She still remembered when he'd bought them back in Cambridge, and how their hands had met in the confines of the paper sack, one of the most thrilling touches she'd ever known.

CHAPTER FOURTEEN

Jane

A week after Jane returned from New York she accompanied Dorothy to the nursing home outside Whitehaven to visit her cousin Ella. Although Jane's relationship with Dorothy remained politely strained, and even more so since she'd gone to New York, she didn't want to miss the chance to meet Ella, and discover any memories she might have to share.

"I don't know how much she remembers about those days," Dorothy warned Jane, "if you're trying to find something out about the vicarage. She's quite forgetful, poor lamb, and yet at other times she's as sharp as a new pin."

"Well, we'll see," was all Jane said, because really, she didn't even know what she would ask. Ella had been housekeeper in the 1950s, a decade after Alice and David James had left the vicarage and, presumably, Goswell. It was highly doubtful that she'd be able to shed any light on the Jameses.

Jane's thoughts were distracted as she drove with Dorothy along the steep, winding road from Goswell to Whitehaven. Last night she'd booked her ticket to New York for the middle of November, although she hadn't told Andrew or the children yet. They hadn't even spoken about it since that one awful, awkward conversation and Jane had gone back and forth in her own mind about whether or not she should go. Then last night she'd seen how low the fares were and recklessly, defiantly even, she'd booked the ticket. She hadn't told Claudia either, though; it was, for now, her own wretched secret, and one she resented feeling guilty about.

A voice kept whispering insistently in her head, *Why should I feel guilty? Why shouldn't I have something just for me?* It was only a month, after all, actually a little less. Three and a half weeks for Andrew and the children to cope without her.

"Here we are," Dorothy said cheerfully, and turned into the car park of a neatly tended building with well-weeded flower beds out front and a dramatic view of the fells from a porch in the back. "It's a nice spot, isn't it," she said, and Jane murmured her agreement.

Once inside, Dorothy kept up a steady chatter with Ella, who sat in a chair by the window of her room, her hands folded neatly in her lap, her wrinkled face tilted towards the sun.

"And this is my son Andrew's wife Jane," Dorothy said in that brisk, cheerful way Jane had noticed people often adopted when talking to the elderly. "She's American, all the way from New York City, but they live in Goswell now, in the old vicarage where you used to be housekeeper. Fancy that!"

"Oh, those were lovely days," Ella said, smiling in memory, her eyes closed, her face still turned towards the window to catch the fleeting sun. "Lovely days. Mr Hawkins was such a nice gentleman – funny, too. Do you know once…" She paused and turned to face Jane and Dorothy, her eyes now bright with remembrance. "I thought I was alone in the house and I decided to slide down the front stair bannister. Oh, I know it was naughty – I polished it every day, you know, and I was just dying to try it." She smiled, and intrigued, Jane leaned forward.

"And what happened?"

"I had a lovely ride – the wax polish made me go ever so fast. And then I got to the bottom, and there was Mr

Hawkins, having come in the front door!" She let out a rusty laugh, and Jane laughed with her.

"What did you do?"

"I apologized, of course. I thought he'd give me my notice right there and then. I was housekeeper, you know, not some young maid with feathers for brains. But he didn't, dear man. He just smiled and said he wished he could slide down it too." She laughed again, in memory. "He was a rather portly gentleman. I think he would have broken the bannister."

"What a wonderful story. I'll have to tell that to my children." Jane sat back, still smiling. She liked the thought of someone sliding down the bannister, laughter ringing through those great big rooms. "Did you know about the vicar before Mr Hawkins, a David James?" she asked impulsively. "He was there during the war, I think."

"During the war?" Ella frowned. "I wasn't in Goswell then, of course, but I do remember the house was empty for a year or so before Mr Hawkins came. It had been bombed during the war, and there was some damage to the out-buildings and a bit of the courtyard wall. You can see it, I'm sure even now, where it's been rebuilt, by the kitchen door."

"Bombed!" Jane said in surprise, for she'd never even considered such a thing. She felt a strange hollow sensation inside, like something had been emptied out. "I didn't think they bombed places like Cumbria." There weren't, after all, any real targets.

"It was unfortunate," Ella said. "The Germans used to target the shipyard down at Barrow, and Glasgow and Belfast as well. People thought a pilot must have just dropped one of his bombs over Goswell on his way back, to get rid of it, you know."

"Was anyone hurt? In the vicarage?"

Ella shook her head. "I don't really know about those days," she said, turning back to the window. "But Mr Hawkins was lovely. Did I tell you about the bannister?"

When Dorothy had driven her back to Goswell, refusing Jane's awkwardly offered cup of tea since she had shopping to do, Jane went straight to the church. She blinked in the dim interior, feeling faintly guilty that she had not darkened the building's doorstep since the last time she'd come in here, looking for answers from Simon Truesdell, the current vicar.

He wasn't in the building now, and she wandered around a bit disconsolately. There was no mention in the history display, she saw, of the vicarage being bombed, which surprised her. Instead the display focused on how the village had hosted several dozen child evacuees from Newcastle and Liverpool.

She'd just stepped back outside into the sunlight when she nearly bumped into him. "Oh, Mr Truesdell! I was just looking for you."

"And I'm happy to be found," he said genially, "but you must call me Simon."

"Simon," Jane repeated, and then felt compelled to say, "I'm sorry we haven't been to services yet. It's been so busy—" Which was, not to put it too baldly, a lie.

"Not to worry," Simon answered with a wave of his hand. "If you'd like, you could join us for the Remembrance service the second Sunday in November. We process out to the war memorial on High Street. It's quite a solemn occasion, and many villagers come along."

"Oh. I'm sure we'd like that." She paused and then began, still a bit awkwardly, "Actually, I wanted to ask you about the war. I was talking to a cousin of my mother-in-law who lived in Goswell in the 1950s, and she mentioned that the vicarage was bombed during the war. Do you know anything about that?"

"I'm afraid I don't." Simon frowned, his forehead wrinkling in thought. "I would have expected someone would remember such a thing. There weren't many bombs dropped around here, although Whitehaven received one, I believe. And a plane, Canadian, crashed there sometime during the war, killing all the crew." He smiled and shook his head. "But a bomb here in Goswell? Well, somebody must remember if it happened."

Jane nodded. She hadn't really expected Simon to know much about it, but she was still disappointed. "Thank you anyway," she said, and turned towards the vicarage.

"Do come to the Remembrance service," Simon called. "We'd be happy to have you along."

Jane promised she would, and then once back in the house she made her way out to the little walled courtyard behind the kitchen. She hadn't been out there much except to empty the rubbish Into the big black wheelie bin, and now she stared around at the little space, studying the walls for a change in the pattern of weathered sandstone.

When she found it, something inside her lurched. She crouched by the back door and ran her fingers along a little uneven rectangle of newer-looking red brick. It wasn't much, and she imagined the outbuildings would have taken most of the damage. The garage and shed next to it that made up one side of the courtyard were both newer, and definitely post-war. Had the original buildings been destroyed? Had Alice James or her husband David been hurt? Crouching there, running her fingers over the patched brickwork, Jane felt a sudden, inexplicable sorrow sweep through her.

She mentioned it to Andrew that evening, after dinner. "Did you know the vicarage was bombed during the war?"

"Was it?" He looked up in surprise from the local paper he'd taken to reading most evenings, despite the fact that the most interesting news was in the nostalgia section, where articles from a hundred years ago were reported. "That's rather unexpected. Cumbria wasn't targeted much by the Nazis, I would have thought. There's not an airfield or shipyard between here and Manchester."

"There's one in Barrow, apparently."

"Ah, Barrow." Andrew nodded. "I suppose some pilot just dropped his extra bombs on the way home?"

"Something like that."

"Who told you this? Mum's cousin? Ella what's-her-name?"

"Yes. I visited her with Dorothy today."

"Oh, good. I'm glad you went." Something about Andrew's approving smile nettled Jane. She turned away, knowing she should mention what else she'd done: book a ticket for New York. Yet somehow the words wouldn't come. "And was Ella in good form?" Andrew asked eventually. Jane saw, with a rustle of his paper, that he'd turned back to reading.

"I think so," she said, and gazed out the window at the endless black of night. "She seemed cheerful enough."

"Good," Andrew murmured, but Jane could tell he wasn't listening. She thought, for only a second, of telling him about the shopping list, and Alice James. But what had she really learned? Nothing of import. Alice remained as unknowable to Jane as she had been when she'd found that old list – and it didn't matter anyway.

Jane pressed her hand against the windowpane, spreading her fingers across the cold glass. For a moment, no more, she had the weirdest sensation that Alice James had once been in this room, had stood at this window just as she had, and had felt the same restless unhappiness that plagued Jane day after day.

CHAPTER FOURTEEN

Alice
Goswell, 1939

"This morning the British Ambassador in Berlin handed the German Government a final note stating that unless we heard from them by eleven a.m. that they were prepared at once to withdraw their troops from Poland, a state of war would exist between us."

Wordlessly Alice and David stared at each other over the wireless set that sat between them in the sitting room. The only sound, for a few seconds, was the buzzy static from the wireless. Then Chamberlain continued, his voice pinched with weary resignation.

"I have to tell you that no such undertaking has been received, and that consequently this country is at war with Germany."

Alice sat back in her chair, her mind whirling, so she barely heard the rest of the broadcast. When it was finished David leaned forward and, grim-faced, switched the wireless off.

"We're at war," Alice said faintly. Outside the sun shone benevolently on an early autumn morning; they'd just returned from church. The only sound now was the twittering of birds, and the faint, plaintive bleating of sheep.

"I knew it would come to this."

Alice knew David had been expecting such news for months, as had, she suspected, most of the country. Yet she hadn't. Tucked away in a land that time itself seemed to have forgotten, she had refused to think about the possibility of war at all.

"What will it mean for us?" she asked, and David sighed wearily.

"I suspect we'll see a whole lot of chaps in uniform, to start with."

Alice had only been six when the last war had ended. She didn't remember much about the actual conflict, but she still recalled the gaunt, blank-eyed veterans who had loitered in the streets afterwards, proud and desperate.

"It's such a shame, to think of the local boys like that," she whispered, and David raised his eyebrows.

"In uniform?"

"I mean… after."

He knew what she meant, and nodded soberly. "War is a terrible thing. A terrible thing." He was silent for a moment, his brow furrowed, clearly lost in thought. "Hitler must be stopped, of course. There's no question."

"Of course." She knew that, even if she didn't like it.

"Alice…" David glanced at her, his expression clearing, something like determination glinting in the hazel eyes she so dearly loved.

"What is it?" she asked, her voice no more than a thread of sound. She knew from that look in his eyes that she didn't want to hear what he had to say. She knew David knew it as well.

"Last time round I was too young," he began, his voice low. "I missed the chance to do my bit—"

"David, you were only fourteen when the war ended."

"And I saw plenty of local lads lose their lives over it," he said quietly. "There was a boy who helped out at the farm, just doing the odd jobs and such. He was a cheerful fellow, always with a kind word for you. You know the type."

Alice nodded, unsure where this sudden confidence was meant to take her.

"He enlisted right at the start, and he survived the whole thing. Came back, and was never the same. Never the same at all." David shook his head, lost in memory.

"Shell shock, you know. He'd been on the front lines for four years. He used to get the shakes, just all of a sudden, there was no reasoning it. And if there was a loud noise, even just an engine backfiring, he'd start to cry. Poor man. He was broken, absolutely broken."

He lapsed into silence for a moment, and then lifted his resolute gaze to Alice. "I told myself back then, when I was just a boy, that if I ever had the chance, I'd do what I could to make sure boys didn't come back like that again, broken beyond repair. Shattered."

Alice felt her fingers curl around the arms of her chair so tightly her knuckles ached. "What are you saying?" she whispered.

"I want to join up, Alice."

"But – but you're a vicar! A man of the cloth. You can't – you can't *fight*."

"As a chaplain."

Wordlessly Alice stared at him. Never had she imagined this. She'd assumed, she'd so naively, blithely assumed, that they were safe. The war might come to England, but it wouldn't come to Goswell. It wouldn't actually come here, to their home, to the small yet happy life she'd built for herself.

"I... I don't know what to say," she finally said unsteadily. "I never expected this." Perhaps she should have done. Now, looking back, she remembered how preoccupied David had seemed, how intently he'd followed all the news, how he'd tried to speak to her, to tell her something, several times, and then changed the subject. She leaned her head against the back of her chair and closed her eyes.

"I'm sorry if I've surprised you," David said. "I can see that I have. But I do feel strongly about this, Alice. I can't fight for my country in the way most men would, but I can do something just as important, perhaps even more so. I can offer those men who do fight hope."

She nodded, for she understood, even if everything in her rebelled against it in a silent scream of protest.

"Perhaps if we – if we'd had children, I'd feel differently, be more cautious—"

Alice let out a little gasp of pain. Even after eight years it hurt, and it hurt more now to think she might have been spared this if her little Rose had lived. Was everything to be taken away from her, piece by precious piece?

David leaned forward and clasped her cold hands. "Oh, darling, forgive me, that was so careless of me, to say it like that. Careless and cruel." He squeezed her hand, and Alice opened her eyes.

"No," she said, and she barely recognized her own voice. It sounded flat and strange. "No, I understood what you meant. You can risk more, can't you, since we don't have children."

"It's not about risk," David said, her hand still clasped tightly in his. "It's about duty."

"I know." And she did. Looking into his dear, determined face, she knew just how important this was to him, and she still hated it. Still railed against the choices she'd never been able to make.

"I'm worried for you," he confessed quietly. "Alone here. I want you to be happy, while I'm gone—"

"That might," Alice said with a barely managed smile, "be too much to ask."

"I was thinking," David said after a moment. "Perhaps you could go to Cambridge, to your father—"

The idea held a kind of desperate appeal. To be safe in her father's house again, to run back to that familiar life once more! Yet even as she contemplated it Alice knew she could not. She was no longer a child, and she could not scurry home like a child to her father's house, even if part of her longed to. "No, David," she said quietly, "my place is here. It always has been, ever since I married you. I'll stay."

She could tell he was glad, even though concern still shadowed his eyes. "I'll worry—"

"Of course you will. And so will I." Alice roused herself enough to speak firmly, with the kind of briskness she usually associated with Mrs Sutherland or Mrs Dunston. "I'm not the childish girl you married, you know. I'm stronger now, and wiser. I'll manage."

Something flashed across David's face, a kind of bittersweet sorrow. "I fell in love with the girl you were," he said with a whimsical smile. "And it was your girlish delight in everything that enchanted me so." He stroked her cheek, his voice turning husky with emotion. "But I'm grateful for the woman you've become, because I know I can go and trust you'll be strong here." He leaned forward and tenderly clasped her face between his hands. "I love you, Alice."

"I love you too." Alice heard the catch of tears in her throat but still she smiled. "So very much."

David smiled back and kissed her. "I'll write to the bishop tomorrow."

And Alice nodded, the last of the smile still on her lips, even as she felt fear claw inside her, for the storm clouds of war had swept over the horizon, through Goswell, and right to their very own hearth.

Three months later Alice stood on Goswell's train platform and smiled with determined cheer as David boarded a train for Barrow. He had joined the Border Regiment, and would be posted initially at an army base in the south, and that was all Alice was to know. It gave her a jolt when one of the young soldiers enlisting called him Padre; she saw him stepping into this new role with enthusiasm and vigour and she could not keep from feeling just a little bit left behind.

He took her in his arms before he left, and when he kissed her his lips were cold. A chilly wind gusted down the rail line and nearly blew off her hat, just as it had when she'd first arrived in Goswell almost exactly eight years ago. Laughing, David righted it again, and she could see from the sparkle in his eyes that he remembered the last time, when everything – the suffering and the joy – had still been before them. Then his gaze turned serious and he stared at her intently as if he wanted to memorize every crease and wrinkle of her face.

"I'm trying to get my fill of you," he said, "but it's impossible."

She laughed and hugged him, and he laughed back, and it felt almost like a regular day, like nothing momentous was going to happen. She clung to that feeling even as he grew serious once more. "I love you, Alice. And I shall pray for you every day. Stay safe for me."

"You are the one who must stay safe," Alice told him, and he smiled and gave her one last kiss.

"I shall. And I shall write to you as often as I can."

"As shall I."

The whistle blew then and Alice stepped back as David boarded the train with a dozen others, all of them looking as exuberant as schoolboys heading off to a cricket match.

The doors closed, and with a puff of white smoke the train pulled away, down the track towards the sea before curving southward towards Millom. The little crew of women and old men who had seen the soldiers off stood unspeaking on the platform, a stunned silence seeming to have taken hold of everyone. They had all said goodbye to someone – a son, a brother, a father, a husband – all of them gone now. Slowly people began to turn away towards their homes; Alice heard a few remarks about how they might be back by Easter, to which no one answered because they all knew it wasn't true.

Alice shivered as another gust of wind knocked her hat once more, and she clapped it firmly to her head before she began the lonely walk to the vicarage.

The house felt unusually quiet as she let herself in, which was ridiculous, since David hardly made much noise. Yet she could feel his absence like a palpable thing, an emptiness in herself. She stood in the front foyer with its drab tiles and soaring ceiling and remembered how cold and unfamiliar everything had seemed when she'd first arrived. It had become home in the last eight years; she had worked hard for it to be so. Yet standing there now, it felt unfamiliar again, and as cold and lonely as it had been that first night.

"Pull yourself together," Alice said under her breath, her tone determinedly brisk. She took off her hat and coat and hung both up by the door. "You cannot go to pieces the moment David's gone. There'll be too much to do to feel sorry for yourself even for a second."

She walked through the house, every room seeming to ring with emptiness, and finally to the kitchen, where Mrs Sutherland was measuring out sugar from the big ceramic jar.

"A half cup to last us," she said grimly, "and I was going to bake a cake."

Alice moved the big brass kettle onto the range. "Why can't you buy more?"

Mrs Sutherland tutted. "Rationing starts next week, don't you know? Bacon, butter, and sugar to start, but who knows what's next."

"Rationing," Alice repeated, rather wonderingly, for she had not thought of such a thing, although she knew she must have heard it on the wireless.

"You probably don't remember it from the last war," Mrs Sutherland said with a sniff. "Started with butter and sugar, just the same, but soon it went to all sorts. Meat, margarine, even cheese and eggs."

Alice had only vague memories of the last war, and she could not remember concerning herself with meat or margarine. Now, however, she recognized she might feel rather differently.

"What is our sugar ration, then?"

"Eight ounces a week for each of us."

"Eight ounces?" Alice shook her head. "We'll have to save up if we wish to eat cake. And I shall stop taking sugar in my tea."

Mrs Sutherland's reply was an eloquent silence, and with a wry grimace Alice knew the housekeeper didn't think much of her sacrifice.

"I've been thinking," Mrs Sutherland said as the kettle began to whistle and she reached for the chipped brown teapot they used only in the kitchen. "It would be good to have a man around here, what with the Reverend gone."

"I suppose," Alice said doubtfully, for she could not see what Mrs Sutherland meant.

"My son Harry is a good boy," the older woman continued. She poured Alice a cup of tea and despite Alice's just-voiced resolution, added two heaped teaspoonfuls of sugar from the jar. Alice did not object. "He's out of work at the moment, and he can't go in as a soldier on account of his feet."

"His feet?"

"Flat," Mrs Sutherland said succinctly. "Very disappointed, he was. But he could do a useful turn around here, I reckon. You know the boy who did the gardening for the vicarage and the church has joined up already?"

"Has he?" Alice had never really concerned herself with the garden, extensive as it was. A boy came in twice a week to weed the beds and trim the lawn, and occasionally when the weather was fine she took a turn about it, but that was all.

"You'll need someone to manage them," Mrs Sutherland pointed out and Alice took a sip of her sweet tea.

"I suppose," she said after a moment. "But won't we turn most of it over to a vegetable garden?" She and David had heard about the new "Dig for Victory" campaign on the wireless only a few nights ago, and David had joked that the churchwardens would make him resign if Alice dug over the church's prized rose garden.

"The royal family has promised to dig theirs over," Alice had replied. "Surely a good example to follow."

Now Mrs Sutherland nodded her agreement. "Certainly we should have a vegetable garden. And we'll want a man around, won't we, for the heavy digging. I'd feel safer too."

Alice nodded slowly. She liked the idea of more company, even the unknown Sutherland boy. Yesterday two of the housemaids had resigned to take up positions elsewhere, one in a munitions factory and one to train as a nurse. Tilly, the last housemaid, would surely leave as well; everyone had a job to do, a part to play in the war effort. Even, Alice thought with a surge of something close to satisfaction, her.

"I suppose it would be nice to have another person about," she said. "Where would he live?"

"Where the last boy lived, in that little cottage in the corner of the church yard."

"Oh yes, of course." She'd seen it, a little stone cottage built right into the corner of the cemetery, rather a rough sort of place. "I suppose your son could have it. But you'll have to talk to the churchwardens about that."

"Oh, I have," Mrs Sutherland said airily. "And what's better, we'll have his ration book as well. So that's twenty-four ounces of sugar a week." And with a rather smug smile she put the jar of sugar back in the pantry.

CHAPTER FIFTEEN

Jane

Jane wandered through the churchyard, the chilly November wind seeming to cut right through her. In just under a week she was meant to leave for New York, and she hadn't told Andrew yet.

She was being ridiculous, she knew, to keep it from him. The longer she waited, the more difficult the conversation would become. And yet Andrew's absolute silence on the matter disconcerted her; he hadn't asked about her plans, or the telephone conversation she'd taken from Claudia a few nights ago, or what the childcare arrangements would be. His silence, Jane realized, felt accusatory; it was as if he were deliberately trying to make this difficult for her.

And it *was* difficult. She felt selfish for wanting to go, and then angry that she did, and then guilty that she was angry. It was a vicious, never-ending cycle of churning emotions. Sighing, she dug her hands deeper into the pockets of her waxed jacket, her head lowered against the wind. She'd learned through her wanderings that the churchyard had a back gate that led to a footpath that went to the beach, and she'd taken to walking it in the morning, after she'd cleared the breakfast things and put a load of washing in.

Her life, Jane thought, most certainly not for the first time, had become almost unbearably mundane. Laundry, dishes, making beds, taking a walk. She still hadn't done any of the painting or decorating that would surely make the vicarage feel more like a home. She'd lugged some paint tins into the dining room, which tended to be the warmest room in the house, but that was as far as she'd got.

If she indulged in a little amateur psychoanalysis, Jane knew she'd say she wasn't doing any decorating because she didn't want to make the vicarage a home. The less she did, the easier it would be to leave it all.

A ridiculous notion, Jane acknowledged with a sigh. Moving back to New York was virtually impossible. Even as she fantasized about it, she knew she couldn't uproot the children again. And as for Andrew… returning to the city was the last thing he wanted.

But what about me? What am I supposed to do?

Resolutely she pushed away those plaintive questions. In six days she'd be in New York, staying with Claudia and helping with the Women For Change fundraiser. Doing what she loved and did best.

And when you return?

Another thought to push away.

She rounded the corner of the churchyard and headed for the gate next to the funny little cottage she'd seen early on in her explorations. It had always looked abandoned, lonely and unloved, so she came to a sudden, shocked halt when the door opened and a man stepped out, squinting in the weak sunshine that filtered through the clouds.

"Good morning." He smiled wryly, accepting her surprise at his presence, and Jane found her voice.

"Good morning. I didn't know anyone lived here. It's looked abandoned for months."

"We just moved in. I'm renting it, for a while at least." He stuck one hand out. "Jonathan Davies."

"Jane Hatton." She shook his hand. He looked to be in

his mid-forties, with untidy, salt-and-pepper hair and pale blue eyes. He wore an old woollen jumper and faded jeans, and after letting go of her hand he dug his own hands into his jeans pockets. "Are you new to Goswell?" Jane asked.

"In a matter of speaking. I grew up here, but I've been living away – abroad, actually – for nearly twenty years."

"What made you come back?"

He smiled wryly and Jane realized the question had sounded rather incredulous, as if she could not imagine why anyone would come back to a place such as this. "My parents still live here, and I wanted to be closer to them. They're getting older, and I'd also like them to spend more time with my son."

From the way he spoke Jane had the distinct sense that there was not a Mrs Davies in this picture. She shifted her weight, another gust of wind seeming to blow straight through her. "How old is your son?"

"He's fourteen. He's over at Copeland Academy."

"Oh, really? My daughter's there too. She's fourteen as well."

"You don't sound like you're from around here."

"No." Jane grimaced wryly. "My husband is originally from Keswick, but we've been living in New York City for the last sixteen years."

Jonathan whistled softly. "A big change."

"Yes." Jane felt a lump rise in her throat and she swallowed hard.

He cocked his head, his smile sympathetic and understanding, and Jane had the absurd impulse to confide in him about how hard she was finding it. She had a strange feeling he would understand.

"Anyway." She cleared her throat, smiled brightly. "You're our nearest neighbour, you know. We live in the old vicarage."

She pointed to the steep, slate roof just visible over the church wall. "Perhaps you'd like to come to supper one evening? You and your son?"

"That would be lovely, thank you."

She felt a little jolt of surprise; she hadn't expected him to accept so readily. She'd made the invitation on the spur of the moment, not really meaning it, yet now she realized she would like the company, and perhaps Natalie and this boy would get along. "Is tomorrow evening too soon?"

"Not at all."

They made the necessary arrangements and then Jane continued her walk towards the beach, feeling a little cheered and yet still anxious about the conversation she knew she needed to have with Andrew.

She told him about meeting Jonathan that night, while they were all eating dinner at the scrubbed pine table in the kitchen. "And his son is in your year at school, Natalie – do you know him? A boy with the last name Davies?"

Natalie just shrugged in reply.

"Well, it will be nice to have some company," Andrew said genially. "I wonder where he's been living abroad."

"He didn't say. I expect we'll find out when they come for supper."

"I'm glad that Jonathan fellow is coming to supper," Andrew said again as they were getting ready for bed. "It's good you're finally meeting people."

Jane prickled instinctively, helplessly. "I've been meeting people all along, Andrew."

He sighed, the sound heavy. "I didn't mean it like that, Jane."

"How did you mean it?"

"Do you know," Andrew answered conversationally, "we

never used to bicker like this. We sound like children."

"You mean I sound like a child."

"*Jane.*" Andrew turned to her, his expression open and earnest and yet somehow bleak. "All I meant was, I'm glad. That's all."

Jane bit her lip. She felt near to tears for the second time in one day. "I'm sorry," she said after a moment. Andrew just nodded, and then, without even meaning to, she blurted, "I've booked my ticket to New York for Monday."

Andrew stilled. "This Monday? As in five days?"

"Yes."

He raked a hand through his hair. "That's rather sudden."

"Is it? I mentioned it weeks ago."

"Mentioned it, yes."

And then realization poured over her as if a bucket of icy water had tipped right on her head. "You didn't think I'd do it," she said slowly. "You were hoping I'd changed my mind. That's why you haven't said anything."

Andrew didn't answer for a moment. "Why haven't you said anything?" he finally asked quietly.

"Because—" She fell silent. "Because it seemed easier not to," she said at last.

Andrew sank onto the side of the bed, his shoulders rounded and slumped. "I wonder," he said, "how it's come to this."

Jane felt her heart lurch against her ribs at the quiet sorrow in his voice. "To what?"

"To us not being able to talk to each other. And when we do…" He trailed off, shaking his head, and Jane swallowed hard.

"Andrew…" But she didn't say anything else, because she didn't know what to say, or how to say it. Apologize? Explain? Attack? Defend?

"Go to New York," Andrew said quietly. "I know it's important to you, and I understand that, I do. So go, and when you come back, we'll talk. Really talk." He got into bed and Jane stood there for a moment, indecisive, unhappy, before she nodded once and climbed into bed beside him.

They lay there in the darkness and the silence, not touching, not speaking, and finally, uncomfortable and unhappy, she fell asleep.

The next day Jane went around the vicarage in a flurry of panicked realization that she could not invite someone to dinner with it looking like they'd moved in mere days ago. At this point she couldn't do much more than move the paint tins and hang a few pictures she'd left propped against various walls. They'd probably stay in the kitchen, anyway, she told herself, where it was warm.

She made a lamb casserole and slow-cooked it in the Aga, feeling almost absurdly domestic, and then attempted a cake which fell depressingly flat. A quick run to Tesco in Whitehaven sorted out the pudding; even though she now lived in the Land of Homemade Baking, she had no shame in serving a store-bought dessert to a man and his son. They were probably subsisting on takeaways and frozen pizza, anyway.

"So who is this guy?" Natalie asked when the children had returned home from school and were making toast in the kitchen, scattering the freshly wiped counter-tops with crumbs and globs of butter and jam.

"His name is Jonathan Davies, and he's moved into the little cottage in the churchyard."

"What little cottage?" Natalie asked in the same surly, suspicious tone, and Jane suppressed a sigh. Every interaction with her daughter had become a battlefield, even when they were just exchanging information.

"I know it," Merrie said. "Sophie and I play near there sometimes, when she's come round. I thought it was abandoned."

"It was, but he's renting it out now."

Merrie shivered with theatrical gusto. "It looks haunted. And dirty."

Jane had to agree on the dirty part, but hopefully Jonathan would sort it out in that regard.

"And his son is in my year?" Natalie asked, and this time her tone was intentionally, and revealingly, casual.

"Yes—"

"Ooh, Nat's got a boyfriend," Ben crooned, and Natalie turned to shove him rather viciously.

"Shut up."

"Oh, don't," Jane said wearily. "I've been running ragged all day trying to get ready for this dinner. I can't take your arguing now."

Natalie turned to glare at her. "You can never take our arguing," she said, and started to slink out of the kitchen.

Jane stilled. "Natalie!" she called sharply. Her daughter paused in mid-slink, her back to Jane, a curtain of dark hair covering her face. "What is that supposed to mean?" Natalie didn't answer and Jane tried to moderate her tone. "I'm serious, I want to know. What do you mean, I can never take it?"

Natalie hunched one bony shoulder in a shrug. "You're always tired out by us."

"Tired *out*—"

"After work."

Jane felt something cold enter her soul. "But I don't work any more."

"Well, whatever you do."

Jane tried to keep her voice light even though her insides writhed with a combination of guilt and resentment. The usual mix. "Are you trying to make me feel guilty?"

Natalie turned back to give her an affronted look. "You *asked.*"

"I know, but—" Jane hesitated, helpless, frustrated. "I'm not tired out by you." She turned to look at Merrie and Ben who were watching this exchange with a kind of fascinated wariness. "You're my children."

"So?"

Natalie's question hung in the air, unanswered. "So?" Jane finally repeated. "I just meant – I love you. You know that, don't you? I mean, really. I love you." She sounded desperate, she realized, as if she were afraid she had to convince them.

Natalie sighed and started to slope off once more. "Yeah, yeah," she said tiredly. "All parents love their children, right?" Which left Jane feeling as if she'd said nothing but cheap words.

She managed to push the conversation to the distant reaches of her mind by the time Jonathan arrived that evening with his son Will, a lanky, semi-spotty fourteen-year-old who had the same slinking, mooching walk as Natalie. They gazed balefully at each other as Andrew took their coats, both of them muttering some form of hello, and Ben eyed the older boy warily while Merrie did so with undisguised, innocent interest.

Eventually they made it to the kitchen for drinks and Andrew ushered Jonathan into the dining room, where he had laid a fire and was now pouring sherry with the enthusiastic bonhomie of a nineteenth-century vicar. Watching him, Jane felt a tug of amused affection and even love she hadn't felt in a long while. Tension had crept into every aspect of their relationship, and for a moment, with the fire crackling and Andrew smiling, she was glad for a little reprieve.

"So, Jane said you've recently moved back to Goswell?" Andrew asked as he handed Jane her sherry.

"Yes… just a week ago, actually."

"Where from?"

"Dubai."

Both Jane and Andrew made suitably impressed noises. "I imagine that makes for even more of a difference than we've experienced," Andrew said with a little laugh.

"The weather certainly does," Jonathan agreed. "No need for a swimming pool here, I'm afraid." Although he was smiling, Jane thought there was a rather grim cast to his features.

"No, no need for swimming pools," Andrew agreed. "Although someone told me there used to be a swimming pool by the beach – filled in ages ago, of course. Health and Safety."

"A swimming pool?" Jane repeated in disbelief. Even in August the weather had been freezing.

"Yes, down by the rocks. It was filled by sea water when the tide came in. I suppose people were hardier a generation or two ago. Didn't mind a chilly dip in the sea."

"Or the pool, as the case may be,'" Jonathan agreed, his expression lightening.

Jane wondered if she were imagining the slight edge to Andrew's tone. Was that remark about being hardy aimed at her – or was she just paranoid?

"So what finally brought you back to Cumbria?" Andrew asked as he refilled everyone's sherry. "Tired of the expat life?"

"Not exactly." Jonathan's mouth twisted wryly and he took a sip of his drink. "My wife and I divorced. She never took to life out there – and I can't really blame her, to be honest. It's so different. She ended up moving back here – she lives in Manchester – and we've worked out joint custody of Will. She has him most weekends and holidays, and I have him the remainder." He smiled, almost in apology. "Perhaps not your usual arrangement, but she prefers city life and the schools are better here. Will seems to be doing all right."

This last bit, Jane thought, seemed almost like a question, as if he were seeking reassurance. Yet neither she nor Andrew answered, for she knew they were both absorbing Jonathan's sad story, and she hoped she was the only one who wondered – however briefly – if their own story might have a similar ending.

CHAPTER SIXTEEN

Alice
Goswell, March 1940

Alice was determined to have a good war. The last few months hadn't been easy, yet she'd found herself almost embracing the challenges of food rations, blackouts, and no help in the house besides Mrs Sutherland.

As soon as the weather turned she was out in the garden with Mrs Sutherland's son Harry, a mostly silent lad of twenty who had taken up residence in the little cottage in the churchyard and helped her dig over the entirety of the vicarage garden. Mrs Dunston had been appalled when she saw the neat furrowed rows where once there had been velvet-green lawn and rose bushes.

"You'd think the vicarage would be spared," she said, a bit resentfully, and Alice had merely smiled and replied, "We must lead by example, Mrs Dunston."

Harry had told her that early potatoes should be planted around Easter, and she shocked the evening congregation when they saw her out in the dusk, dropping seed potatoes into the soil. Mrs Sutherland silently handed her a mug of weak tea when she came into the kitchen afterwards, every taut line of her body radiating disapproval that Alice had worked on the Sabbath.

Later that night Alice confessed her Sabbath-day labours in a letter to David, admitting that she was not perhaps as repentant as she should be. *There's just so much to do,* she wrote, the words coming fast on the page, her ink blotting. *And for once I feel able to do it.*

She became friends, of a sort, with Harry; he never said much, but he'd show up at the kitchen door with a seed catalogue or a new cutting, and Alice would exclaim over it as if he'd given her a rare treasure, and usher him in for a mug of tea at the kitchen table.

"I didn't expect to take to gardening," she told Mrs Sutherland one evening as she paged through a catalogue, marking the things she wanted. "I'd never done it before."

"Needs must," Mrs Sutherland replied, and Alice couldn't tell if she approved or not.

"They do, indeed," she answered cheerfully. "Harry says we could do the walled garden over in potatoes – it would be enough to last us all winter."

"The walled garden," Mrs Sutherland repeated, and now Alice could tell she disapproved.

"Why not? It's just a few twisty old fruit trees now, and we can plant around them."

"It was an orchard back in my day," Mrs Sutherland said with a sniff. "As lovely as you could wish. Mrs Sanderson always used to come in first in the competition for best damsons at the fete."

"Perhaps that was more on account of her being Mrs Sanderson rather than her damsons," Alice answered a bit tartly, and Mrs Sutherland shot her a suspicious look.

"What do you mean? They were lovely, those damsons."

"I'm sure they were. And the potatoes will be lovely too, especially when we're eating our fill of them in January."

To this Mrs Sutherland only sniffed, but Alice was impervious. The garden had fired her imagination as nothing else had yet in Goswell, and she was determined to make a success of it.

As April came to a close she heard of another way to serve her country; Goswell would be receiving a trainload of child evacuees from Liverpool.

"Who will take the children?" she asked Mrs Sutherland, who gave a typical sniff.

"Farmers, most like. They need help with the work."

"But some of the children will be little—"

"Who wants another mouth to feed in these days? And *some* of those children – most, I'd say – will be dirty and ill-mannered. You have no idea what city children are like."

"Neither do you," Alice pointed out reasonably, to which she got precisely no answer. "I'd like to take one," she said after a moment and Mrs Sutherland stared at her in disbelief.

"You? Take a child?"

Alice bristled at the housekeeper's incredulity. She was nearly thirty years old, and certainly capable of taking care of a child. "Why shouldn't I?" she asked, striving to stay reasonable. "I certainly have the space. With all the housemaids gone, there are nine spare bedrooms."

"Still. A woman alone..." Mrs Sutherland shook her head. "I don't know."

"There are plenty of women raising children alone," Alice returned with spirit, "what with their men off to war." She added quietly, needing to say it, "I would have been raising a child or more alone if Rose had lived." Mrs Sutherland didn't answer, and Alice continued briskly, "I should certainly take a child – it's practically my duty. When are they arriving?"

"On tomorrow's night train." Mrs Sutherland parted with the information reluctantly. "Around six o'clock, or whenever it comes. You can't count on anything these days."

All the next day Alice thought about meeting the child evacuees. She would like a little boy, she decided, about five or six years old. A girl would be too hard; she'd be reminded of her baby daughter. But a boy... a boy with David's impishness, with tousled hair and muddy knees...

She felt a brief blaze of pain for the kind of child she'd never had, and she told herself sharply to stop that nonsense, because taking in an evacuee was no replacement for being a mother, and she knew that.

Yet still she dreamed.

At half past five Alice left the vicarage and walked down the main street to the train station. The sky was a pale, fragile blue and the sheep, recently deprived of their lambs, bleated plaintively.

A few people were milling around, hunched in their overcoats and scarves because even though it was the end of April the wind was, as always, bitter.

Alice only half-listened to some of the mutterings about the dangers of taking in a child from the city slums; horror stories of being poisoned by strychnine or murdered in your bed by some unfortunate, urban child.

A few of the men from the outlying farms drove up in their wagons, surveyed the crowd impassively and sucked on their teeth as they waited for their newest labourers.

The train didn't pull in until a quarter to seven, and by then everyone was restless and numb with cold, the wind blowing far fiercer now, and they tucked their hands under their armpits and stamped their feet, impatient to get what they came for and go home.

Alice watched the first children come off the train, their faces city-pale and smudged with coal dust. They wore woollen coats with gas masks round their necks and pitifully thin cardboard suitcases bumped against their knees. Labels bearing their names were pinned to their backs, and a harassed and tired-looking woman herded them off the train and towards the village hall. Alice saw that some of the little ones were crying quietly, their grubby faces made even grubbier by their tears, and she felt a lump rise in her throat.

"Poor little things," she whispered, and Flora Welton fell into step beside her.

"I hope they go to good homes. I can't bear to think of my Jamie as alone as all that."

"Will you take one, Flora?"

"If only we had the space! Mum's house is fit to burst as it is, and Jamie shares with me." She shook her head regretfully. "But you will, won't you, Mrs James?" In all their years of friendship Alice had never been able to get Flora to call her by her Christian name.

"I hope so. I'm all alone up at the vicarage. It seems a shame to waste the space, and I'd like the company."

"I'm sure you would, what with the Reverend gone. Is he well?"

"Yes, he's well." David was, as he'd been during their courtship, a champion letter writer. He wrote two or three times a week – long, newsy letters with stories that made Alice laugh aloud and almost feel as if he were right in the room with her. Sometimes she would look up from reading one of his letters and blink in surprise that she was alone, the house yawning in silent emptiness all around her.

Now she and Flora followed the rest of the crowd to the village hall. By the time they arrived the billeting officer, a thin, sharp-looking woman Alice didn't recognize, had lined up the children on the stage where the band usually was for the occasional ceilidhs. They looked even paler and dirtier under the bright electric lights, and the officer cried out, "Pick which one you like. Quick, now, it's getting late."

Alice stood there, frozen in an awful indecision while others started forward. Some smiled kindly at the children, others simply grabbed them by an elbow and marched them off. The sturdy-looking older children went first to the farmers, and Alice watched as a pair of spinster sisters picked two angelic-looking twin boys, no more than five or six.

"You'd best hurry, or there will be none left," Flora said with a little laugh and with a jolt of surprise Alice realized she was right. She'd been so horrified by the thought of having to actually pick a child – and thus *not* pick another – that they'd almost all gone by the time she approached the stage.

In fact there were only two children left, a brawny looking boy with freckles and large ears who looked to be about nine or ten, and a scrawny, surly-looking girl of about twelve who scowled at everyone she met, her thin arms crossed over her chest.

"Hello," Alice said shyly, addressing them both, but one of the farming men strode forward and jerked his thumb towards the boy.

"I'll take you as well. Be quick about it."

The boy scrambled off the stage and Alice was left staring at the girl, who glared back at her with insolent defiance.

"I'll take you, then," she said as cheerfully as she could, and the girl lifted her chin.

"Didn't have much choice, did you?" she drawled, her Liverpudlian accent so thick that it took Alice a moment to decipher what she was saying.

"Well, never mind that. My husband David always says God's design can be seen in everything, even the mistakes."

The girl raised her eyebrows, her mouth twisting in a sneer. "So I'm a mistake, then?"

"No, of course not," Alice said hurriedly. "Never that. I'm glad to have you." She smiled and stuck out her hand. "My name is Alice James. What's your name?"

The girl didn't answer for a moment, just let her gaze wander up and down Alice, so she felt as if she were the one being inspected – and coming up short. "Vera," she finally said. "Vera Miller."

"Well, Vera, I live in the vicarage down the road. Let's get you settled, shall we, because it's rather cold and dark out, and I'm sure you need a nice hot meal."

Vera didn't answer, just sloped off the stage and followed Alice towards the doors, her suitcase banging against her scrawny knees. Alice spoke to the billeting officer and then she was released, with Vera, into the night, her heart thudding hard as she wondered just what she had got herself into.

They walked in silence down the street to the vicarage, and it was dark when they arrived. Mrs Sutherland had left an hour ago, and Alice only hoped she'd left something warm on the range for supper.

"You must be hungry," she said to Vera as they stepped inside the foyer, and Vera shrugged, then shivered.

"Cor, it's cold in here."

"I'm sorry about that. The vicarage is terribly draughty and I'm afraid coal is in short supply these days. We spend most of our time in the kitchen."

"You'll want me in there anyway, won't you," Vera said and Alice glanced at her in surprise.

"What do you mean?"

Vera hunched her shoulders. "To work and the like."

"I didn't bring you here to be some kind of unpaid

servant," Alice said gently. She laid one hand on Vera's pitifully thin shoulder and felt the girl tremble underneath her touch. "I brought you here because I would like you to have a nice, warm, safe place to stay, and because I'm a bit lonely now my husband's away."

"Is he the vicar?"

"Yes, and he's gone to be a chaplain with the army." Alice smiled and dropped her hand from Vera's shoulder. "I miss him very much. Come into the kitchen where it's warm."

A few minutes later they were both settled at the pine table with plates of Mrs Sutherland's lamb stew in front of them. It was hot and filling, which was about all that could be said for it, but Vera ate like she hadn't seen a hot meal for a week. Alice felt cheered by this, even though the girl barely said two words to her over the course of the meal.

"You must be tired," she said when Vera had scraped her plate clean. "Come upstairs and I'll show you your room."

She'd picked the bedroom over the kitchen for Vera, for it was the warmest room in the house. Vera stood in the doorway as Alice laid her case by the bureau. It was smaller than the other bedrooms, but cosy, and she'd picked a vase of daffodils and put them by the washstand.

"This all for me?" Vera asked disbelievingly, and Alice smiled and said, "Of course it is." Vera gave her a contemptuous glance, as if she couldn't believe how daft Alice was, giving her a room all to herself. "I hope you like it," Alice added, and Vera just snorted and went over to her suitcase.

"It's all right, I s'pose."

Alice nodded, and then after a moment when neither of them said anything at all she nodded again and said, "I'll leave you to it then, Vera. Do let me know if you need anything." Vera didn't answer, and Alice left the room, closing the door behind her.

She'd known it might not be easy, she told herself as she got ready for bed. It was bound to be uncomfortable and awkward at first – and yet. She still felt disappointed and uncertain, and despite the addition to her household, lonelier than ever.

She let out a little sigh as she stared out at the endless darkness, the only sound the rattle of the windowpanes and the mournful bleating of sheep. Nothing in life, she supposed, ever turned out the way you expected or even hoped it to. She'd learned that lesson many times already, and it seemed as if God wished to teach it to her again.

Jane

The day after Jonathan and Will came to dinner, Jane told the children about New York. She wasn't sure what to expect, and so she kept her tone and expression determinedly cheerful as she explained it all after school, over toast and tea at the kitchen table.

"You mean you'll be gone for nearly a month?" Merrie said in a small voice and Jane only just kept her smile in place.

"More like three weeks." Three and a half, but three sounded better.

Merrie bit her lip. "You'll miss the carol concert down at the lifeboat station. I'm singing. My whole year group is."

"Oh – well, Daddy will go, won't he? And when I come home you can tell me all about it."

Merrie didn't answer, and Jane fought the guilt that had started rushing through her, an unrelenting river of unwanted emotion.

"What about after school?" Ben asked. "Who will be here?"

"You don't really need anyone, do you?" Jane said, trying now for a kind of jocularity. "You're nearly twelve, Ben – Merrie will go to Sophie's until you and Nat come home."

"So I'm supposed to be Merrie's babysitter every day until Dad comes home?" Natalie said with a sneer, the first words she'd spoken since Jane had begun the conversation.

"Merrie's hardly some toddler you need to chase after," Jane said as reasonably as she could. She glanced at Merrie, who was looking pale-faced and possibly near tears.

"What about dinner?" Ben asked. "Dad can only do pasta or eggs."

Jane felt the anger start to rush in with the guilt. "I've made some casseroles for the freezer," she said, still hanging onto her cheerful tone, if only by a thread. "And you can all chip in, you know – Natalie makes a mean hamburger."

Natalie made a sound close to a snort. "So I'm supposed to watch her and make dinner? What am I, a slave?"

Merrie made a small, hurt sound and rushed out of the room. Jane lost the cheer.

"Natalie, why do you have to talk like that? Merrie's no trouble – and if making dinner turns you into a slave, then obviously I am one too."

"You've been making dinner for, like, a *month*," Natalie snarled. "And you're already tired of it. Some slave you are."

"Is that what you want?" Jane demanded, her voice rising shrilly. "For me to be some kind of domestic servant to you all?"

Natalie's face had turned red with anger and her eyes glittered with tears. "I want you to be a *mom*," she shouted, "but that's something you've never wanted to be."

"That is completely unfair—" Jane shouted back, stopping when Natalie stomped from the room. She turned back to Ben who was picking at his rather dirty fingernails, his face averted from hers. "Ben – you don't believe that, do you? You don't think that?" She sounded, Jane thought, desperate. Uncertain.

Ben just shrugged. "Dunno," he said, and then he sloped off upstairs too.

Jane sank onto a chair, her head in her hands. Her mind was spinning with the accusations Natalie had hurled at her. *I want you to be a mom.* But she'd always been that. She felt the injustice of it burn inside her. In this day and age, couldn't a woman have a career and a family? Why were her children – and, if she were honest, her husband – determined to drag her back to the Dark Ages, with a frilly apron tied around her waist, chained to this damned Aga?

Resolutely she rose from the table and went to find Merrie. She'd deal with them, she decided, from youngest to oldest.

Merrie was huddled on her bed, her nose buried in a book with a bright pink cover.

"What are you reading?" Jane asked as she came to sit on the edge of the bed.

Merrie didn't look up from her book. "Just something I got from the library," she mumbled.

"Merrie..." Jane took a breath and hesitantly touched her daughter's soft, dark hair, where it curled around her forehead. "Going to New York for a little while has nothing to do with how I feel about you," she said, the words coming slowly, awkwardly. "You know that, don't you? I love you, and I'll miss you very much when I'm away."

Merrie didn't answer, and her face stayed determinedly behind the book's pink covers. Jane sighed and stroked her daughter's hair, tucking a lock behind Merrie's little ear. "Say something to me, sweetheart. Tell me what you're feeling."

Merrie's fingers tensed on the book cover. "I don't want you to go," she finally said in a voice so small Jane had to strain to hear it.

"Oh, Merrie..." Jane sighed, not knowing how to answer, or what comfort she could give.

Merrie finally looked up from her book, her eyes seeming huge in her face, and glassy with tears. "Why don't you like it here, Mummy?" she asked.

Jane felt as if her heart had frozen in her chest. Her hand stilled on Merrie's hair. "I'm not going to New York because I don't like it here," she said finally, and Merrie just stared at her, waiting. Jane knew her daughter deserved more of an answer. All of her children did. "Merrie, it's not as simple as liking or not liking a place. I admit, I do find it difficult to adjust to life here. I don't have a school to go to like you and Ben and Natalie do, and I'm used to working all day long. It's been hard for me, but that has nothing to do with you, or how much I love you."

"But you'd still rather go back to New York."

Yes. Jane smiled, or at least tried to. "I'm going back to help out a friend," she said after a second's pause. "And just for a few weeks."

"And after that? Will you keep going back to help out?"

"No—" Jane heard the waver of uncertainty in her voice and her hand dropped from Merrie's head. Did she really want to make that promise? "Probably not," she amended, and Merrie returned resolutely to her book.

The conversations with Ben and Natalie didn't go any better; if anything, they were worse. Ben just answered monosyllabically to Jane's by-the-book assurances that she loved him, she'd miss him terribly, and she was doing this to help a friend.

He barely looked up from his DS the entire time, finally raising his head only to say, "I get it, Mom. You do whatever, OK?"

Natalie didn't speak at all. She sat curled up on a corner of her bed – her room, Jane saw, was a complete sty – picking flakes of black nail varnish off her nails.

"Natalie, my going to New York isn't about me wanting or not wanting to be a mom." Silence. "I love being a mom.

Your mom." Jane took a breath, fighting the impulse to take her daughter by the shoulders and shake her. "But like I told Merrie, it's been hard for me to settle into life here. It seems like it's been hard for you too, so I hope you can understand a little bit of what I'm feeling."

Natalie finally looked at her, her stare malevolent. "I'm not going back to New York."

"Because you have school—"

"I don't *want* to go back to New York," Natalie cut her off icily.

Jane sighed. "It's only for three weeks."

"Whatever."

Not trusting herself to say anything else, Jane turned and left the room. She started towards the kitchen, intending to make dinner, but suddenly she couldn't stand the thought. All she'd done since she'd moved to this awful place was housework. Chores. Cooking, cleaning, making sure everyone else's lives ran smoothly.

And what about mine?

Without even thinking about what she was doing, she grabbed her coat and headed outside. It was just after five o'clock and already pitch black. She dug her hands into the pockets of her coat and struck out towards the village, turning abruptly to the beach road. She didn't want to see anyone.

She walked quickly, her head down against the wind, empty of thoughts or any emotion except for a blind, pulsing anger. Eventually she ended up at the beach; the tide was out and the sand stretched away into the darkness so she couldn't even see where the water began.

She stood for a moment on the concrete promenade that ran along the beach, the wind whipping her hair about her face. She didn't know how long she stood there, or what she thought or even felt; everything in her, from her toes to her heart, seemed to have gone numb.

Eventually she realized it must have got quite late, and she turned around and headed back to the house. By the time she came to the church lane she saw the house blazing with lights and Andrew's car in the drive.

Steeling herself for whatever came next, Jane let herself into the house.

She stood for a moment in the vestibule, quiet and cold, and took off her coat and boots. She could hear, faintly, sounds from the kitchen, a clank of pans, a sudden, surprising burst of laughter, and bizarrely, unfairly, she felt hurt. Left out, even though she'd excluded herself.

Slowly she walked towards the kitchen and stood in the doorway. Merrie was laying the table, and Ben and Natalie were bickering good-naturedly by the sink. Andrew stood by the Aga, flipping pancakes.

The room fell to silence, or at least it seemed so to Jane, when they saw her standing there, her hair still wind-blown, her cheeks red with cold.

"Did you have a nice walk?" Andrew finally asked in what Jane thought was an overly pleasant voice.

"Fine." She couldn't think of anything else to say. Andrew turned back to the Aga and Merrie laid another plate. Ben stared at Jane for a moment before he snapped a dish towel at Natalie and she grabbed it; a second later they were involved in a tug of war. Jane thought about remonstrating with them, but then wearily, she decided there was no point. Everyone was getting on with things without her, so without another word she turned around and left the room. She didn't come down for dinner.

She stayed in her bedroom, like a scolded child, while Andrew sorted the children out with homework and bedtime.

Eventually, sometime after ten, he came into the room and Jane could tell by his very precise movements that he was angry.

"Are you ill?" he asked after he'd taken off his shoes and tie and was unbuttoning his shirt. "Is something wrong with you?"

Jane rolled over onto her side, away from him. "I'm on sabbatical," she said and she heard Andrew's cufflinks clatter onto the top of the bureau.

"I thought that was next week."

"Maybe it starts now."

"Jane." The bed creaked as he sat down on it. "Can you please tell me what's going on? I came home tonight to a dark house and the children not knowing where you were. Merrie's only eight, you know."

"You think I don't know my own daughter's age?"

"She was scared."

"I was gone for less than an hour."

"Without any warning—"

"I *know*, Andrew." She swung up from the bed, stared at him rather wildly. "I know, OK? I was fed up. I'd told them about New York and they were all angry, saying I wasn't a good mom—" Her voice broke and she lay down again, curling into a ball, her faced pressed into the pillow. She felt Andrew's hand on her shoulder. "You don't think that, do you?" she asked in a low voice. "You don't believe I'm a bad mom just because I liked my job?"

"No, of course not." He squeezed her shoulder. "But if you're asking if I think that both of us working full time had an effect on the children, then the answer is yes."

"I didn't ask that," Jane said, rolling over to gaze at him wearily. "But it's good to know what you think."

"Don't you think it had an effect, Jane? Honestly?"

"I suppose." She knew she couldn't really deny it, yet

everything in her resisted, because it felt like a judgment on her.

"At least you're not getting migraines or ulcers now," Andrew continued. "I know you miss your job, but it was practically killing you. All those last-minute emergencies, worries about donors – I could see it, Jane, even if you couldn't."

"I suppose," Jane said after a moment, her voice toneless, "it's hard to go from a hundred to zero."

"I understand that."

"Going back to New York is just a compromise, Andrew. It's a way for me to adjust. Do you understand that?"

He didn't answer for a moment, and she knew he didn't understand it. And maybe she was deceiving herself, thinking that going back to New York could in any way help her adjustment to life here in Goswell. "If I stay here, I'll go mad," she said quietly, and Andrew's hand dropped from her shoulder.

"I didn't realize it was that bad," he said stiffly, and Jane sighed.

"I'm sorry. I didn't mean to sound melodramatic."

They were both silent, and Jane felt as if nothing had been resolved.

CHAPTER SEVENTEEN

Alice
Goswell, April 1940

Since it was Mrs Sutherland's day off Alice woke early to stoke the range and get the kitchen warm and cheerful for Vera, despite it being another grey day with raindrops spattering the windowpanes. After a good night's sleep she felt less dispirited and more determined to make this work, to welcome Vera properly and help her to settle in. She'd start with a fry-up.

Fortunately, living in a farming community meant they had plenty of eggs and milk. One of the local dairy farmers had taken it as his God-given duty to keep the vicarage supplied with both, and now Alice hummed under her breath as she fried several eggs and cut thick slabs of bread for toast. She brewed a pot of tea and set the table for two, even going out in the garden to pick a few late daffodils to make things nicer for the young girl. She took a moment to survey the garden she and Harry had worked on all spring, the potato plants coming up in proud, neat rows, along with some early lettuce. Harry had told her it was best to wait until May to plant things like peas and carrots, maybe when they had a nice warm spell.

"Whenever that will be," Alice had teased, and Harry, a normally taciturn young man, had cracked a rare smile.

Back inside, she finished her preparations and then went upstairs to fetch Vera. The house was almost eerily quiet, and when Alice poked her head into Vera's room she was surprised to see the bed empty and unmade. Frowning, she straightened the covers and went back out into the hall. Perhaps the girl had decided to have a little look round. What child could resist exploring a huge house like this?

She peered in a few of the other bedrooms, but they were all empty and silent. Then she heard a footfall from her own room, and her heart gave a funny little lurch. She walked quickly to her room, and saw Vera spin around in front of her bureau, her furtive expression becoming at once both guilty and defiant.

"Vera—"

"What?" The girl lifted her head in challenge. "I was just looking around."

"I can understand that, but you should ask first," Alice said quietly. "I wouldn't go poking through your things, you know."

Vera just shrugged, her dark eyes still sparking defiance, and Alice's heart sank. It did not seem a particularly good beginning to their first day together. "I've made breakfast," she said, trying to inject a more cheerful note into her voice. "Why don't we go down to the kitchen."

With another shrug Vera slunk past her, and that was when Alice saw her slip something into the pocket of her dress. Her heart sank further, as if a stone had lodged in her chest. Had Vera actually taken – *stolen* – something from her bureau? The thought filled her with a kind of weary despair as well as a personal hurt.

Telling herself not to be so suspicious, she followed Vera downstairs and attempted to keep up a steady stream of chatter as she served out the eggs and toast and even a few precious rashers of bacon she'd saved for this occasion. Vera barely spoke at all.

After the nearly silent meal Alice suggested she show Vera the garden. The rain had cleared and a pale, fragile-looking blue sky had emerged from behind the shreds of cloud, the spring sun shining benevolently upon the still-wet grass.

Outside Alice breathed in the clean smell of dirt and grass and rain, and turned to Vera with a smile. "We've started our own Victory garden," she said, gesturing to the half-acre of lawn that was now freshly turned earth. "We've planted potatoes and lettuce so far, but Harry – that's the gardener, and Mrs Sutherland's son – has plans for loads of things. Carrots, peas, parsnips, beans…" She trailed off, because Vera was glaring at her as if she'd said something particularly offensive.

"So that's why you brung me here, then."

"Brought," Alice said automatically. "And I don't understand what you mean."'

"To work all this." With one contemptuous sweep of her arm Vera gestured to – and seemed to dismiss – Alice's prized plot.

Alice felt her cheeks heat as a surprising spurt of anger surged through her. "We all work alongside each other here, Vera," she said evenly. "So yes, I'd expect you to help. But if you think I've brought you here to act as some unpaid skivvy, then you're quite mistaken." Vera said nothing, just folded her arms across her skinny chest and looked mutinous. "It could be fun, you know," Alice said in a gentler tone. "I'd never gardened before, but I do like growing things now. Seeing something you planted yourself come to life—" She pointed to a pale green shoot of a potato plant. "It's amazing, really." And it restored her faith in a benevolent and sovereign God. Vera still said nothing, and Alice suppressed a sigh. This entire morning had clearly got off to a rather dreadful start.

"Look," she tried again, "I don't want to argue. I'd like you to settle in here and enjoy yourself. Tomorrow I'll show you around the village school."

Vera thrust her lip out. "I'm too old for school."

"At twelve?" Alice tried to hide her dismay. "I should hardly think so. Wouldn't you enjoy being in school and learning things?" Vera just shrugged. Alice forced herself to smile. "Well, we'll have a look round tomorrow. Why don't we go inside, because it looks like it's going to rain again."

Sure enough, the fragile blue sky had darkened ominously, and the first raindrops spattered against the windows as they came into the front vestibule.

Vera went upstairs to her bedroom and after tidying up the breakfast things, Alice decided to slip out and go to the church. She was reluctant to leave Vera alone in the house, especially considering her earlier snooping, but since David's departure she'd taken to slipping into the church and breathing in the comforting scents of incense and dust, sometimes going to his vestments and touching them; they still smelled, ever so faintly, of his aftershave.

Now she stood in the dim silence of the church and blinked hard, for just managing the morning with Vera had tried her more than she'd expected. If David were here, he would know exactly how to handle her, she thought. With his customary firm gentleness and wry humour, Vera would have been won over in minutes.

She went into the vestry and opened the cupboard containing David's vestments, but as she leaned in to breathe in their scent she could only smell beeswax. Someone must have polished the cupboard door, and the comforting smell she associated with David was gone.

She closed her eyes, a stab of disappointment piercing

her so sharply it almost took her breath away. Losing this little bit of David, as silly as it might have seemed, made him feel farther away than ever, and her lonelier than ever.

With a little sigh she closed the door and turned around, suppressing a gasp of dismay as she saw that the church silver had been left out on the table instead of locked away in the safe. The church had some lovely pieces of communion silver from the 1600s, and they had been one of David's pride and joys. John Bearman, the retired clergyman who had taken over as vicar while David was away, was, Alice knew, quite absent-minded, and must have left it out after the midweek communion.

Sighing, she took it from the table and put it on top of the safe, where at least it was mostly hidden. She didn't possess a key, but she would talk to the Reverend Bearman at the first opportunity. Goswell was a safe place, but it didn't bear thinking about how awful it would be if the church's most precious possession went missing.

Back outside the sky had cleared once more and Alice's spirits lifted a little. Perhaps this afternoon she could do some baking with Vera; she'd saved two weeks' coupons of sugar for such a purpose.

"Alice, my dear girl!" Alice turned to see Mrs Dunston, the wife of one of the churchwardens, walk briskly towards her. "I must say I was completely shocked when I heard you were taking in one of those wretched evacuees. Are you quite sure you know what you are doing, my dear?"

Mrs Dunston's tone clearly indicated that she did not think Alice knew at all. "Perfectly sure, Elizabeth," Alice answered pleasantly. "I have eight bedrooms going spare. It's only sensible to make use of one of them."

"But an evacuee from who knows where—"

"Liverpool," she interjected, but Elizabeth Dunston simply forged on relentlessly.

"And you all by yourself, with the vicarage so remote – anything could happen—"

"I'm hardly all by myself. Harry Sutherland has taken the groundskeeper's cottage, as you know, and Mrs Sutherland comes in most weekdays. I'm sure I'll manage quite well."

"And does David approve?"

Alice bristled. She was not a child, to be so reprimanded, even if when she'd first arrived in Goswell she might have acted a bit like one. She was twenty-eight years old now, living on her own, and she was quite finished with Elizabeth Dunston treating her as if she were dim-witted. "I have not yet had the opportunity to inform him," she replied coolly, "but I assure you, he will be pleased I am doing my Christian duty."

"But you can't trust those city children," Elizabeth protested, and she almost sounded afraid. For a second Alice felt a flicker of sympathy for the woman. Elizabeth Dunston had been born and bred in Goswell, and had most likely never met a city child in her life, yet she seemed to genuinely believe what she was saying. "I've heard they're all thieves, or worse."

"I assure you, I am fine," Alice said, and with a curt nod of farewell, hurried back to the vicarage. She didn't regret taking Vera in, but as she recalled how the girl had slipped something into her pocket after leaving her bedroom, Alice wondered disconsolately if there might be some truth to Elizabeth Dunston's words.

Back inside, Alice found Vera in the girl's bedroom once more, flipping through the pages of a rather lurid-looking film magazine she must have brought from Liverpool. She didn't even glance up when Alice appeared in the doorway.

"Well, then," she said in a voice full of brisk cheer, "I thought we could do some baking today. Do you like scones?"

Vera did not lift her gaze from the magazine. "I s'pose."

"Or what about biscuits?" When Vera still did not look up Alice almost twitched the magazine from the girl's nail-bitten fingers, but she resisted. "What would you like to bake, Vera?"

Finally the girl glanced up. "I dunno how to bake."

"Did you never help your mother in the kitchen?"

The girl's mouth twisted sardonically. "My mum never spent much time in the kitchen."

Gingerly Alice took a step into the room. "Tell me about her," she invited. "And your life back – back in Liverpool. Do you have brothers and sisters?"

Her expression still darkly guarded, Vera shook her head. "Mum didn't even want me, so she made sure not to have any more, didn't she?"

"And what about your father?"

"I dunno who he is."

"Oh – oh." Alice tried not to blush, although she was shocked. Perhaps Mrs Dunston had a point, if a rather unfair one. City children were rather different. Then she remembered that Jamie Welton was just like Vera, born without knowing his father, and Flora was as lovely a person as Alice had ever known. "Well, I'm sorry for that," she said with a kindly smile. "But I do hope, in time, you might come to see Goswell – and me – as part of your home and family."

Vera simply stared at her disbelievingly, and this time Alice did blush. She felt, with that simple statement, that she'd revealed more about her own unhappy state than Vera's.

CHAPTER EIGHTEEN

Jane

Remembrance Day Sunday dawned bright and cold, and the mood in the ancient church was sombre as Jane entered with Andrew at her side and the children falling in behind them. The pews were full; everyone had come out to remember the dead, dressed in dark clothing, their faces serious or contemplative. A line-up of various village groups, from the Rainbows and Cubs to the few remaining veterans, were getting ready to process down the aisle.

As Jane waited for the service to begin her mind drifted to Alice and David James. Strange to think Alice must have sat in one of these pews, listened to her husband preach. Had her children lined up next to her in the pew, proudly turned out? Jane had never learned if she'd had children.

When she got back from New York, she'd have another go at finding out more about Alice, she decided. She could ask around the village; Ellen's family had been living here for generations, and she was bound to know something.

Jane knew she hadn't told anyone about Alice because she had felt, bizarrely and inexplicably, like her own secret. Her own secret friend, which was ridiculous and rather pathetic, yet still she felt it. She and Alice had both lived in that huge, draughty house. They'd both stared out the window at the bleak sheep pasture, had listened to the wind rattle the windowpanes, had sat in the kitchen, huddled by the Aga, and made shopping lists, and it almost felt like her own melancholy was an echo of Alice's.

She really was being fanciful.

The service started and Jane stood up.

She didn't think about Alice again as she paid attention to the service; at one point in the sermon her mind drifted and she thought about how she had to finish packing before she took the two o'clock train to Manchester that afternoon. Ever since she'd told the children about going to New York, they'd seemed sulky, although Jane didn't know if she were simply being paranoid. She felt racked by guilt and resentful that she did, torn between wanting to please her children – and Andrew – and wanting to please herself. Why, she wondered, hardly for the first time, did those two desires have to be at such odds?

In any case, she'd spent the last few days making casseroles to freeze and catching up on laundry, laying out school uniforms and writing lists about reading diaries and Merrie's swimming lessons and milk money. Everything was arranged, ready, and yet sitting there listening to the choir sing a melancholy anthem, Jane realized she didn't feel ready.

She almost – *almost* – didn't want to go.

A sudden silence in the service brought Jane back to the present. Everyone was processing out of the church, following Simon, and with a startled glance at Andrew, she followed.

"We're going to the war memorial," he whispered. "The vicar will read the names of all those fallen in the wars."

She nodded her understanding, and followed the rest of congregation down the drive, through the church grounds, and then out onto the main street. There was something both stoic and solemn about the silent procession, with Simon holding the cross high above, the shape of it dark against a lowering grey sky.

He stopped in front of a weathered stone memorial that Jane had passed every day on her way to Merrie's school, but had never paid much attention to. Now she saw it was a war memorial, with the names of all of Goswell's dead engraved upon it.

In a loud voice Simon read the names. "Timothy Abbott. Walter Anderson. James Bettinson..."

The wind swept straight from the sea and a shiver moved through the group. Jane found her thoughts drifting again, only to return to the present with a sudden, inexplicable apprehension.

"Henry Hepworth. Oliver Himes. Albert Huggins..."

She stilled, her heart starting to beat hard, although she couldn't say why. Simon's voice continued, solemn, sonorous. '*David James...*'

She let out an involuntary gasp, and Andrew glanced at her in both surprise and concern. Jane just shook her head, and Simon continued reading the names.

David James. David James had fallen in the war – how? He'd been a vicar. And he must have, Jane thought, joined up as a chaplain. Unless he'd died in that stray bombing Ella had told her and Dorothy about? But she knew instinctively there had been no casualties from that; it surely would have been mentioned somewhere in the church history. Simon would have known—

And Alice James had been a widow. How old had she been? Had she had children to comfort and surround her? Now, more than ever, Jane wanted to know the answers to those questions.

Five hours later she was in the airport, waiting to board the flight to New York. Andrew and the children had seen her off at Goswell's little station, and they'd been a sullen, mostly silent group. Jane had felt wretched, and no more so than when Merrie had thrown her arms around her waist and whispered against her stomach,

"I don't want you to *go*."

"Merrie," Jane had said helplessly, and Andrew had stepped forward to pry Merrie's arms from around Jane.

"Now, now, Merrie, we'll have a splendid time. And Mummy will be back before you know it, and with presents too." He'd spoken cheerfully, but Jane still felt a censure from him — or was it from herself?

Why was she doing this?

As soon as the plane took off she powered up her laptop and pulled up the spreadsheet for Women For Change's donations for the month of October. Within minutes she was absorbed and almost happy. Only a small part of her remembered Merrie's plaintive wail, Natalie's sullen silence, Ben's seeming indifference — and ached to be back with them, even in Goswell.

Three days later Jane was settled at Claudia's apartment and pulling her usual ten-hour work days. At first she'd been buzzing, the city's energy firing her forwards, filling her up. Now, sitting in her old office, the sunlight streaming through the dusty windows as she sipped a *vente latte*, she had to admit she was just a little bit tired. Exhausted, really, and yet happy — but still with that awful mother-guilt.

"The sun shines so much here," she said wistfully. While enduring Cumbria's weather, she'd literally forgotten how it felt to enjoy a crisp, sunny day, to take it as routine.

Claudia laughed. "Poor Jane. That place is really getting to you, isn't it?"

"No," Jane said automatically, because she didn't want to give in to that old despair — and complaining to Claudia about her life in Goswell felt disloyal not just to Andrew but to her children and even herself. "I just forgot, that's all."

Yet three days in – three days of back-to-back meetings, phone calls, and event planning, and nights made sleepless by a combination of jet lag and worry – Jane almost wanted to go home.

Or perhaps she wanted this to be home again, a desire she fought against because it was so obviously impossible. Walking down Broadway one evening after meeting with the caterer, she tried to imagine that she was walking back to their old apartment, rather than Claudia's modern one-bedroom. Yet as she pictured it she felt an all-too-familiar cramping in her stomach, her heart rate accelerating with stress. She imagined the mess and chaos that would greet her on arrival, pictured herself scrabbling for takeaway menus as Ben whined about his DS and kept the TV on too loud and Natalie disappeared into her room, headphones securely in place, while Andrew texted her to say he'd be late again, marking papers...

No, she didn't want that life again. She certainly didn't want to fantasize about it now.

Then, out of the ashes of one dream, her subconscious gave birth to another and she began to imagine that she was walking back to her own apartment, some cute little pied-à-terre near Columbus Circle, convenient for work and transportation. She'd live there for two weeks out of every month, and then fly back to Goswell to be with her family. The best of both worlds.

And since I'm such a lousy mother, maybe it's the best solution.

She stopped right there on the Broadway, hardly able to believe that she'd actually fantasized about such a thing, even for a moment. That even now, with realization trickling coldly through her, she still wanted it – and didn't want it, all at the same time.

I don't belong anywhere, she thought as she started walking slowly once more, people pushing past her with an impatient hiss of breath or sometimes a swear word. She didn't want to live in New York, and she couldn't honestly say she wanted to live in Goswell. She was emotionally homeless.

"Why don't you give it a year?" Claudia suggested one evening when they were both curled up on the sofa in her apartment, after she'd asked Jane about her life – or lack of it – in Goswell. "Tell Andrew he can have his English experience, and then you want to move back."

"That seems rather cold—"

"*Cumbria* seems rather cold, sweetie—"

Jane shook her head. Claudia was both single and single-minded; she had no idea what kind of cost such a decision would have on her marriage, her family, and even herself. "I couldn't do that. A year isn't long enough, anyway, to decide if you like a place. And I could hardly pull all the children out of school once they're settled—"

"*Are* they settled?"

Jane considered this for a moment. "I think so. It takes time, of course, and we've only been there for two months—" *Two months.* It was such a short amount of time, and yet to Jane it had felt like forever.

"But you're not settled," Claudia observed and Jane bit her lip.

"I don't think I've really tried," she confessed. It *felt* like a confession; despite the tension between her and Andrew, her insistence about how hard it was and how hard she was trying, Jane knew then that she hadn't been – not as she should have, or even could have. Some part of her had deliberately, determinedly dug her heels in and refused to adapt – and she knew Andrew had seen that, felt it.

"I'm not sure why you should try," Claudia said robustly. "Honestly, Jane, don't you think Andrew is asking too much of you? To leave your job, your friends, your family—"

"He did it," Jane answered quietly. She knew that was why she had first agreed to the move, even if she'd resisted and still was. Andrew had left all those things for sixteen years. How could she insist he continue to do so?

"It was his choice," Claudia argued. "All those years ago – he came to the States before he even met you!"

"I know." She'd told herself the same thing more than once. Jane let out a tired laugh. "You're like a devil's advocate, Claudia. I've said all those things to myself, in my more self-pitying moments."

"It's hardly self-pity. I don't see why you shouldn't have the best of both worlds. Couldn't you come to some arrangement? Live in Goswell and New York?"

"They're kind of far apart."

"So? Lots of people do a transatlantic commute. Two weeks there, two weeks here… we'd snap you right back up, you know."

Jane shook her head, smiling faintly. It was her fantasy brought to life… and yet that's all it was. A fantasy.

Yet the next day she found herself slowing in front of a trendy-looking real estate agent. One of the placards in the window detailed a studio on Sixty-ninth and Columbus, "a bijou property for the career-focused", and before she could think better of it, or anything at all, she was opening the door to the agent's and going inside.

A receptionist greeted her and she asked about the studio, and just two minutes later a thirty-something man in an expensive and hip-looking grey silk suit came out of his office, all smiles, and told her he could take her to view the studio himself right now.

"I'm really just looking," Jane felt compelled to admit, because in the space of a few minutes she felt like her reckless impulse had taken on a life of its own.

"Aren't we all?" the man answered with a sideways smile and led her outside. "Are you in a rush? We can take a cab."

It was a beautiful, crisp sunny day and the studio was only a few blocks away. "Let's walk," Jane said, because she didn't want the expense of a cab on her conscience as well as the waste of this man's time.

"I'm Peter Lanfer," he said, shaking her hand. His grip was warm and dry.

"Jane Hatton."

"You've been in the city long?"

"Sixteen years," Jane answered, and left it at that. She felt vaguely guilty for not explaining about England and Andrew and her three children, yet somehow she couldn't bring herself to.

"Long time. I've been here for ten. Love it, though. Couldn't ever leave."

Jane smiled weakly. "Me neither," she murmured and Peter grinned. He had very straight, very white teeth.

"And where you do you live now?"

"Ah…" Her guilt intensifying, she gave the address of their old apartment. "Ninety-Third and Central Park West."

"Great location," Peter enthused as they turned onto Sixty-Ninth Street. "But I suppose you want to be closer to work?"

"Ummm… yes." About 4,000 miles closer.

Peter kept up a steady chatter about the apartment, the location, the great restaurants on Columbus, the proximity to Lincoln Center. ("Do you like the opera? I've just been for the first time in my life, can you believe it? Puccini. I didn't understand a word.")

"Well, it is Italian," Jane offered diplomatically, and he grinned, flashing her those white, white teeth again.

"But they have those little translation screens right in front of every seat! I mean, what are we, Philistines?"

And she laughed, appreciating his easy charm. Something in her wilfully relaxed. She'd just go with this. It was one afternoon, one *hour*, for heaven's sake, and she'd indulge in her absurd little fantasy and then go back to reality, which was that the first week of her three-and-a-half-week hiatus was almost over, and this time next month she'd be back in Goswell, learning how to live there forever.

"Here we are," Peter said, and unlocked the door of a smart-looking Brownstone in the middle of the street. He held the door open for Jane, and she stepped into a small but gracious lobby with a black-and-white marble-tiled floor and an old-fashioned elevator with polished wooden doors.

"It's lovely," she said, charmed again, and Peter nodded.

"Old-world elegance, this place. I know it sounds like a line but apartments in this building are snapped up very quickly."

"That is most definitely a line," Jane answered with a laugh as they stepped into the elevator. It was quite small, and her shoulder brushed Peter's. "I've lived in this city for twenty years, and I've been through half a dozen apartments in that time. I've heard all the lines you real estate brokers trot out."

"You real estate brokers?" Peter repeated, clutching his chest theatrically. "You wound me."

The elevator doors swooshed open on the fourth floor. "But I'm right," Jane said, and stepped into the hallway. She was uncomfortably aware that this came close to flirting, which was, of course, ridiculous. Peter Lanfer had to be ten years younger than she was. He probably treated all the old ladies this way.

"So here we are," Peter said, and unlocked the door to the studio. Jane stepped into the room which was no more than fifteen by fifteen feet, a tiny box of an apartment, and yet it was charming. French windows overlooked the street and from this height she could see the stark branches of Central Park. She walked slowly around the little space, taking in the fireplace, the en suite bathroom, the built-in cupboards, the kitchen in the corner with a tiny slice of granite counter top and a two-burner stove. For a tiny space, it was beautiful.

Peter stood by the door and let the apartment soak into her, wisely saying nothing. She was, Jane thought with a rueful sigh, already sold. And it was pointless, ridiculous... wasn't it?

"There's laundry facilities in the basement," Peter said after a few minutes. "And the super lives on site. He's very good. I've dealt with him before."

"I'm really just looking," Jane said, helplessly, and Peter nodded.

"Of course. But how about we grab a coffee and I can tell you a little bit more about the apartment?"

"I don't want to waste your time—"

"It would be a pleasure," Peter said, and somehow she was swept along, outside the building and then down the street to a little French patisserie with tiny wrought-iron tables. Peter ordered them both cappuccinos and a couple of fruit tarts, which happened to be one of Jane's favourite pastries.

She nibbled at it nervously, conscious that this really had most assuredly got out of hand.

"So you like the Upper West Side?" he asked and she nodded, knowing she needed somehow to come clean, and yet feeling unable to begin. "I like the East Village myself. Although I could see once I had a wife and a couple of kids, I might want to move uptown." He smiled boyishly, and Jane simply sat there, frozen, having no idea what to do. "What line of work are you in?" he asked, and they talked about Women For Change and charity work in general for a few minutes, and then Peter gave her "the deets" on the property and possible financing and Jane listened, letting it flow over her and wondering how to tell Peter she really had no intention of buying the beautiful pre-war studio on Sixty-Ninth and Columbus – didn't she?

For a second, as Peter kept talking, she pictured how it could work. They could afford the studio if they basically liquidated their savings. She could commute just as Claudia had suggested, as she had fantasized. A week in New York, three weeks in Goswell. With the children in school full time they would barely miss her, and she'd have the best of both worlds. She could keep her career, her life, and still be there – mostly – for Andrew and the kids.

Why shouldn't she? *Why shouldn't she?*

"Jane?" Peter's friendly voice broke into her thoughts. "You want me to go through that again?" She heard a note of laughter in his voice and she blushed.

"Sorry... I was just thinking everything through. What were you saying?"

She ended up taking an application and promising to be in touch with Peter soon. As she walked back to Claudia's apartment her mind spun and whirled with ideas, with possibility, with hope.

Maybe... just maybe... she could actually do this. She could have everything she wanted.

CHAPTER NINETEEN

Alice
Goswell, May 1940

It was a lipstick. It had taken Alice a while to realize just what Vera had taken, because she never wore it and wouldn't have missed it in the first place, which made the whole thing all the more difficult.

She was tempted simply to overlook it, to try to forget and move on, forging a good relationship with the girl. Yet how could they possibly have a good relationship that was based on such deceit on both sides? And if she did overlook it, Vera might be tempted to try to steal again, and where would that lead either of them? There could be no trust, and without it, no possible relationship.

Still she let a few days pass as she considered what to do. She longed for advice, yet she was not about to admit what had happened to the likes of Mrs Sutherland or Mrs Dunston, both of whom, she knew, would sniff self-righteously and ask her what she'd expected of an evacuee.

Alice thought about writing to David, but it would take weeks for the letter to reach him and an answering one to reach her, and she knew the situation required far more urgent attention than that.

So what to do? She was still morosely pondering the question when she came across Flora Welton outside the butcher's on Lowther Street.

"Queued over an hour for this bacon," she told Alice with a wry smile. "And it won't be more than a few mouthfuls for Jamie and me."

"It's hard, isn't it," Alice said in sympathy, although she knew her situation was far easier than Flora's. Several of the local farmers still put bits aside for her, and she often found something on the vicarage steps, whether it was a bag of winter vegetables or half a dozen eggs.

"It is, at that," Flora agreed. "But never mind." She smiled, cheerful as always. "How are you getting on with that evacuee of yours? She looks about Jamie's age, I reckon."

"She's twelve," Alice confirmed, and realized with a sudden surge of warmth that Flora was exactly the kind of person she could talk to about Vera. "She's a bit surly," she continued, "but I suppose that's to be expected. It must be so strange for all these children, coming so far away."

"Terrible," Flora agreed, her smile fading. "I can't imagine what it must be like for the poor mites, especially the little ones. They're barely more than babies."

"I know."

"But your girl will settle in, I'm sure," she continued with more cheer. "She's bound to."

"Yes—" Alice hesitated, then plunged ahead. "It's only – something's happened, and I'm really not sure what to do about it."

"Oh, aye?"

Quickly Alice explained about the snooping and the lipstick. "I'm just not sure what to do. I don't even care about the lipstick, it's not that—"

But Flora was already shaking her head very firmly. "You mustn't let her get away it, Mrs James, it's not a kindness. Take a firm hand, although I know it's hard. I do hate disciplining

Jamie, but he'd be half-wild if I didn't, and it's hard enough for him already in this village."

"Is it?" Alice asked, although she knew of course it had to be, with Jamie having no father to speak of. "It's not as though it's his fault."

"No, but it doesn't matter." Flora's mouth tightened before she shook her head and smiled once more. "You must be firm with her. Kind, too, but then you always are. Tell her she mustn't ever do it again, and send her to bed without any supper."

Alice drew back, appalled. "Oh, I couldn't! She's half-starved as it is—"

But Flora refused to relent. "How else is she to learn? If it doesn't hurt, it won't matter to her."

"It just seems cruel."

"Cruel to be kind, then. You won't do her any favours in this life, Mrs James, letting her get away with something like that. If she pinches something down the road, it will be a lot worse for her than a missed supper."

Alice walked back to the vicarage slowly, her mind and heart heavy with dread. She knew Flora was right, but the thought of being so strict with Vera went against everything in her nature.

Slowly she opened the vicarage door and headed back to the kitchen with her parcels. Mrs Sutherland sniffed at the amount of coffee, but took them all the same.

"Have you seen Vera?" Alice asked, and Mrs Sutherland sniffed again.

"Upstairs, I should think, loafing about."

"Thank you, Mrs Sutherland," Alice answered, a bit severely, and the housekeeper simply sniffed a third time.

Alice found Vera in her bedroom, lounging on the bed with her shoes still on, flipping through one of her film magazines.

"Vera, I'd like to talk to you," she said, and heard how wavery her voice sounded. Vera didn't even look up from the magazine. "Get your shoes off the bed," Alice said in something of a snap. "You'll get mud on the coverlet." When Vera still didn't move or acknowledge her at all Alice lifted her feet herself and dropped them unceremoniously on the floor. She twitched the magazine from Vera's hands and tossed it onto the bureau. "Please afford me the respect of looking at me when I'm talking to you," she said stiffly, and Vera fixed her with a stony expression.

She'd gone about this all wrong, Alice thought hopelessly. Already Vera was set against her, and she hadn't even mentioned the lipstick yet. Trying for a more conciliatory tone, Alice sat on the bed next to Vera. "Vera, I believe you've taken something of mine and I'd like it back." No answer, no change in the girl's expression at all. "The other day you went in my room without asking and now a lipstick's missing from my bureau."

Vera's lip curled. "And so you think I nicked it, o'course."

"It's a reasonable conclusion to draw," Alice answered steadily, "especially since I saw you slip something in your pocket as you left."

Vera tilted her chin. "Wasn't nothing but a handkerchief."

Alice had never seen Vera use a handkerchief, much less possess one. "You stole that lipstick, Vera," she said, and heard a quaver in her voice. "I'd like it back, please." As steadily as she could she held out her hand and kept her gaze on Vera.

A full minute ticked by with neither of them speaking or moving. Alice felt her jaw ache with tension and her hand started to tremble. Then, just when she thought they'd be sitting there locked in a glare forever, Vera got off the bed and went to her bureau. She rifled through the top drawer for a moment before tossing the lipstick at Alice; it landed on her lap.

"There you are. I didn't like the colour, anyway."

"Thank you, Vera," Alice said with as much dignity as she could muster. "For punishment you will stay in your room all afternoon and have no supper."

Vera's jaw tightened and her dark eyes snapped but she said nothing.

"I hope this never happens again," Alice said as she stood, the lipstick clenched in one hand. "I do so want you to be happy here."

Vera still didn't speak and Alice left the room and sagged against the door, her eyes closed, her legs shaking. That had been far harder than she'd expected, and she had no idea what would happen now.

Mrs Sutherland made no comment when Alice informed her Vera would not be down for supper, although Alice sensed a certain smug satisfaction in the older woman's countenance as she took a place away from the kitchen table. After the housekeeper had left and Alice had spent a quiet if rather distracted hour reading in the dining room – the warmest room downstairs – she decided to talk to Vera again. She wouldn't apologize, but perhaps they could come to some kind of understanding.

She mounted the stairs with a hard-beating heart, for she had no idea what she would say to the girl, or how Vera would respond.

In the end, she wasn't given a choice. She knocked once on the door to Vera's bedroom and then opened it, but the room was empty. Vera had gone.

Alice stared at Vera's empty bed with a kind of numb disbelief. Where could the girl have possibly gone? The simplest explanation was that she was somewhere in the house; perhaps she'd gone and hidden as a way to frighten her.

Turning quickly on her heel, Alice left Vera's bedroom and began a methodical search through the rest of the house, even the now-unused and draughty maids' bedrooms on the top floor. Vera wasn't to be found.

She went back downstairs, her heart starting to beat hard. It was early May and although there was a chill in the air, the sun had not yet set, and vivid streaks of pink and orange lighted the horizon. Alice decided to look outside.

She walked through the garden first, and then the church's gardens, and finally the churchyard itself, the mossy headstones now lost in shadow as twilight settled upon the earth. She came upon Harry's cottage in the far corner of the yard, a tumbledown place with broken roof-tiles and one of its windows papered over. Alice had never been to his cottage before, had never had any reason to go. Now, acting out of desperation, she hammered on the door.

Harry opened it with a look of blatant surprise, blinking rather owlishly at her.

"Mrs James—"

"Vera's gone missing, Harry. Can you help me look for her?"

"Vera?"

"The girl staying with me," Alice explained, impatience and even fear sharpening her voice. "I sent her to her room with no supper and now she's gone and left." She blinked back sudden tears. Clearly her stern handling of Vera had backfired – perhaps disastrously.

"She can't have gone far," Harry said and Alice shook her head.

"But I can't *find* her."

He nodded slowly. "All right, then," he said, and went

back inside for his coat and boots. Alice stood in the doorway, trying not to notice the untidy sprawl of clothes, boots, and dirty dishes that made up Harry's living area. Though he was meticulous about his garden rows, he was not quite as neat in his personal life.

A few minutes later they were methodically combing through the churchyard, calling Vera's name, but the only answer was the howl of the wind that had picked up since the sun had set. It was dark now, and far colder, and Alice quaked to think of the girl out alone in this. Even a May evening in Cumbria could be cold and harsh.

"Maybe she's gone into the church," Harry suggested, and Alice nodded with a kind of desperate, frantic relief.

"Yes – she wouldn't want to be out in the dark and cold. Let's have a look."

Harry possessed a key to the church even though Alice did not, since part of his responsibilities was to maintain the building both inside and out. As soon as they stepped into the dusty, dark interior Alice knew Vera wasn't there. Still she looked, half-hoping to find the girl curled up on a pew or in a corner of the vestry.

She muttered under her breath as she saw Reverend Bearman had left the silver out again. "I'll have to speak to him again," she said to herself, and turned to Harry who was standing in the doorway, watching her.

"You don't have the key to the safe, do you?"

He shook his head. "No, only the Reverend's got that."

"Well, then." As before, Alice put the silver on top of the safe and then covered it with one of the linen napkins used to cover the communion bread. "That will have to do." She turned back to Harry. "Where should we look for her now, do you think?"

Harry shook his head slowly. He wasn't, Alice knew, the cleverest of men, although he was a solid, stolid worker. "I don't rightly know. Maybe she's gone off to the beach?"

"The beach…" Alice tensed at the thought. If the tide was in, the beach could be a wild and rough place, with the surf pounding right over the cliffs. She shuddered to think of Vera, a city child, out alone in all of that wildness.

"Else she's wandering through the village?" Harry suggested, and Alice bit her lip.

"We'll have to try both. Will you walk up the high street, Harry, and look for her? She doesn't even know anyone yet, so she has to be out somewhere… I'll go to the beach."

Harry shrugged in acceptance, and after getting a torch from the house Alice headed down the footpath that led right to the beach. The sky was black and starless and the wind was picking up, the lonely mournful sound of it in the trees replaced by the relentless crash of the surf as she approached the sea.

The tide had started to draw in, and as Alice came closer to the verdant cliffs that fell steeply to the sand, she could see the spray being flung across their tops with each roar of the waves, and shuddered. She hoped Vera was somewhere warm and dry and *safe*… wherever she was. She hoped she could find her, and said a quick, fervent prayer to that end.

She walked along the cliff top, the wind whipping her coat and skirt against her body. Surely Vera wouldn't have come this far. She was a city child, unused to the ways of the waves and wind – which made the possibility of her coming this way such a danger.

Alice was just about to turn back towards the village when a figure caught the corner of her eye. She stilled, then saw the woebegone form huddled amid the rocks below, by the old swimming pool that had been cut into the cliffs ages ago. On a calm day it was filled by the tide and children swam in it, but tonight the waves flung themselves against the sides and foamed over the top, and Vera stood stock-still, her scrawny arms wrapped around her body, clearly petrified by the incoming surge of the sea.

Alice hurried towards the footpath that wended its way down the steep side of the cliff. In the dark, with the spray of the waves wetting the shallow, rocky soil, it was a treacherous course even for her, who had taken the path many times. For Vera... she could not imagine. How desperate had the girl been?

Carefully Alice picked her way across the sea-slick rocks until she was close enough to call to the girl.

"Vera," she called softly, and even with the roar of the wind and the waves she knew the girl had heard her, by the way her huddled figure tensed. "Come with me. I'm so glad I found you."

"Are you?" Vera managed, defiant despite her fear. Alice almost laughed at her spirit.

"Of course I am. I've been terrified that something had happened to you—" She stopped, not wanting to make her feel guilty. "Please come home with me now."

She edged closer and reached for Vera's hand; it was cold and stiff but Vera still let her take it and lead her away from the pool. The tide had drawn in closer and Alice's shoes and stockings were soaked – as, she saw, were Vera's. Still holding her hand, Alice led her up the footpath, slipping once and falling hard to her knees. She managed to keep Vera upright, however, and finally, after what felt like an interminable length of time, they reached the top of the cliff.

"Thank God," Alice murmured, and started walking towards the road back to the vicarage. As soon as they were away from the cliffside, however, Vera yanked her hand away and Alice felt an arrow of hurt. After all that, Vera was still going to stand on her prickly pride.

She had hoped this experience might provide a breakthrough for her and the girl, or at least a truce, but as Vera stalked ahead of her, her head held high, Alice feared that nothing had changed.

CHAPTER TWENTY

Jane

Jane stared at the application she'd filled out for the studio on Sixty-Ninth Street. It had been burning a hole in her bag for the last ten days, and Peter Lanfer had called her three times, offering some friendly chat as well as a warning that several other interested parties had looked at the studio and were seriously considering making an offer.

I'm insane, Jane told herself, *even to think of it.* To think it could work… and yet why shouldn't it work? Money would be tight but not impossible. She'd already discussed the details with Claudia about coming back on a part-time basis, and she was thrilled.

"This is just what we need, Jane. And honestly, I think you need it too."

And Jane had agreed, and repeated that to herself, like a promise or a prayer. *I need this. This is reasonable, because I need it.*

Now she just had to tell Andrew. She tried to imagine the conversation, how it could begin, how it could end, and failed on both counts. Then she told herself it would be better if she had concrete information about the apartment, flights, salary. She spent half a day (which she should have spent solidifying arrangements for the fundraiser) making spreadsheets and compiling a file of data that she could present to Andrew. She called Peter Lanfer and told him she wanted to see the studio again; he said he'd meet her there.

The studio was just as lovely, a little jewel nestled near Columbus Circle, as before. Her heels clicked on the shiny parquet floor as she walked around the room, asked a few unnecessary questions.

"Is it a noisy building? Are there many – families?"

"No, it's mostly professionals and singles." He gave her a knowing smile. "You don't want some bratty kid keeping you up at night with their wailing, right?"

Jane smiled tightly and turned away. *I can do this,* she told herself. *I need this. That makes it fair. It makes it right.*

Taking a deep breath, she turned back to Peter. "I've filled out the application. I'd like to make an offer."

"Fantastic." He took the sheaf of papers from her and deposited them in his leather attaché without a second glance. The smile he gave her was warm, almost admiring. "How about I take you out for a drink to celebrate?"

Jane stared at him, felt as if someone had dumped a bucket of cold water right over her head. She was icy with shock. "A... drink?"

"There's a nice little wine bar right around the corner. It could become your local."

Standing there, Jane felt reality rush in – cold, hard, unwelcome and yet so painfully necessary. What was she doing? What on earth was she doing, standing here, pretending to be someone she was not, someone single and footloose and free? She knew Peter was asking her out on at least a semi-date, and the thought made her feel sick. She wanted to blurt "I'm married!" but the shame went too deep. She could not believe she'd let it get this far. She'd let her fantasy run away with her, and now she was ashamed that she'd even had it in the first place. What would Andrew have thought, if he'd known? If she'd actually told him, presented all this to him as so very reasonable?

"I'm sorry," she finally managed through numb lips, trying to smile although she wasn't sure her mouth was working properly. "I'm short on time. But... thanks for the offer."

Back at the office she shredded all her meticulous spreadsheets and deleted the files on her computer, flushed with guilty shame. She was just finishing an email to Peter Lanfer, withdrawing her application, when Claudia popped her head into the office.

"Did you make an offer on that studio?"

Jane looked up with a sigh. "Yes... and no."

"What do you mean?"

"I changed my mind, Claudia." She swivelled in her chair to face her friend. "I woke up."

"You mean you got cold feet."

"I appreciate your support," Jane said wryly, "but it wasn't going to work. It wouldn't have been fair on Andrew or the kids."

"And what about you? Who is fair to you, Jane?"

"Andrew's been fair," Jane said quietly. It hurt to admit it, to at least attempt to let go of the resentment and blame she'd been feeling for so long. "I just haven't tried. I've been fighting this move tooth and nail, even if I've said I wasn't." As she spoke the words she knew they were the truth and that hurt too. It all hurt: admitting her own failings as well as the loss of a pipedream. She turned back to the computer and resolutely pressed "Send". "I don't want to fight any more."

"You want to give up."

"I want to try," Jane corrected. "Something I haven't done yet. Andrew – and my kids – deserve at least that much."

Claudia folded her arms. "And what if you try, and six months or a year down the road, you're still miserable?"

"Then I suppose I'll need to think about what I can

change." Jane gave her friend a rather wobbly smile. "I know you're disappointed, but try to understand, Claudia."

"I am disappointed," Claudia admitted with a sigh. "But maybe you'll change your mind."

Jane knew she wouldn't.

A week later, the day before the fundraiser, Andrew rang her. They'd only spoken a handful of times since she'd been in New York, and then mainly to exchange relevant information, rather than actually chat. Now the sound of his familiar, affable voice gave her a sudden, surprising rush of homesickness.

"How's the Big Apple?" he asked, keeping it light, and Jane managed a little laugh.

"Oh, the same as ever. I don't think it ever really changes."

"Are you enjoying your lattes?" he continued with a teasing lilt. "And takeaways at any hour of the day or night, delivered right to your door?"

"The convenience is nice," Jane admitted, "but I miss you." She felt an ache rise in her throat, making it difficult to speak. She blinked rapidly. "I miss the kids. And I think I even miss that draughty old house." The realization surprised her.

"It misses you," Andrew answered quietly. "We all do."

"Oh, Andrew." Jane tried to swallow past that ache. "Maybe it was a mistake coming here."

"Why do you say that?"

"Because... because..." *Because, just like you said, it will make it harder to go back. I ran after something I thought I wanted, and I'm not sure I want it any more... but I don't know what I want.* "I don't feel the way I expected to," she said after a moment. "The way I wanted to."

"Maybe that's a good thing," Andrew said slowly. "Maybe it was something you needed to realize, and going back to the city was the only way you could."

She almost snapped back that she didn't need some sort of life lesson, but something kept her from it. The old Jane, the resentful, embittered one, would have made that snippy retort. Now she stayed silent, and let the resentment fade away.

"Jane?" Andrew asked quietly. "I'm glad you're there. You're needed, you know. The charity needs you, Claudia needs you. You're doing a good work."

Jane swiped at her eyes. She was an emotional wreck, she thought wryly, which was so unlike her. "Thank you," she said when she trusted herself to speak. "I think you're right. I suppose I did need to come here, at least for a little while." She'd needed the wake-up call. "Now tell me what's going on there. How are the kids?"

"Oh, fine," Andrew answered. "Ben's playing football on Friday evenings down at the rec ground by the beach. He comes home absolutely filthy, but he loves it."

"And Natalie?"

"She seems all right. Not much of one for talking, but she and Will have been walking to the bus together. And no complaints from her about much, which is something."

"What about Merrie?"

"As cheerful as a cricket, as she always is. Hanging around with Sophie all the time. They went to visit Sophie's great grandfather the other afternoon. Ellen took them."

"Her great grandfather? He's still alive?"

"He's about eighty-five, apparently, but still sharp as a new pin. Lived through the war, of course. I'm sure he has some stories to tell."

"Yes…" Jane thought of Alice and David James. Ever since she'd learned of David's death she'd felt a bit melancholy, fighting a kind of absurd grief for someone she'd never even known. She shook it off suddenly, jolted by something Andrew said as he continued to chat about Merrie's visit to Sophie's great-grandfather.

"Did you say *Welton*?"

"James Welton, yes. That's the name of the chap."

"Ellen's grandfather is a Welton?" Jane repeated incredulously, and Andrew let out a little laugh.

"This means something to you, obviously."

"Well, no, it's just… I suppose it does, in a way." Hesitantly she told Andrew about the shopping list, and what little she knew about Alice and David James.

"Fascinating," Andrew said slowly. "But you haven't found anything else about them?"

"Only his name on the War Memorial, and the list. Other than that it's like they didn't exist."

"I suppose that happens to us all," Andrew said with a sigh. "How much of a legacy does any average person leave? But it is so interesting to think of the people who've lived in our house, made it their home. You should talk to this Welton fellow. He might even have known them. He was around when they were, anyway."

"Yes—" For the first time Jane felt her spirits lift at the thought of returning to Goswell. "I'll do that, when I get back."

"I love you, you know," Andrew said, and Jane heard the note of vulnerability in his voice. She blinked hard.

"I love you too, Andrew. And I'll be home in a couple of weeks." As she hung up the phone she realized it was the first time she'd actually, and unthinkingly, called Goswell home.

It was early December when Jane returned to Goswell, exhausted from her work with the fundraiser but strangely grateful to be back in Cumbria with her family. The fells were white with frost, Derwentwater sparkling under a winter sun as Andrew drove her back from the airport.

"I have a bit of a surprise for you," he told her as he turned onto the A595 towards Whitehaven.

"A surprise?"

"It's not much. I just thought I'd do a little work for you." He smiled rather mysteriously and Jane smiled back, shaking her head.

"A little work? Did you paint the living room?"

"Not that kind of work."

"Oh." She sat back and laid her head against the seat as a wave of jet lag swept over her. She must have dozed, for soon they were driving down the steep, winding road that led into Goswell, the sea sparkling in the distance, the huddle of houses and cottages a cheering sight, even if Jane could already hear the mournful howl of the wind.

"Do you know, New York actually seemed quiet at night?" she told Andrew as she straightened and rubbed the sleep from her eyes.

"Quiet? That's a new one."

"No wind. The windowpanes didn't rattle."

"I bet you didn't miss that," he said with a chuckle and she laughed back.

"I don't know if I did or not. But I had trouble sleeping."

The next few hours were taken up with a boisterous reunion, as Andrew made tea and toast in the kitchen and the children, even Natalie, regaled Jane with tales of every single thing that had happened while she was away.

"All right, now," Andrew finally said when there was nothing left but empty mugs and toast crumbs. "Your mother's flown all night and is exhausted. I'm sending her straight to bed, and you lot can do your homework." They went off with loud, theatrical moans, and Jane smiled at Andrew gratefully.

"I am rather tired."

"Why don't you sleep for a few hours? I'll wake you for supper, so your body clock won't be off too much."

"All right. Thank you." She hesitated, wanting to say something of all she'd realized in the last few weeks, all she'd missed, yet somehow the words wouldn't come. "What was this work you've done for me, then?" she asked instead.

"Oh, just a bit of snooping around on the internet," replied Andrew modestly, but Jane could see he was bursting with excitement.

"The internet?"

He reached for a sheaf of papers on the kitchen counter; Jane saw it was a bunch of print-outs from various websites. "I did a bit of research on your Alice James," he said, and for a reason she couldn't fathom at all Jane felt her heart sink.

"Oh?"

"Yes, and with a bit of digging, I found out quite a lot." Andrew slipped on his reading glasses and rifled through the papers. "You know the vicarage was bombed in 1941?"

"Yes, your mother's cousin had said—"

"No one was hurt, apparently. There were no bomb casualties in this part of Cumbria at all. But David James died in November 1943, of pneumonia, poor chap. His funeral was here at the church, but he was buried in Keswick, where he was from, originally."

"Oh," was all Jane could think to say. Her mind was whirling and she had a sudden, desperate impulse to tell Andrew to stop but he kept on, cheerfully oblivious. "Alice had to leave the vicarage, of course. She moved back to Cambridge in 1943 – that's where she was from. It's amazing what you can find on these genealogy sites."

"I'm sure it is," Jane whispered.

"She died in 1995, and she's buried there. I even managed to find out what was written on her headstone – that took a phone call to the church, but the secretary was ever so helpful."

"Really—"

"'Beloved by Vera', it said. Who do you suppose she was?"

Jane shook her head. "I have no idea."

"They didn't have any children, by the way, as far as I can tell." He glanced up, beaming. "So that's all I've found out. Nothing much happened here during the war, it seems, although James Welton might say differently. The most exciting thing was a Canadian fighter crashing in Whitehaven, and the church silver was stolen from here. It was really good stuff, apparently, from the 1600s. It was replaced in the 1960s, some modern pieces, not at all the same." He stopped suddenly, frowning. "Jane? What's wrong?"

She shook her head, fighting back tears, knowing she was being ridiculous. "Nothing. I'm just tired—"

Andrew took his glasses off slowly. "I've done this all wrong, haven't I? You didn't want to know it all, not like this."

"It's not that," Jane explained awkwardly. "I do want to find out about Alice. But hearing it all stated so matter-of-fact – I don't know, it makes her less real, somehow."

"*Less* real?"

"Or maybe more real, I don't know. She's not this woman in my imagination, who I sometimes feel just stepped out of the kitchen, or wrote that shopping list a moment ago. She's just a woman who lived a long time ago and has been dead for nearly twenty years. A woman who doesn't matter any more." She blinked hard.

"She does matter," Andrew said quietly. "She mattered to

her husband, and to this Vera. She might have lived a quiet, forgotten life, but she was important in her own time. Who knows what she accomplished, or whose life she changed?"

Jane nodded and sniffed. "I'm sorry. I'm being horribly sentimental."

"And I'm being horribly insensitive." He sighed and put the papers down on the table. "Jane, I know I haven't handled this whole move properly. I should have realized how hard it would be on you, how much you'd be giving up. I was just carried away by my own excitement – and, if I'm honest, a bit of self-righteousness. I felt like it was my turn."

"It is your turn, Andrew," Jane answered. "You lived in New York for sixteen years—"

Andrew shook his head. "A marriage doesn't work in turns. You're both in it together, the whole time. And if you're really unhappy here in Goswell, then we need to figure something out. I'm not sure what, but I don't want to go on if it's not what you want."

"I know you mean that." Jane brushed a tear from her eye. "But that's not what I want. We've only been here two months, Andrew, and I know I haven't really tried. Not like I could have, or should have."

"There's a reason for that—"

"Not a good one." She leaned forward and kissed him softly. "I want to start over. I want to try, properly this time, to settle here and be happy."

His arms closed around her and she heard his little sigh of relief as he drew her head to his shoulder. "I want you to be happy too," he said softly. "I want us all to be happy, Jane, so much."

And as she returned the embrace Jane offered a silent prayer that Andrew's wish might be granted.

CHAPTER TWENTY-ONE

Alice
Goswell, September 1941

It had been four months since Vera had arrived – four long, difficult months. Alice kept trying to find a way to reach the girl, but Vera remained stubbornly sulky and independent, if not outright defiant.

She went to school but seemed to make no friends; she ate her meals in silence, Alice's friendly questions drawing out only the barest of monosyllabic answers. Alice had insisted that Vera help in the garden over the summer months, thinking that the shared work and the satisfaction of a harvest might draw her out, but Vera laboured in grim silence, making Alice feel almost like a slave driver.

She thought they'd experienced a moment of sympathy when Alice first harvested the potatoes. Scrabbling in the earth with childish excitement, she triumphantly dug up four lumpy, misshapen potatoes.

"We shall eat these for supper," Alice announced, and Vera glanced at them dubiously.

"Ones from the shop look better."

"But these will taste better," Alice assured her. She sat back on her heels, unmindful of the turned-up soil, and gazed up at the fragile blue sky, with white wisps of cloud streaking the horizon. "Isn't it amazing, Vera," she said, "that things grow? That you can put a seed in the earth and get a potato?"

"I dunno," Vera said after a moment. "I never thought of it before."

"Neither did I. I never thought of it at all; I just took it all for granted. I suppose I took a great deal of things for granted, really." Alice stared up at the sky for a moment longer, thinking of both the joys and the disappointments that had made up her life, and how so often she'd let the latter dim the former.

She felt Vera step nearer. "Maybe I'll have a go, then," she said, and with something approaching wonder Alice watched her prod the dirt dubiously before coming up with another lumpy potato. Alice clapped her hands in victory and Vera offered her a shy, hesitant smile. At that moment Alice felt nearly completely happy, and she thought Vera was finally overcoming her sullen resentment, but as soon as they were back in the house, Vera sloped upstairs and was as sulky as ever at dinner, when Alice served up the potatoes roasted and crispy.

She began to despair of ever truly getting on with the girl, and she'd said as much to David in her letters, who wrote back encouraging missives advising patience and care, both of which, four months on, Alice was finding in short supply.

One cold, windy morning in September – they were predicting a particularly frigid winter throughout England and all of Europe – Alice made her way up the high street to queue at the butcher's. The last few months had made both her and Mrs Sutherland even more careful with their food supplies. They bulked out most meals with potatoes from the garden and made hearty vegetable stews and soups flavoured with a small bit of bacon.

Together Alice, Vera, Mrs Sutherland and Harry had sixteen rashers of bacon a week, and enough coupons for at least one or two cheap cuts of meat. It was more than many people had, and yet both Vera and Harry ate voraciously, and Alice often felt the hollowness of her own stomach.

She missed the days of thick beef roasts and Yorkshire puddings dripping with rich gravy, and then sponge cake or treacle tart for pudding, covered in cream. Those days were long gone, and sometimes she wondered if they would ever be back. The face of the world, it seemed, was changing forever, and when she thought about it too much, Alice felt frightened of what lay ahead, of the uncertainty that shadowed all of their lives.

Now she banished such thoughts and took her place in the queue outside the butcher's.

"What are we queuing for today?" she asked Flora, who was huddled in the line, her normally cheerful countenance looking rather pinched.

"Who can say? I heard there was pork but it might just be a rumour."

There was a bitter edge to Flora's voice that Alice wasn't used to hearing, and she saw how drawn and exhausted her friend looked, her shabby coat pulled tightly around her thin frame.

"Are you all right, Flora?" she asked. "Is anything the matter?"

Flora shook her head. "It's not for you to worry, Mrs James."

"You're my friend, so of course it's my worry," Alice answered staunchly. "What's going on?"

Flora pressed her lips together and shook her head, and Alice feared she'd get no more out of her. Then in a rush of words she confessed the truth. "My mum's sister's come to live with us. She lived down in Barrow and she's been bombed out. With her and her son, there's no room for Jamie and me."

"No room," Alice repeated, appalled. "But surely—"

"Mum says she's done well by me for long enough," Flora said bleakly. "And I can hardly blame her, can I? I've brought shame to the family, after all."

"Oh Flora, don't say that."

"It's true, right enough."

Alice shook her head. "It's not. You're such a good mother to Jamie—"

Flora sniffed, blinking back sudden tears. "You're too nice, Mrs James, to everyone."

Alice suddenly felt near tears herself, first from the strain of dealing with Vera's sullenness and now Flora's predicament. "What will you do?" she asked, trying to be practical, and Flora shrugged.

"I don't rightly know. I might find a place in Whitehaven—"

"In Whitehaven!" Alice repeated, appalled. "You can't leave Goswell."

"No one's got room for the likes of me," Flora answered.

"I do," Alice said firmly. Flora gaped at her. "Even with Vera I've got six empty bedrooms – the pair of us are rattling around in that vicarage!" The idea bloomed inside her, warming her from the inside out. "Of course you must come live with us."

"I couldn't," Flora protested, and Alice knew she meant it. Flora had always been far more conscious of the social distance between the two of them than Alice. Even though they'd been friends for years, Flora still wouldn't come to the vicarage for tea, and she'd accepted Alice's dinner invitation with the utmost reluctance, only agreeing when David had spoken to her personally. Most of their conversations took place in the street, and several times Alice had coaxed her to the tea shop by the beach.

"You could—" Alice began, but Flora cut her off.

"What would the churchwardens say? Or any of the congregation?" Flora shook her head, her eyes wide with apprehension. "And what of the new Reverend, or the diocese? There might be *laws* about it—"

"There are no laws about things like that," Alice said firmly. At least, there were no such laws that she knew of, and she didn't care about them anyway. It was wartime, and she intended on doing her Christian duty.

"What would Mr James say?"

"I would have his full support," Alice answered with complete certainty. "You know that, Flora. David has always been fond of you and Jamie."

Flora's face crumpled and she fished for her handkerchief, pressing it to her damp eyes. "You're too good," she sniffed. "The both of you. Too good for me."

Alice smiled and shook her head. "I'll allow that David might be, but I'm really not. I'm only doing what I want to do, Flora – really, I'm very selfish! Having you and Jamie as company for Vera and me seems to me the most wonderful thing." She reached over to squeeze Flora's hand, determined for the other woman to accept her invitation. "I won't take no for an answer, I absolutely won't. And I also insist that you finally start calling me Alice."

Flora wiped the tears from her eyes with a tremulous smile. "All right, then. We'll accept. And I thank you from the bottom of my heart for your kindness... Alice."

A quarter of an hour later Alice was walking back to the vicarage with six ounces of pork shoulder and a new lightness to her step. What *would* Mrs Dunston say to Flora and Jamie coming to live with them? Alice wondered about this as she came to the level crossing by the now bleak-looking rail station; all the signs had been removed, and the few trains that rattled through Goswell were sorry affairs, with blackout curtains tacked across their sooty windows.

What would Mrs Sutherland say, for that matter? Alice could already imagine the eloquent sniffs the housekeeper would give when she told her the news. She stiffened her shoulders as well as her resolve. She didn't care what anyone said about having Flora and Jamie to live with her. It was wartime, after all, and she couldn't think of better company to share the vicarage with her. Even with Vera she felt lonely.

She'd just turned down the twisting church drive when a low whine turned into a full roar and a plane soared straight above her, its dark wings almost seeming to clip the tops of the trees.

Alice's heart seemed to freeze right within her, for she recognized a German bomber. German planes didn't often fly over Goswell, although enough had on their way to Belfast or Barrow to necessitate the building of an air raid shelter behind the school fields in the middle of the village.

Most people had learned to recognize the far-off drone of the German bombers and head for shelter before anything was directly overhead, but Alice had been too lost in her thoughts to notice the approaching threat.

Now she instinctively put her hands over her head and ducked as the plane flew low directly over the vicarage, and then she screamed when the outbuildings between the church and the house suddenly exploded into flame.

Smoke and dust rolled towards her in a thick wave and, coughing and choking, she started to run to the house – and Vera.

She dropped her parcels, even the precious pork, and wretched open the gate to the kitchen courtyard; coal dust had blackened the air and splinters of wood rained down. Through the cloud of debris she could see that the bomb had hit the outbuildings, including the wood and coal shed, and she stumbled back as she saw the flames licking at the buildings and their flammable contents.

She felt a hand on her shoulder and turned to see Harry, shaking his head. "Don't go any closer, Mrs James. The fire brigade is coming."

"Vera—"

"She'll be inside. Don't look like the house was too badly hit. Come back, now."

Alice let Harry lead her out of the courtyard, her eyes streaming and coughs wracking her frame. In the distance she could hear the clanging bells of a fire engine.

"I need to find Vera," she said when her coughing had subsided and Harry nodded.

"I'll stay here."

She hurried around to the front of the house, wrenching open the door. The vestibule felt dim and quiet after the chaos of the bombing, and her heart pounded so hard her chest hurt.

"Vera!" The house was silent; Alice knew Mrs Sutherland had gone to Whitehaven today for a doctor's appointment. "Vera!" she called again, desperation and the effect of the smoke making her voice hoarse.

Then she heard a small sound from the kitchen, something between a moan and a sob, and she ran towards it.

The house might not have been directly hit, but the force of the bomb had caused the kitchen windows to shatter, and shards of glass littered the floor.

Alice's heart seemed to leap into her throat as she saw Vera crouching under the kitchen table, her eyes wide and terrified, blood trickling down her cheek.

"*Vera!*" Alice dropped to her knees, heedless of the glass, and without even thinking she held her arms out to the girl. Vera threw herself into Alice's embrace, her thin body wracked with sobs.

"I – I thought I was going to die," she sobbed against Alice's shoulder, and Alice stroked her hair, making soothing sounds as she held her close.

"I'm just so glad you're safe."

Vera's arms tightened around Alice. "I'm sorry," she whispered. "I'm sorry for everything."

"It doesn't matter," Alice answered, but her heart swelled at Vera's words. *Finally!* Had this tragedy finally broken down Vera's defences? Despite the disaster outside, Alice prayed it was so.

CHAPTER TWENTY-TWO

Jane

As winter deepened its hold on the Cumbrian countryside Jane dived into her new life with determined cheer. No longer was she going to resist every change or inconvenience, bemoan the lack of local amenities or the endlessly grey weather. She stopped fantasizing about a decent takeaway and disciplined herself not to check the weather in New York, or compare it to the dark, windy days in Goswell.

Instead she busied herself with all the tasks she'd put off: she painted the entire downstairs in bright, cheerful colours, and rearranged the furniture in the sitting room. She hung pictures and bought curtains for the long, sashed windows, which helped with the endless draught. She bought a tumble dryer and had it installed in the tiny utility room off the kitchen; it meant squeezing around it to get to the back door, but the convenience was certainly worth it.

With the downstairs in a mostly decent state, she turned to matters of the hearth. She bought an Aga cookery book and made warming soups and hearty stews for supper, presiding over the table with determined pride. Admittedly, Ben fished all his vegetables out of whatever he was eating, and Natalie sulked when the meal contained meat, as she'd recently and inexplicably become vegetarian, but Andrew and Merrie ate them all up with gusto.

She made a deliberate effort to be available and present when the children were home; she checked their homework and read aloud with Ben and Merrie. She tried to engage Natalie, but her oldest daughter regarded these attempts with obvious suspicion.

"Why are you so interested?" she practically snarled when Jane had asked several seemingly innocuous questions about her daughter's day.

"Because I'm your mother and I love you—"

"You never asked before."

Never was a bit harsh, but Jane accepted this as her due, her penance. "I'm asking now, Natalie," Jane said quietly. "I'm trying."

"Why?"

"Because—" Jane stared at her helplessly. She had a feeling there was a right answer to this question, and for the life of her she didn't know what it was.

"I don't want you to *try*," Natalie said, stalking past her up the stairs. "I don't want it to be some *effort*."

"When you're this charming," Jane snapped back before she could help herself, "it generally is."

The only response was the slam of Natalie's door, and Jane groaned aloud. She'd thought, naively she saw now, that once she'd accepted her life was here, once she *tried*, everything would fall into place. She'd assumed only her attitude needed changing. Clearly that wasn't the case.

Still, there were other opportunities, and Jane approached them with the same determined cheer with which she'd tackled the sitting room and the Aga. She volunteered for the Village School Association, which conveniently met at the pub, and signed up at the first meeting to bring two tray bakes to a coffee morning at the school.

"What is a tray bake, exactly?" she asked Ellen as they walked down the high street after collecting Merrie and Sophie from school one wintry afternoon.

Ellen laughed. "You've agreed to something without even knowing what it is? It's just a tray of cakes – brownies or what have you."

"I figured as much," Jane said, her confidence restored. She could bake brownies.

"So Andrew was asking about Granddad," Ellen said with a sideways smile. "You've been doing a little sleuthing, apparently, into the history of your house?"

"He has," Jane answered. She still felt a strange sting at the new knowledge Andrew had gained about Alice and David James; she didn't like to think about the rest of Alice's lonely-sounding life or her headstone in some Cambridge churchyard. "But it *is* funny that your maiden name is Welton—"

"Is it?" Ellen raised her sandy eyebrows. "How so?"

With a little laugh Jane explained about the shopping list she'd found. "I know it's nothing much—"

"But it's fascinating," Ellen interjected, her eyes sparkling. "You wouldn't know, of course, but I've got a bit of a chequered past."

"Chequered?"

"My great-grandmother, Flora, was an unwed mother, which of course was shocking in that time. My grandfather never knew who his father was – Flora wouldn't name him."

Jane slowed her pace, her insides flaring with a sudden spark of interest. "Really… why do you think she wouldn't?"

"Honestly, I don't know. Of course, everyone assumed the worst. They said he was married, or disreputable, or worse. But no matter what the gossip, she never breathed a word."

Jane stopped right there in the street, Merrie and Sophie dancing along ahead of them. "So who were the Weltons who came to dine at the vicarage?"

"That's puzzling, isn't it!" Ellen exclaimed. "I don't think my grandmother would have ever been invited to the vicarage, based on the simple fact that she was an unwed mother."

"Would the Jameses have been so snobbish?" She couldn't help but feel a little needling of disappointment. The picture she'd created in her head of Alice James did not include socially snubbing a single mother.

"I don't think it was a matter of snobbery," Ellen replied. "I doubt it would have even occurred to them. And if it did, I doubt my great-grandmother would have accepted."

Jane shook her head. "But it did occur to them. The proof of that is in the shopping list."

Ellen shook her head. "It's so odd… I wonder if my Granddad would know? I've never really talked to him about his childhood," she confessed with a guilty smile. "When I was younger, well, you just don't think of it, do you? The past seems completely irrelevant. When I fell pregnant Granddad told me about his mum having him – a kind of solidarity, I think. I never knew her, you know. She died before I was born."

"It *is* fascinating," Jane murmured. "I never really thought about who the Weltons might be. I was always just wondering about Alice."

"You should talk to my grandfather. I'm sure he'd love to regale you with tales of his childhood."

"I'd love to hear them," Jane said sincerely. "Especially if he remembers anything about the Jameses."

"Well, he might do," Ellen said as they both quickened their pace to catch up with the girls cavorting ahead of them. "Especially if he'd been invited to Sunday dinner at the vicarage!"

Jane laughed, even as she acknowledged that there was in fact every possibility James and Flora Welton had been invited to dine at the vicarage. She wondered if they had accepted, and if so, what the experience had been like.

"But enough talk about the past," Ellen said when they'd reached her house and she'd plonked the kettle on the stove. The girls had scampered upstairs and Jane sank into a chair at the scrubbed kitchen table with a grateful sigh. "How are you doing? You've been like a whirling dervish since you got back from the States – cleaning, painting, volunteering for every committee—"

"Just the VSA," Jane protested with a smile. "But I am thinking about joining the running club – I could use the exercise."

"You're going to wear yourself out."

"I'm fine," Jane said firmly. "I like being busy. I need it."

"Do you?" Ellen gave her a speculative look as she handed her a mug of coffee. "*This* kind of busy?"

Jane tensed instinctively. "What do you mean?"

Ellen shrugged. "I'm glad you're getting involved, but you don't have to prove anything to anyone."

"I'm not," Jane said, and heard how stiff her voice sounded. She took a sip of coffee. "What would I be proving, anyway?"

"I don't know." Ellen smiled, her eyebrows raised teasingly. "That you can be the perfect village wife and mother? We all feel that pressure sometimes."

"I'll never be that," Jane answered with a laugh, but it sounded a little hollow even to her own ears. She felt a bit hurt by Ellen's comment, which seemed like a criticism, even as she wondered if there was any truth in it. Was she trying to prove something – to Andrew, to the other school mums, or maybe just to herself?

"The point is," Ellen said, drawing her back to the conversation as she fetched the biscuit tin, "that you need to do the things that make you and your family happy. Not the things you think you should do, or that you think other people expect you to."

Jane took a sip of coffee, her mind spinning. At this point she didn't even know what made her happy. *Was* she happy, racing around, baking and cleaning and volunteering? She felt more productive, at least, than she had moping around the vicarage and thinking about Alice James. But was that enough?

"It's a work in progress," she finally said, and reached for a biscuit. "*I'm* one."

"Aren't we all," Ellen agreed, and took a biscuit herself.

Christmas in Goswell was, everyone told her, a wonderful affair. Jane admired the fairy lights that were strung along the high street, and the wreaths that graced nearly every door. Andrew had, as she would have expected, got into the spirit of the thing, and bought both a wreath and outside lights for the vicarage; he and Ben spent a precarious hour stringing them on top of the gabled windows.

For her part, Jane attempted mince pies – something she'd never done in sixteen years of marriage – although she cheated and bought the mincemeat from a jar and the pastry from the chilled shelf of the supermarket. Still, Merrie enjoyed cutting them out with childish care and dusting the tops with icing sugar.

The vicarage, Jane supposed, would have been a fantastic house to decorate for Christmas, with its many fireplaces and the sweeping staircase that called out for garlands of evergreen and holly. She gazed down at their one sorry little box of Christmas decorations and ornaments and knew it would barely kit out the sitting room.

"We'll have to get a real tree," Andrew said when he and Ben came in from putting up the lights. "At least nine feet tall. We could get two, couldn't we – one in the dining room as well."

"We could," Jane answered, "but I don't see why we should. Trees are expensive, Andrew." She knew she sounded prissy, but she was tired and frazzled by the thought of Andrew's mother and sister and her family coming for Christmas – Dorothy, she knew, would expect the vicarage to look like something out of *Cumbria Life*, and would be quizzically disappointed when it wasn't.

"Well, we are having guests this Christmas," he said mildly. "It would be nice to have the place really festive."

"I suppose." Issuing the invitation to Dorothy and Trisha had been all part of Jane's embrace-life-in-Goswell plan, yet the thought of decorating the whole house properly, never mind feeding and entertaining an extra five people, only exhausted her.

Annoyed with herself, she put another tray of mince pies in the oven and slammed the door. What was wrong with her? She'd put her moping days behind her, and yet ever since Ellen had asked her if she were happy, she'd felt decidedly disgruntled. Why did anyone ask that question, she wondered grumpily, since its obvious implication was that you weren't, or didn't seem like you were?

And *was* she happy? She still didn't know. Some days she wondered if she kept herself so busy bustling and baking and signing up for everything on offer because if she stopped and let herself be still, she'd know the answer to that question all too easily.

It wasn't fair. She was making an effort, and it still didn't feel like enough. Her family was certainly happier; Andrew beamed when he saw her stirring a big pot of something on the Aga, and only last night Merrie had put down her spoon after eating a large helping of bread-and-butter pudding (straight out of Jane's new cookery book) and said with her eyes shining, "I *love* living here."

Ben had happily sloped into a gang of village boys who all hung around the rec ground on weekends and kicked a football, and fortunately didn't seem to get into too much trouble.

As for Natalie… she seemed happier too, Jane acknowledged, except with her. Every effort Jane made was treated with silent contempt or eye-rolling, and after several tense verbal battles Jane had decided to ignore it. At least Natalie was doing well in school and had friends, Will being the chief one. Last Saturday she'd gone to the cinema in Workington with two girls from her year, and whenever Will was mentioned she went suspiciously silent and red.

Jane supposed most fourteen-year-old girls didn't get along with their mothers, but it still made her feel frustrated and even hurt. Didn't Natalie see she was trying? And what had she meant, she didn't want Jane to try? What else was she supposed to do?

In any case, Natalie was happy enough, if not with her. Jane knew she was the only discontented one, despite her determined appearance otherwise. She was the only one who, having accepted the wind and rain, the cold and isolation, still felt like she wasn't home. She wasn't herself.

And she had no idea how to change things.

Maybe it would just take time, like Andrew had said. Everyone always said how stressful moving was. Maybe if she was just patient, and kept at it, eventually she'd look around – look inside herself – and realize she was both happy and home. Maybe it didn't happen with a switch or click, but rather a gradual dawning, the way sunshine crept over the fells.

By the time Dorothy and Trisha arrived with family in tow – two children, three dogs, and Trisha's husband Dan – Jane had organized the vicarage into a fairly decent, Christmassy display. She'd found evergreen to decorate the bannister and mantelpieces, and had agreed to Andrew's second tree, all nine and a half feet of it. She'd made more mince pies and had the children make salt-dough ornaments for the tree, painted a variety of garish colours, including one that Ben said was a vampire, with blood dripping from its fangs.

"Nice Christmas spirit, Ben," Natalie had said with a roll of her eyes, but she was still smiling and her brother just laughed. The children hadn't bickered as much here in Goswell as they did in New York, Jane realized. Perhaps it was having more space to themselves, or the fact that they all really were happier. She doubted she had anything to do with it.

They got along well with their cousins Chloe and Oliver, and the children all disappeared upstairs rather quickly, with accompanying thuds and shouts. Jane hadn't spent much time with Trisha or Dan, but she got along with them well enough and they enthused about the house – "So much atmosphere!" – and raved about the Aga.

"I've always wanted one of these," Trisha said as she stood by the Aga's warmth. "And Goswell is so beautiful – like a postcard. Here I am, living in a three-bedroom detached in a faceless suburb – you're so *lucky*, Jane."

Jane smiled weakly and took another batch of mince pies out of the oven.

A few minutes later Dorothy breezed in with several tins of homemade cakes and Jane felt herself tense. She and her mother-in-law had never really cleared the air after that argument several months ago. Despite a couple of trips to Keswick and the visit to the nursing home to see Ella, Jane felt the same stiffness she always had with Dorothy.

Now, as Dorothy unpacked all the things she'd brought, Jane kept a smile on her face despite the fact that she was feeling both determined and exhausted, as well as decidedly on edge, all of which annoyed her. It was *Christmas*, for heaven's sake. Why couldn't she let go of this irritating anxiety, this skittish fear that she was unhappy, that this still wasn't working? She wanted to relax and enjoy everything, and yet she felt wound up so tightly she didn't even know how to begin.

"Oh, mince pies," Andrew said with a delighted smile as he took the lids off one of Dorothy's many tins. "My favourite. No one makes mince pies like you do, Mum."

Jane watched from by the Aga as Andrew bit into one of his mother's homemade pies, complete with star-shaped top and tiny silver-ball decorations – everything homemade, of course, from the mincemeat to the pastry. She'd probably even made her own suet.

Andrew hadn't, Jane noticed, eaten one of her practically store-bought mince pies. Next to Dorothy's, they looked very sad indeed.

It wasn't a competition, she told herself, even as she acknowledged that some part of her felt like it was – and one she was bound to lose.

Was *that* what was making her so on edge? Was she trying to turn herself into *Dorothy?* The question didn't bear answering.

With the flurry of activity around Christmas – the midnight service, stockings and presents and an enormous dinner followed by a walk down to the beach with Dorothy's dogs – Jane didn't actually get a chance to talk to Dorothy, or anyone, until Boxing Day, when she was putting away the leftover ham and wiping down the kitchen surfaces.

Dorothy appeared in the doorway with two glasses of cream sherry. "I thought you could do with one," she said, handing Jane one of the glasses. "You look shattered."

"Thank you," Jane answered, deciding to ignore the "shattered" comment. She felt shattered, but she still didn't appreciate Dorothy saying so. Everything that came out of the woman's mouth felt like a criticism, an insult.

"You seem to have settled in here, after all," Dorothy said, leaning against the Aga's rail.

"After all?" Jane repeated. "What do you mean?"

"It wasn't easy, was it?"

Another observation she could have done without. Jane took a deep breath and focused on wiping the sink down yet again. She was tired and irritable and not in the mood to have a conversation with Dorothy where she felt patronized for trying to be what everyone else seemed to want her to be.

"Thank you for the sherry," she said when the silence had stretched on, and Dorothy sighed.

"I can see I've offended you. I seem to have the knack."

Jane didn't answer. Dorothy sighed again. "All I meant to say, Jane, was that I appreciate all the effort you're making. The children seem well settled and Andrew looks more relaxed than I've seen him in years. And the house is beautiful – I love the colours you've chosen for the walls. You need that brightness in this climate, don't you?" Tentatively she laid a hand on Jane's shoulder. "I know we haven't always seen eye to eye, but I'm proud of you, Jane. You've done a brilliant job – with everything."

Jane turned to give her mother-in-law a watery smile.

She could tell Dorothy was being sincere, and she appreciated everything she'd said. She *did*.

With a motherly pat on her shoulder Dorothy turned and left. Jane stood in the sudden quiet of her kitchen and let out a shuddering breath. Then she took a large gulp of sherry.

"Jane?" Andrew appeared in the doorway. "Why don't you leave all this? We're playing Charades in the sitting room." He smiled, his face flushed from the fire or the sherry, a bit of tinsel stuck in his hair.

Jane opened her mouth to answer that she'd come right along – and burst into tears.

CHAPTER TWENTY-THREE

Alice
Goswell, February 1943

"Alice, someone is cycling up from the station."

"From the station?" Alice looked up from the paper where she'd been jotting ideas for this summer's garden. She wanted to plant more potatoes, of course, a whole field of them in the walled garden behind the roses. And Harry had promised her he'd rig up some kind of greenhouse, so she could try tomatoes and cucumbers. This would be the third summer she'd done her garden, and every year it had been bigger and better. "Who is it, I wonder?" she asked Vera.

"It looked like Billy Biggs," Vera said quietly, and Alice felt her heart still inside her, seeming to hang suspended and silent in her chest. "It could be anything," Vera continued quickly. "Anything at all."

Alice just nodded. Her heart had started beating again, harder than ever, so every thump hurt. Everyone in Goswell knew that Billy Biggs delivered telegrams from the office attached to the rail station, and everyone also knew that telegrams never meant good news, not during wartime.

Vera had been living at the vicarage for nearly three years now, and Flora and Jamie had been there for over two. It had been a delightfully happy household, at least after those first awkward and uncertain interactions had taken place, with Jamie and Vera glaring warily at each other, and Flora fluttering about, acting more like a servant than a friend.

"You live here, you know," Alice had said in exasperation when Flora had jumped up from a chair as soon as she'd entered the dining room. "You're not my maid, Flora."

"I just want to be a help—"

"You are a help. And I want you to relax and feel comfortable here, as much as you can, anyway. I'd like you to think of the vicarage as your home."

To Alice's surprise Flora went very pale, her eyes glassy with tears as she shook her head. "I could never think that."

Alice frowned. "Why not?"

Flora shook her head again, moving around the room, picking up little objects and setting them down in a state of obvious agitation. "Because... oh, because." She looked up miserably. "I'd rather not say, to be honest."

"You don't have to, of course," Alice replied. "But I must confess I'm at a loss." She sat down in the chair across from Flora's and picked up a pair of stockings that had been the subject of her mediocre darning. Flora continued to move restlessly around the room, and Alice decided to wait in silence and see if her friend would finally confess whatever was bothering her.

"No one knows about Jamie's father," she finally said abruptly, with a wary glance at the closed door. It was after nine o'clock and Mrs Sutherland had gone home, the two children in bed.

"And you don't have to tell me," Alice answered swiftly. "Although I can't see what Jamie's father has to do with the vicarage feeling like your home."

Flora gave her a glance of weary despair. "Can't you?" she said and Alice went still.

"Are you... are you saying... Jamie's father...?" She

faltered and then stopped completely, unable to put into words what Flora seemed to be implying.

"Mr Sanderson, the last vicar," she whispered. She sat down again and buried her face in her hands. "I'm so ashamed."

Alice's mind spun. "He was married," she said slowly, and Flora let out a muffled sob. "Oh, Flora, I'm sorry. I didn't mean it that way. I was only being stupid and thinking aloud."

"It was just before he retired," Flora said with a sniff, speaking through her fingers. "A choir party. I used to be in the choir, until – well, you know." She let out a shuddering breath. "It was just the one time. He was a bit tiddly with sherry and I was – oh, I don't know what I was. Star-struck, most like. He – he reminded me of my grandfather." She let out a hiccuppy laugh. "That sounds mad, I know."

"Sad, perhaps," Alice said quietly. Her heart ached for Flora.

"He was horrified afterwards, of course. Said he'd never done anything of the like before – and of course I hadn't either. He left the village soon after, and I never got a chance to tell him I was expecting. Not that I would have. What could he have done?"

"Provided for you," Alice suggested with a touch of acid. She felt a surge of anger for the former vicar. He must have been past sixty, and Flora only just out of her teens.

"It would have ruined him, and his family, and the whole village. Everyone loved Mr Sanderson so, and he was ever such a nice man, if a little…" She sighed and finally dropped her hands from her now-blotchy face. "Weak. And they wouldn't have thanked me for it, either."

"Well," Alice said after a moment, "I suppose I can understand why you're uncomfortable in the vicarage."

"You won't think differently of me, will you?" Flora asked anxiously. "Because – him being the vicar—"

"Oh, Flora." Alice shook her head. "I never minded who he was. I've only wanted to be your friend." She reached out to clasp Flora's hand and from that moment on Flora lived in the vicarage as if it were her home rather than a grand house she didn't belong in, unless it was to tidy and dust there.

Jamie and Vera settled into a friendship of sorts, two misfits at school who banded together, and the following years, despite the never-ending ache of David's absence, were some of the happiest and busiest Alice had ever known.

She enjoyed Vera and Jamie's help in the garden, now willingly given, and they'd all just about split their sides laughing when they used an old silver-wheeled pram left in one of the outbuildings to wheel an enormous marrow to the summer fete. Vera had perched an old baby's bonnet on top of it and Alice had, for once, not felt the usual pang of sorrow for the children she'd never had. They were all immensely proud when the marrow won the second prize.

Alice treasured Flora's company during the long, dark evenings, when they often sat by the fire in the dining room, which was smaller and easier to heat than the sitting room, and chatted while they darned stockings or knitted socks for soldiers.

After the vicarage had been bombed and Vera had cried in Alice's arms, something had changed between them. Vera's brittle edges had smoothed and softened, and her sulky defiance had only reared itself on infrequent occasions, usually with Jamie, but he just laughed it off.

Mrs Sutherland had, predictably, been eloquently silent (save for a few sniffs) about the new arrivals. Others had offered opinions without being asked, and Alice had endured a fifteen-minute lecture from Mrs Dunston about what was appropriate for residents of the Vicarage (with a capital V), before she was finally able to get a word in edgewise and tell her, as politely as she could, to mind her own business.

The only opinion she really cared about was David's, and he'd been, as she'd first told Flora, firmly on her side. *Dearest Alice,* he'd written, *after ten years of marriage I certainly trust your intuition and wisdom, and most of all your kindness. I do hope this doesn't make things harder for you, or Flora, but I'm heartily glad you have a kindred spirit for company.*

Alice had even shown the letter to Flora, who had wept once more into her handkerchief, calling herself a ninny afterwards. "It's just so unexpected," she'd said, "and yet why should it be? Mr James has always been the kindest man."

"He has," Alice had agreed quietly, an ache in her words, for she hadn't seen David in over a year and just the thought of his dear face, his winsome smile and sparkling hazel eyes, always ready to see the humour or good in any situation, made her heart twist inside her.

He'd come home on leave last Christmas for four wonderful days, accepting the fuller household with cheerful alacrity, but since then she'd had only his letters to rely on, and those didn't come as frequently as she would have liked.

And now a telegram. Alice stood up from the kitchen table and wiped her damp palms along the sides of her dress. Her stomach churned with sudden nerves before it hollowed out completely and she had a strange sense of unreality as she went to answer the door, almost as if she were floating above herself, watching everything happen.

"Good morning, Billy." Somehow her lips curved into something like a smile as she greeted the unhappy-looking young man in front of her, his bicycle leaning against the side of the vicarage, his cap twisted between his nail-bitten hands.

"Morning, Mrs James. I'm sorry to deliver this to you." With a look of abject apology in his eyes he handed her the telegram, a single piece of paper that Alice knew would change her life forever.

"Thank you, Billy." She still felt as if she were floating high above, removed from this terrible scene unfolding like some maudlin radio drama with rote lines and wooden acting. She couldn't think of anything else to say; her mind and body were both numb, and so with a final nod of acknowledgment she closed the door.

She heard Billy fetch his cycle and the crunch of gravel as he pedalled down the church lane. The telegram lay in her hand, its edge sharp against her palm. Vera came into the vestibule, her shoes clicking on the tiles. Every noise seemed amplified, hurting Alice's ears.

"Alice?"

Alice didn't answer. She felt now as if she was stuck up there on the ceiling, watching this all take place yet unable to do anything at all. Frozen. If only she could remain so, if only she didn't have to march relentlessly forward with time, each endless moment sure to hold discovery and pain. "Do you want me to open it?" Vera asked gently, and finally Alice shook her head.

"No," she said, and her voice sounded strange and distant to her own ears, almost cold. "No, I must do that."

She walked slowly to the kitchen, part of her taking in every innocuous detail of the moment: the ticking clock, the gentle hiss of the range, the pale winter sunshine streaming through the windows and gilding the kitchen in fragile gold. She catalogued them in her mind, felt they were precious, for she knew with a bone-deep certainty that this was the last moment she would know any kind of peace, any sort of hope. The last moment of any possible ignorance or innocence.

"Alice—" Vera stopped, her narrow face pinched with anxiety. In the nearly three years since she'd lived with Alice she'd matured into a young woman, fifteen years old, whip-thin, with a sallow face and a sudden, beautiful smile. Now she bit her lip and looked at Alice with huge, tear-filled eyes.

"It's all right," Alice said, and strangely, she felt that it was. That it would be, with time. She felt almost as if David were telling her it would be, as if she could hear his voice, steady and even-tempered and yet full of hidden laughter.

"Are you going to open it?" Vera whispered. Alice stared down at the single slip of paper. "It might not be bad news," she continued in a rush. "Or, not the worst news. Perhaps he's ill or—"

Alice just shook her head, silencing the girl. The military didn't send telegrams just because someone was ill. She ran her thumbnail along the edge of the telegram, and felt the sudden, sharp sting of a paper cut. The pain, minor as it was, jolted her out of the numbness she'd been instinctively cloaking herself with, and for a moment she couldn't breathe as pain swamped her, worse than anything she'd ever felt before.

"Oh, *Alice*—" Vera choked, one hand stretched out towards her.

Alice opened the telegram.

It was incredibly brief, horribly succinct. *Regret to inform you Rev David James has died in service. Letter to follow.*

That was all. Two short, unemotional sentences, and her world collapsed around her as if a Nazi plane had dropped a bomb right there in the kitchen, turning everything she'd ever known to rubble and dust.

"Is it—?" Vera asked, her voice filled with tears, and Alice didn't answer. Her mind buzzed and her vision tunnelled into darkness and for a moment she thought she might faint or collapse; surely she couldn't just go on standing here, breathing and being, not when David was dead, had been dead for days, maybe even weeks—

"*Alice*," Vera said, and this time it was a sob, and she put her arms around her. Alice accepted the embrace instinctively even as her mind hammered absurd denial. *This can't be true. If it were true, I would have known. I would have felt something, some shift in the air, in my soul. I would have felt the loss of him inside me.*

And yet she knew now, from the emptiness that howled through her, colder than any Cumbrian wind, that it was true. David was gone.

CHAPTER TWENTY-FOUR

Jane

It had been three weeks since Andrew had walked in on Jane in the kitchen, looking completely flummoxed to see her in tears. She never cried. In fact, the more emotional she felt, the brisker she became, as if she could reason herself out of sorrow or will herself into joy. Neither worked this time, and the tears streaked down her face unchecked.

"Jane—" Andrew held his hands out in helpless appeal. "What's wrong, darling? Has something happened?"

"No." She shook her head and wiped her face. She hated crying in front of anyone, even the man she loved most in the world. It was so horribly revealing, so humiliatingly weak. "I'm just being stupidly emotional. It's the season, you know." She tried to smile.

Andrew's brow creased and he drew her into his arms; Jane came with a bewildering combination of relief and reluctance. "Emotional about what?"

"Everything, I suppose." In truth she didn't know why she'd started crying. What was she so upset about? She might have been wondering if she were truly happy, but she hadn't actually thought she was *sad*. Not this kind of sad, anyway.

"But…" Andrew stroked her hair, his arms secure around her. "I thought everything was going so well."

"It was. It is." She sniffed and drew back, trying to reassemble her dignity. "I'm not having a breakdown, honestly, Andrew. You just caught me at an emotional moment. It *is* Christmas."

The smile he gave her was both crooked and worried. "You don't have emotional moments."

"I must be changing." She smiled back, sort of. "Maybe it's the menopause."

"You're a little young for that, I think."

She shrugged, then drew in a rather ragged breath. "Don't fuss. And don't worry. I'm fine."

But fine, she thought now, three weeks after Christmas, wasn't the same as happy. She shouldn't be navel-gazing so much, she acknowledged irritably as she drove to Endsleigh on an unusually sunlit morning, the frost glittering on the fields. If she just got *on* with things, she wouldn't have time to wonder if she was happy or not. And there was plenty to be getting on with; even though Christmas had passed and the days were short, dark, and cold, family life churned on relentlessly.

Only last night Natalie had asked if she could go to the cinema in Workington with Will; Andrew had been about to agree when Jane had asked,

"Just the two of you?"

A dull flush had crept up Natalie's face. "Well, yeah," she said, scuffing her toe along the kitchen floor and not meeting either of their gazes. Andrew had glanced at Jane, bewildered, and she'd almost laughed. Clearly he had no concept that at nearly fifteen Natalie might think of Will as more than a friend.

"I think you're a little young to date, Nat," she said as mildly as she could, and her daughter's dull flush turned a bright, mottled red.

"It's not like that," she blustered. "We're just *friends*."

Jane hadn't answered. She'd seen the way Natalie looked at Will when he wasn't noticing and she had a feeling it was exactly like that, at least on Natalie's side. Andrew, predictably, was simply gaping at the two of them, slack-jawed and bug-eyed, as if it were just occurring to him that Natalie was not in pigtails and a pinafore.

"I'd rather you went with some friends," Jane said firmly. "It's better to go out in groups at this age, Natalie, honestly."

Natalie glared at her. "I liked you better before, when you didn't have time for us," she snapped, a comment Jane knew Natalie meant to wound. Still she held the line and Natalie flounced upstairs in a major huff, the door slamming in the distance.

"I can't believe she wants to date," he said in a hollow voice, and Jane patted his hand.

"She is almost fifteen, Andrew."

"Will's a good lad," he said cautiously and Jane shook her head. It was ironic that she was the one coming down hard now, when last year in New York, when Natalie had got in trouble for being at a party where some kids had been drinking, Jane had been the one who had wanted to cut her some slack.

Now, she supposed, she felt differently, because she'd had more time with Natalie, both alone and with Will, and she wasn't distracted and even consumed by work. She saw things she hadn't even bothered to look for before, and she made her decisions not out of impatience and irritation, but a quiet, if rather sad, certainty.

"Natalie cares too much," she said quietly. "It would be better if they didn't go out alone."

And I care too much, she thought. *I care that my daughter seems to hate me, that nothing I do is right.*

Now as Jane drove to Ben and Natalie's school she wondered about her son. Ben's teacher had rung yesterday and asked for a meeting, and Jane's stomach had clenched. Ben had been tested for learning disabilities back in the autumn, and he'd been diagnosed with a reading disability. It wasn't, his teacher had explained earlier, dyslexia but rather a difficulty with comprehension that could be addressed with learning support.

Jane had thought he was making good progress, but now she wondered. Why else would his teacher call her into school on a Wednesday morning?

Ben's teacher Sara met her in the reception area, looking too cheerful for it to be really bad news. Jane smiled back in greeting, and Sara led her to an empty classroom, the scent of books and unwashed PE kit mingling in the still air.

"Sorry we don't have a nice lounge with a coffee machine," she said, making a face. "This is it, really. And I'm sorry for dragging you out here – I just wanted to talk to you in person about Ben."

"Is everything all right?" Jane asked, hearing the anxiety in her voice.

"Oh, fine. Everything's fine. Brilliant, in fact – Ben is doing so well with learning support, and his reading comprehension is coming on loads."

"Oh. Good." Jane sank back against the plastic chair, relief coursing through her. She realized then just how worried she'd been, now that the knot of nameless anxiety always inside her had loosened, just a little bit.

"Sorry if I panicked you. I was actually wanting to talk about an opportunity for Ben – the college is starting a scheme of teens reading to elderly residents of the nursing home outside Whitehaven."

Jane nodded slowly; it was the same place Dorothy's cousin resided. "Yes, I know it."

"I thought Ben would be a great candidate for the programme," Sara continued, her voice bright with enthusiasm.

"It's simple, really. It's just a couple of pupils going once a week to read to the residents, and then discuss the passage. I think that kind of thing could be really helpful for Ben's comprehension skills, and I know the residents would love his energy."

"Would they?" Jane smiled weakly. She imagined Ben careening about the lounge of the home, knocking into wheelchairs and making far too much noise.

"Oh, yes." Sara nodded. "Ben is always so cheerful, enthusiastic about everything – it would be a fantastic fit, I know."

And not one she ever could have imagined, Jane realized. She was grateful to Ben's teacher, to his school, for understanding him in ways she never had and giving him opportunities she had assumed he couldn't handle.

Her mind buzzed with new and uncomfortable thoughts as she drove back to Goswell. The sun was, amazingly, still shining, every blade of grass and leafless tree glittering and bright. The world felt fresh and clear and cold, and when she thought of everything that had happened, all the good and even wonderful things, she wished this knot inside her wouldn't just loosen a little, but dissolve completely.

What's wrong with me?

The question – as well as that frustrating knot – remained with her as she walked down to the beach, determined to enjoy the sunshine, and then went back to pick up Merrie from school before Ben and Natalie came home.

She'd met a handful of mums now, knew them well enough to chat with in one of the tight little clusters at the school gate that she'd gazed on with such despair at the beginning of the school year.

As usual, Ellen fell in step beside her as they walked down the steep little lane that led from the school to the high street.

"I've talked to my grandfather about visiting with you," Ellen said, hitching her bag higher on her shoulder. "I almost asked him about the vicarage, but I thought you'd want to do that."

Jane smiled, touched that her friend had understood that – even if she didn't completely understand it herself. "That would be fantastic," she said. "When's a good time?"

"How about tomorrow afternoon?"

"Perfect."

Jane told Andrew about Ellen's invitation over dinner that night.

"I wonder what he'll tell you about Alice James," Andrew said, smiling, and Natalie looked up from her dinner.

"Who's Alice James?"

Rather self-consciously Jane told her children about finding the shopping list and learning a little bit about the Jameses.

"So they lived here? Way back then?" Natalie sounded more interested than Jane would have expected her to be.

"You found a shopping list right in there?" Ben waved towards the larder with his fork. "Maybe it's a secret code and she's trapped in time and asking for help…"

Natalie rolled her eyes. "This isn't an episode of *Dr Who*, Ben."

He shrugged, grinning. "But that would be so cool."

"What's cool," Jane answered, "is you being selected to take part in this new reading programme at the residential home. Your teacher said she talked to you about it?"

Ben blushed and hung his head. "Yeah…"

"That's great, Ben," Andrew exclaimed, his voice brimming with enthusiasm. "Really well done."

Natalie punched his arm lightly. "Not bad," she said, which was high praise indeed coming from her. Jane smiled at them all, felt that knot inside her loosen a little bit more. But it was still there.

Later she lay on her bed with Merrie tucked under her arm, reading a *Famous Five* book with the duvet drawn up nearly to their chins. Even with the fire Andrew had laid that was now crackling merrily in the fireplace, the room was cold.

"But we're cosy," Merrie said, when Jane said as much, snuggling in closer to her.

Jane smiled and turned a page. "Yes, we're cosy indeed."

She read a few pages, enjoying the solid warmth of Merrie next to her, the crackle of the fire and even the rattle of the windowpanes, reminding her that just as Merrie had said, they were cosy inside, sheltered from the cold and the wind.

Then Merrie placed her hand on the page to stop Jane reading and turned to her with a serious look, her wide brown eyes dark, her mouth pursed in thought.

"Merrie…?"

"Why don't you work, Mummy?"

The first thing Jane registered was the *Mummy*. Merrie really was beginning to sound British. She smiled and brushed her daughter's silky fringe away from her eyes. "Why don't I work? What do you mean?"

"You worked when we lived in New York. Why don't you now? Isn't there a Women For Change here?"

Jane smiled at the innocence of the question even as that knot tightened and solidified inside her. "No, there isn't. And I – I wanted to take a break from working, to spend more time with you and Natalie and Ben."

Merrie frowned. "But we're at school all day."

Jane closed her eyes for a second and summoned strength. Children had such innocently pointed questions. They cut to the quick, to the bone.

"Sophie's mummy works," Merrie continued. "While we're at school."

"I know that." Ellen had a part-time job with the council.

"Do you not want to work any more? Is that why you stopped?"

"Well—" Jane broke off before she'd even formed a reply because the truth was, she didn't know what to say. *Did* she not want to work any more? Certainly not the crazy, consuming hours she'd had in New York, but forget work completely? Forever?

"I stopped because we moved here, Merrie," she said at last, keeping her voice cheerful and mild. "And I'm glad for the break."

"But you'll go back? One day?" Merrie sounded anxious, and Jane couldn't tell if it was at the thought of her going back to work – or not going back.

"I don't know. I don't know if I could find the kind of job I'm suited for here." West Cumbria wasn't exactly brimming with employment opportunities.

Merrie snuggled even more against Jane, her elbow digging into her mother's side as she laid her head on her shoulder. "I hope you do, Mummy. I hope you find something. I think you're happier when you work."

From the mouths of infants, Jane thought rather numbly, and turned back to the *Famous Five*, where life was far more exciting, but also a lot simpler.

CHAPTER TWENTY-FIVE

Alice
Goswell, March 1943

"The post has come."

Vera stood in the doorway of the dining room, watching Alice with anxious eyes. It had been four weeks since the telegram had come with the news of David's death, and after the bustle of arranging the funeral and his memorial in the church, Alice had spent most of that time right here in the chair by the window, gazing out at the frost-tipped garden and letting her mind wander through the years and then into comforting numbness.

Now she turned to Vera, tried to summon the energy to respond. "Is there anything of note?"

Vera stepped into the room and held out a letter. "It's from the bishop."

"The bishop," Alice repeated, remembering how Henry Williams had taken David's funeral service, and spoken so sensitively about how women bore the brunt of war – the sorrow and the separation that would, in many cases, last throughout their lives.

She'd sat there numb and yet still aching, and when afterwards he'd clasped her hand between his own and murmured how sorry he was, Alice had managed to reply, although she could not recall what she'd said.

Now she roused herself enough to take the letter and open it, scanning the lines without much surprise or emotion.

"Well?" Vera asked, chewing her lip. "What does he say?"

Alice lowered the letter to gaze for a moment around the room, with its faded chintz chairs and the big mahogany table from David's parents' farmhouse; once she'd imagined their children seated around it, but that dream had faded long ago, along with others. She turned to Vera.

"He says I must vacate the premises by the first of May."

"Vacate the premises?" Vera stared at her in confusion and Alice managed a wry smile.

"Leave. The house doesn't belong to me, Vera. It's the church's, or the diocese's, really. The next—" She paused for a second to summon that necessary numbness once more. "The next vicar will need to take up his place."

"Oh." Vera's eyes widened and her face paled. Alice felt a needling of guilt; she should have explained matters to her before this. In truth, she hadn't even thought about it. The letter hadn't surprised her, precisely, but she had not yet had the energy or interest to think about the future, whether it took place here in Goswell or—

"Where will you go?" Vera asked, and Alice heard a trembling note of anxiety in her voice.

"I don't know." Upon David's death she'd received a small pension as a war widow, and another small sum from the church. There had been a bit of savings as well, and cobbled all together she would manage. But where? "I suppose," she said slowly, "I shall return to Cambridge." Earlier in her marriage, when she'd first arrived in Goswell and then when her baby daughter had been stillborn, she'd longed for the comforting familiarity of the tall, narrow house on Grange Road.

Now she didn't know how she felt about it, or anything. She could not imagine living there again, in those gloomy rooms, once again fetching for her father, who was elderly now and more forgetful than ever, and talking over the teapot with Mrs Chesney, choking down her awful cooking, everything the same as if these twelve years in Goswell had never been, as if her marriage, as if David had never been.

Alice closed her eyes.

"And what about Flora and Jamie?" Vera asked.

With effort Alice opened her eyes again. She must shake this dreadful lethargy, she thought. It wasn't fair to the others for her to simply sit all day, staring into space and thinking of the way things used to be, how she still so desperately wanted them to be.

"I don't know," she admitted. Flora had been wonderfully kind since David's death, never asking too many questions, always ready to listen, pouring a cup of tea and simply leaving it by Alice's elbow. Often it went cold and untouched but Alice still appreciated her friend's gestures.

"And what about me?" Vera asked in a small voice. She tried to smile, but it wobbled and slid right off her face. Alice's heart lurched and she straightened in her chair.

"*You*—" She must come to terms with all of this, she told herself severely. She hadn't even considered that Vera wouldn't have a place to go; she'd assumed it would be with her. "I won't leave you with nowhere to go, Vera." Tears thickened in her throat. She did not want to leave the girl. She couldn't.

"They'll re-home me, I suppose," Vera said, and Alice could tell she was doing her best to put a brave face on it. "Someone else in the village could do with a girl around the house, no doubt."

"I won't have you being someone's skivvy," Alice answered. It was what Vera had thought she wanted of her all those years ago. "And there's no reason why you should be re-homed—"

"You think the new vicar will want me?" Vera asked, and Alice heard the awful mix of hope and fear in her voice.

"Vera, *I* want you. I don't want to leave you here. You're not some kind of unwanted parcel, you're almost like a daughter to me. I'd take Flora and Jamie with me if I could, but I know they wouldn't want to leave Goswell."

"You mean… you mean you'd take me to Cambridge?"

Alice sank back in her chair, her initial burst of fiery determination spent. "I don't know. I don't know if I can. I suppose the best thing to do is to write to your mother and see what she thinks. She might want you back, you know."

"She never wanted me in the first place." There was no bitterness in Vera's voice, just fact. "But I'll write to her."

"It's a start," Alice said quietly. Even if she didn't want to start this new chapter of her life, she knew she needed to, and not just for her own sake.

She told Flora about the letter from the bishop that evening, when Vera and Jamie were in bed. Flora bit her lip, glancing down as she threaded her needle with more concentration than was surely needed.

"I knew it would happen, of course," she said, still looking down. "But I hoped… oh, I suppose I hoped that they'd wait until this awful war was over. Reverend Bearman is doing well enough, and I hate the thought of you being turfed out like that—"

"I've a place to go," Alice answered. "It's you and Jamie I'm worried about. Will you go back to your mum's?"

Flora looked up, her eyes clouded with doubt. "It's

still packed like a tin of sardines over there. I don't know if there's room."

"There's always room—"

"Well," Flora answered, her tone practical, "I don't know if Mum would say there's room." She sighed. "Don't worry about me, Alice. Jamie and I will find a place."

"You could always come with us."

"What? To Cambridge? I've never been farther south than Preston."

"There's always a first time," Alice said with a small smile and for a moment she thought Flora would consider it. Then her friend shook her head.

"I couldn't. I know Mum can be as cross as two sticks but she'd still miss Jamie if I went so far away." Tears filled Flora's eyes and she blinked rapidly. "But I'll miss you, Alice. Dreadfully. You've been the best friend I've ever had, you know, and for longer than you even know. I don't know what I'll do without you."

"And I without you," Alice answered, her voice rough with emotion. "For I could say the same, Flora. You've been such a good friend to me." She reached over and clasped her hand, and the two women remained silent, caught in their own grief and sympathy, as the wind howled outside and the fire crackled in the hearth.

Roused finally from her lethargy, during the next few weeks Alice set about arranging matters. She wrote to her father, and received his reply that of course she must come and stay with him once again; the house would be hers eventually – a prospect Alice did not want to consider just now.

She parcelled up her things and arranged for the larger pieces of furniture she couldn't take with her to be given away.

She offered Mrs Sutherland two weeks' severance, which the older woman took with a sniff of gratitude.

"I don't suppose I'll stay on and see if the new vicar wants me," she said with a shake of her head. "I've a sister in Millom, and this cold has got into my bones. I've a mind to go there."

"And Harry?" Alice asked.

"He's been talking about starting over as well," Mrs Sutherland answered. "Maybe in Barrow, or even Manchester. There's more for a lad to do there."

Alice nodded, saddened to think of their household, strange as it had been, breaking up in such a fashion. But that was what war did, she supposed. It came and took and destroyed. It was up to them to rebuild as best they could.

A week before she was meant to leave the vicarage, with the first tulips poking their shy heads from the flowerbeds, Vera still hadn't heard from her mother.

"I won't leave you here," Alice said firmly. "You can come with me, and any news from your mother can be passed on. There's no reason to do otherwise."

"But what if someone says—"

"Who is this someone, I wonder?" Alice teased with a smile. "You've been living with me for three years and you'll continue to do so, at least until we hear from your mum. It's as simple as that."

"Thank you, Alice," Vera whispered and Alice shook her head.

"I should be the one thanking you, Vera. I couldn't do this on my own."

A knock sounded at the door, and Alice went to answer it, since Mrs Sutherland was elbow-deep in flour in the kitchen.

"Mr Dunston—" She rarely talked to the sober-looking churchwarden; he always seemed so serious and preoccupied, and she felt as if even her shy hellos were wasting his time. Now he looked unaccountably grim. "Is something wrong?"

"I'm afraid so, Mrs James. Something is very wrong indeed."

Alice felt a tremble of fear even as she fought the sudden, absurd urge to laugh. What, she wondered, could be more wrong than what had already happened?

"What is it?" she asked and Mr Dunston shook his head, the gesture one of bleak judgment.

"The church silver has been stolen. And we think your girl has stolen it."

CHAPTER TWENTY-FIVE

Jane

Jane came into the cheerful sitting room of the residential home in Whitehaven where James Welton now lived, glancing around at the different people seated about the comfortable space. Some played cards, some read, and some simply sat and chatted.

"There he is," Ellen said cheerfully and waved at a white-haired man in a dark green jumper and worn cords. His hair was sparse and thin but his eyes glinted cheerfully as he rose from his seat to bid them welcome.

"Ellen's told me about you," he said as they settled into chairs on either side of him. "You've taken over the old vicarage."

"I have," Jane confirmed, smiling. She liked James Welton immediately; there was something so friendly and approachable about him, so open and honest.

"It's a nice house," James said. "Although it can get rather cold, can't it just, in winter." He smiled knowingly and Jane leaned forward.

"Have you been inside it?"

"Have I been inside! I only lived there for near on two years."

"Lived there!" Jane stared at him, dumbfounded. Ellen, she saw, looked shocked too.

"You never told me that, Granddad," she said in a tone of faint reproach. Previously seeming so open and honest, James now suddenly looked a bit shifty.

"It was a long time ago."

"Even so—"

"I had good memories there," he said, and Jane could understand how he might want to keep those precious.

"Did you live with the Jameses?" she asked and James nodded.

"Just the Mrs James. The Reverend was away as an army chaplain."

"Why did you live there?" Ellen pressed. She still looked flummoxed. "I thought you grew up in your grandmother's house."

"I did, save those two years. But Granny's sister came to stay after her place was bombed and there wasn't room for us. I was a bit of a terror." His eyes glinted and Ellen smiled.

"Now that I can believe."

"It was kind of Mrs James to take us in," James continued. "Not everyone approved, you know, on account of my mother not having wed. But Mrs James was determined – Mum told me that, after. She tried to refuse but Mrs James wouldn't hear of it."

"Of course not," Jane said softly. She couldn't believe she was actually sitting and talking to someone who had known Alice James, who had talked to her. For so long Alice had been like a ghost, a shadow, unknown and unknowable. Yet now Jane had the chance to find out who she really was, what someone had thought of her. The realization filled her with excitement and also a ripple of something like fear in case Alice didn't live up to her expectations.

"So it was just you, Flora, and Mrs James living in that big vicarage?" Ellen asked.

"And Vera," James answered. "Along with the housekeeper. I don't remember her name, but she wasn't the cheerful sort."

"Vera!" Jane leaned forward again. "Beloved by Vera" had been engraved on Alice's headstone. "Who was Vera?"

"An evacuee from Liverpool that Mrs James took in. She was my age, and she wasn't the easiest character, but Mrs James kept with her. It's a shame how it all ended."

Jane's heart lurched. "What do you mean? How did it end?"

"Vera was accused of stealing the church silver. She was a bit rough, I'll grant you, but Mrs James had done so much for her. That didn't seem to matter to some, though. I don't rightly remember the whole of it, but I know some were baying for blood – Vera's, it seemed – and she was that scared they'd put her into one of those homes for bad girls. You know, a reformatory."

"Did they?" Jane asked in a whisper. Even Ellen seemed transfixed by the story, leaning forward, her gaze fastened on her grandfather.

James shook his head. "No, they dropped it all in the end. Never really knew why, or how. They never found out who stole the stuff, that I know. Mrs James left right after it all happened – the Reverend had died a few months before, I think, and she took Vera with her. They went back to Cambridge – we kept in touch through letters for a while, but then…" He shrugged and spread his hands. "You know how it is."

"And what was Mrs James like?" Jane asked. She felt a strange tug of sadness that she would never know this for herself. "What do you remember of her?"

"She was quiet," James said after a moment. "And sometimes she seemed a bit – sad. She had no children, so that might have been part of it. She loved her garden – a Victory garden, it was. She got everyone mucking in, digging potatoes.

We wheeled a marrow in a pram, once, to the summer fete." He let out a reminiscent sigh. "She was lovely, and gentle with everyone. I know Vera adored her, even if she didn't say so. And I was rather fond of her myself, to be honest. There was something so… *sincere* about her, I suppose. You know the kind of person who you can always tell is really listening?"

Jane nodded. "Yes," she said. "I know."

Jane's mind was still buzzing with the new information about Alice when she returned to the vicarage. She stood in the driveway, dusk just beginning to settle, and felt as if she saw everything a little bit differently now. James had told her that the walled garden behind the roses that was now nothing but bramble had been a field of potatoes. Alice had apparently dug over the entire lawn to plant vegetables – much to the consternation of the churchwardens. The thought of her Alice, who had been so gentle and quiet, showing such spirit and initiative made Jane smile.

And yet she'd had so much sadness in her life – no children, her husband dying while she was still a young woman, the trouble with Vera. Still she'd persevered, had kept going on even when things were uncertain, or hard, or lonely.

Alice had made a difference, Jane thought, without making a fuss about it. Surely that quiet strength was an example she wanted to follow, a lesson she could take to heart?

She heard the creak of the church door opening and turned to see the current vicar, Simon Truesdell, leaving the church. Impulsively she started forward.

"Hello, Simon."

He smiled and raised a hand in greeting. "Hello, Jane. Nice to see you. Not minding this cold too much?"

"At least the sun's been shining." She took a breath. "I

know this might seem a bit odd, but I wondered if I could ask you about the church silver?"

"The church silver?" Simon's eyebrows headed towards his hairline. "Now that's not a request I get every day. What about it?"

"I heard it was stolen back during the war?"

"That's right. I don't know too much about it, to tell you the truth. It was the good stuff, from the 1600s, very valuable."

"And they never found it? Couldn't you trace that kind of thing?"

"You'd think you could, but who knows? It was wartime, after all. In any case, no one saw or heard of it again, as far as I know."

"And no one had any idea who stole it?"

"Not that I've heard. It's a shame, really. The communion silver we have now is decent, but nothing like that."

"May I see it?" Jane asked.

Surprised, Simon nodded. "Another request I don't get very often. But come on, I'll show you."

The inside of the church was cold and dark, and the electric light in the vestry that Simon switched on bathed one corner of the soaring space in a rather sickly yellow light.

"Here it is," he said, unlocking a safe and bringing out a few pieces of well-polished, simple silver. "Rather modern and plain, which I don't mind, frankly. But some people miss the old stuff."

"Yes…"

Simon handed her the plain communion chalice and Jane held it up to the light, studying it closely as if it could offer some insight on what had happened all those years ago. Who had stolen the original silver? And how had gentle, quiet Alice helped Vera to escape the punishment others had wanted for her? She knew instinctively that it was Alice who had helped Vera, and kept her out of some awful reformatory. Yet how?

"A funny thing in the records," Simon continued conversationally. "This silver was bought right when the last bit was stolen, around 1943, I think. But it wasn't paid off until 1955."

Jane looked up. "Was it that expensive?"

"No, that's the thing. The church bought it, and someone paid them for it, like a debt. Regular instalments every month for twelve years, all made in the ledger." He shook his head. "Makes you wonder, doesn't it?"

"It does," Jane said softly, gazing down once more at the chalice. She knew instinctively that it was Alice who had paid that money for the silver, who had paid the debt. It was Alice who had, despite the disappointments in her own life, saved someone, and done it with such little fanfare or fuss that no one even knew.

"Jane?" Simon sounded startled and when she looked up she saw him gazing at her in consternation.

"Yes…?"

"It's just…" He gestured helplessly. "You're crying."

"Am I?" Jane touched her damp cheek and let out a shaky laugh. She realized that for once she wasn't even embarrassed; she didn't mind these tears. "Sorry. I've been a bit emotional lately. It's just… she was a remarkable woman, wasn't she? And no one ever even knew."

"She?" Simon repeated blankly, and Jane realized he didn't even know who she was talking about.

"Never mind," she said quietly, and handed back the chalice.

CHAPTER TWENTY-SIX

Alice
Goswell, April 1943

"What do you mean, he's gone?"

Mrs Sutherland wouldn't quite meet Alice's eye as she busied herself about the kitchen, wiping the already clean table-top and shuffling the teapot and cups around needlessly.

"I told you before. He'd a mind to go to a city, Carlisle or Manchester—"

"I thought you said Barrow before," Alice said. "And in any case... he's just gone?" Alice felt a ripple of unease at the way Mrs Sutherland moved around the kitchen, her voice sounding brisk and even shrill. "I thought Harry would have said goodbye, after all—"

"Well, he's a man, and he's busy. You know how it is."

Alice supposed she did. Things could change so quickly, and without any warning; look at her own situation. Sighing, she reached for her tea. "Where has he gone, then?" she asked. Mrs Sutherland hesitated, and Alice put down her tea. "You do know where he's gone, don't you?"

"Of course I do," Mrs Sutherland answered, and now her voice really did sound shrill. "He's gone to Carlisle." She whisked away her teacup and put it in the sink, her back to Alice.

"Carlisle? Has he got a job there, then?"

Another telling hesitation and Alice felt that unease deepen. Something wasn't right about what Mrs Sutherland was saying –

or rather, what she wasn't saying. Yet Alice had too many other things to worry about to consider what Harry might be up to.

In the three days since the church silver had been stolen, the pressure to blame Vera had only intensified. Both of the Dunstons had very nearly quivered with moral outrage, and Mrs Dunston had pointed out, quite rightly, that Vera had stolen before.

Alice had stared at her, utterly heartsick. "What do you mean, before?"

Mrs Dunston had lifted her chin. "From your very own bureau, wasn't it?"

Alice hadn't told anyone about that long-ago episode save Flora, and she couldn't believe Flora would have said a word to Mrs Dunston – so how had the woman known?

"You don't think Vera stole the silver, do you, Mrs Sutherland?" she asked and saw the housekeeper stiffen, her back to Alice.

"I don't suppose it much matters what I think."

"You've been in this house with Vera for three years," Alice persisted. "Surely you don't think she's capable?"

"I know she's capable," Mrs Sutherland answered flatly and Alice stilled.

"What do you mean?"

"What do you think I mean?" Mrs Sutherland turned around, and Alice saw to her surprise that the woman was trembling from head to toe. "She stole that lipstick right off your bureau, didn't she?"

"How did you know about that?"

"Miss Welton told me."

Oh Flora, Alice thought disconsolately. She could see how it might have happened; Flora would have assumed Mrs Sutherland already knew, and must have said something about how well Vera had come on since then... yes, she could see just how it could have happened.

"And you told Mrs Dunston, didn't you?" Alice said heavily and the housekeeper bristled.

"And what if I did? The girl's a thief, isn't she?"

"She is not!" Alice rose from the table, suddenly feeling quite terrible with rage. "She took one lipstick, and she gave it back. And that was three years ago, Mrs Sutherland! How could you hold it against her, when you know how she's helped us all this time? How she's like a daughter to me?" Too late Alice realized tears were spilling down her cheeks and she wiped at them angrily.

"Someone took that silver," Mrs Sutherland said, and though she sounded stubborn Alice saw she was near tears herself.

"Yes, someone did," she answered slowly. "And it wasn't Vera." And Harry had left so suddenly – he'd been in the vestry with her all that time ago when Reverend Bearman had left it out, most likely knew he left it out more often than not. Mrs Sutherland was acting strangely, trembling and near to tears – that was so unlike her...

"Mrs Sutherland," Alice said clearly, "do you know who stole it?"

"Of course I don't." Mrs Sutherland's voice shook. "But it stands to reason it's a girl who's already shown she'll take something that isn't hers."

Alice took a deep breath. "Why has Harry gone off so suddenly, you don't even know where, with no work to speak of?"

Two angry red splotches of colour appeared on Mrs Sutherland's wrinkled cheeks. "Mind what you say!"

The two women held each other's gazes for a long, tense

The Vicar's Wife

moment. Then Alice let out her breath in a sigh of weary despair. "You know," she said quietly, "they want to send Vera to a reformatory? Her mother hasn't written back and if she's died in a bombing—"

"That's not my concern."

"Is it not?" Alice shook her head sadly. "Have you no Christian charity?"

Mrs Sutherland recoiled as if she'd been struck. She turned back to the sink and busied herself with the teacups; Alice watched her with a sense of hopelessness. If Harry had stolen the silver and gone, there would be no way of proving it. No way of clearing Vera's name.

After several minutes when the only sound was the clink of the cups in the basin Mrs Sutherland put her hands flat on the counter, her back still to Alice and radiating tension.

"He's my son, Mrs James," she said quietly and Alice's heart ached.

"I know," she answered. She didn't say anything else; what could Mrs Sutherland do, at any rate? Strangely, in that moment she felt more sympathy for Mrs Sutherland than she ever had before. "I know."

Alice took a deep breath, her fingernails digging into her palms, before she reached for the doorknob to the sitting room. Behind her she could hear Mrs Sutherland coming with the tea tray, laid with the best china. Mr Dunston, the other churchwarden Mr Sidwell, and Henry Williams, the Bishop of Carlisle, were all on the other side of the door waiting to discuss the stolen silver – and Vera.

Alice had tried to keep the wardens' suspicions from Vera, but she'd found out anyway, probably from Mrs Sutherland. She'd been distraught, although she'd hidden it well. It was only when Alice had heard her sobbing wildly on her bed that she realized how upset and afraid Vera truly was.

"They'll send me away, won't they?" she'd asked when Alice had come in and sat on the edge of her bed. "To some kind of prison for girls."

"No, they won't, Vera."

"Mum won't care," the girl sniffed. "If she's even alive. She hasn't written, has she? She never cared about me. Me leaving was the best thing that ever happened to her."

"And the best thing that's ever happened to me," Alice answered quietly. She reached over and stroked Vera's hair. "I won't let them blame you for this, Vera."

Vera raised her tear-stained face from her pillow. "You believe me, then? That I didn't take it?"

"Of course I do."

"Even though I took your lipstick?"

"You gave it back, and that was years ago. You've changed, Vera. And I love you. I won't let anything happen to you."

An incredulous light dawned in Vera's reddened eyes. "You love me?"

"Of course I do." Alice gathered the girl in her arms. "I told you, you're like a daughter to me. I'll take care of you, I promise."

Promises, Alice thought bleakly as she opened the door to the sitting room, were all well and good, but could she really keep them? Vera's fate was not in her hands... but rather the hands of the men waiting in this room, all of them looking exceedingly dour.

"This is a serious business, Mrs James," the bishop said when Mrs Sutherland had served them all with cups of tea and then, with one anxious look at Alice, had departed. "A serious business indeed."

"I know, Bishop," Alice answered. "And I'm very sorry the silver was stolen. David always thought it the most beautiful craftsmanship."

"And so it was. And very valuable."

"A fifteen-year-old girl would hardly be able to appreciate the value," Alice said as evenly as she could. Her hands were trembling and she put her teacup back down in its saucer. "Much less find a place to sell it on."

"She's from Liverpool," Mr Dunston said darkly, as if that explained everything. "She knows all sorts of people, I've no doubt."

"But she's been living in Goswell," Alice reminded him. "And there is no reason to think she stole anything—"

"She stole before," Mr Dunston said flatly.

"A lipstick, and she gave it back—"

The bishop was shaking his head, and already Alice could feel the conversation slipping away from her. They wanted someone to blame; Vera, still an outsider, was the easiest candidate.

Alice knew she could tell them about Harry Sutherland leaving Goswell so suddenly. It would surely cast doubt on Vera's guilt, and yet still she hesitated. She didn't know for certain that Harry had taken the silver, and they might not even believe her. Besides, casting suspicion on Harry would hurt Mrs Sutherland dreadfully, and perhaps even affect her standing in the village.

She and Vera were leaving in a few days, God willing, and she didn't mind what anyone here thought of her. She just wanted her freedom – and Vera's.

"We need to take action," Mr Dunston said with decision. "The girl is the obvious candidate. She needs to be dealt with."

Henry Williams raised his shaggy eyebrows. "What are you suggesting?"

"She doesn't belong here. We might not get the silver back but the girl belongs in a—"

"But why shouldn't you get it back?" Alice pressed. "Where could she have put it?" She turned to the bishop in desperate appeal. "Surely you can see that if she took it, it would be found somewhere. In her room or—"

"She probably passed it on," Mr Dunston said grimly. "The girl's a menace, always has been. She spoke back to Mrs Dunston once and is always giving her looks."

Alice bit her lip. She knew Vera could be a bit... sharp, but was Mr Dunston really going to make a few surly looks his reason for putting Vera in a home?

"Her own mother doesn't want her," he continued with a kind of grim triumph, and Alice felt fury bubble up inside her.

"I want her, Mr Dunston. Vera has been wonderful to me, and I know she didn't take that silver. By having her put in a reformatory you are proposing to ruin a young girl's life on mere hearsay." She turned to the bishop, leaving the churchwarden blinking in surprise. "Bishop, I've lived here quietly for twelve years, and I leave for Cambridge in a few days. I am hoping to take Vera with me, and offer her the kind of love and opportunity that would not be found if she were sent to a girls' home." She took a breath, steeling herself to continue without breaking down in tears, as she felt perilously close to doing.

"As Christians we are meant to practise forgiveness and exhibit love. I ask you to be merciful to both me and Vera, and allow her to return to Cambridge with me. She didn't steal the silver, but I know I can't prove it, and if people want to see her tried and found guilty, they will have it done." She spread her hands wide. "I can't return the silver, or pay for it, as I know it is irreplaceable, but I will offer to replace it with what is available."

"Even that would be terribly expensive," Mr Sidwell, who was the church treasurer, offered dourly. "The church can't even afford it."

"I'll pay it in instalments, then," Alice said, desperation edging her voice. "As long as it takes. We can come to some arrangement, surely."

The bishop stared at her for a long, fathomless moment. "This girl means that much to you?"

"Very much so."

He nodded, and Alice held her breath, waiting. Finally he spoke. "Very well. So be it. The silver will be replaced, and the girl will have a home." He turned censorious eyes towards the churchwardens. "I believe in second chances, gentlemen. As does God."

CHAPTER TWENTY-SIX

Jane

Everything felt different somehow, now that she knew more about Alice. Jane couldn't explain it to herself, much less anyone else, yet after talking to Simon she walked through the rooms of the vicarage, now with their bright paint and modern furniture, as if in a trance.

This was Alice's house, and yet it was her house, or at least it was becoming her house. Living here in windy, desolate Goswell was becoming her life, just as it had been Alice's. Jane had never been one for sentiment, had never believed in ghosts or auras or any of the other far-fetched things people believed in these days... and yet she felt a connection, a kinship to Alice, and had done ever since she'd first picked up that shopping list.

How did she explain that? And never mind explaining, what did she do with this new understanding she had of Alice James, and the life she'd lived with quiet, forgotten dignity?

Jane ended up in the garden, now stark and bare, and gazed at the thorny branches of the neglected roses and imagined Alice here, digging with quiet determination, making her garden. She pictured Vera and even James with her, and his mother Flora, all ploughing for potatoes, weeding carrots. It was hard to imagine such a scene, even though she could feel the echoes of it. There was certainly no sign of any of it now.

"You won't believe the people I've talked to who remember your Alice James," Ellen said the next morning, when they'd dropped Merrie and Sophie at school and were walking back down the high street.

"My Alice James," Jane repeated with a shake of her head. "Who else remembers her?"

"My neighbour Dorothy Burton, for one. Said Mrs James always visited her gran, and she had the kind of voice you could listen to for hours. She said she always liked it when Mrs James came to visit."

"Did she," Jane murmured. It gave her a strange feeling to think of all these memories surfacing, like pieces of a puzzle slowly being fitted together, and the whole image finally taking shape.

"Yes, though the funny thing is, she didn't even remember who Alice James was, until I mentioned the vicarage and the war and all of it."

That was, Jane thought, not all that surprising. "She did live a quiet life."

"Yes… she didn't remember Vera, though, at least not specifically. Said there were evacuees all over the village. Goswell took in near to fifty."

That evening Jane sat at the kitchen table and gazed at her family surrounding her; Merrie was dreamily twirling her pasta around her fork and Ben and Natalie were bickering, admittedly good-naturedly, about *X Factor*. Andrew was smiling with a benevolent bonhomie and Jane's heart swelled, the knot that had been so long inside her seeming, for the moment, to dissolve.

"I was thinking," Andrew said, "we ought to get a dog."

The children all fell silent before they erupted into squeals and shouts, and then suggestions for names and breeds.

"A dog," Jane repeated, surprised she wasn't as opposed to the idea as she once might have been.

"Yes, I like to imagine myself traipsing through the fells with a nice Labrador at my heels," Andrew said with a grin. Jane raised her eyebrows.

"As I recall, you haven't done any traipsing through the fells since we arrived."

"No, but if I had a dog… this house was made for a dog. This life was."

Jane couldn't help but smile at his infectious enthusiasm. "I might be persuaded," she said, which gave rise to more squeals and shrieks from the children.

After dinner, as Jane was clearing up the kitchen and humming under her breath, Natalie appeared in the doorway. Jane tensed, for conversations with her daughter still felt like battles, daggers drawn.

"Do you need something, Nat?" she asked lightly when Natalie hadn't spoken for a few minutes.

"I… I just wanted to say I'm sorry," Natalie said in a rush. She looked down, her dark hair swinging in front of her face, one foot scuffing the floor.

"Sorry?" Jane stopped wiping the table, her face set in a frown. "What for?"

"For being… you know… stupid," Natalie mumbled.

"You haven't been stupid."

Natalie looked up, blinking from behind her fringe. "I've been kind of horrible to you," she said, and Jane gave her a small smile.

"I know I haven't been the easiest person to get along with sometimes." She sat down at the table and beckoned Natalie forward; her daughter came reluctantly, slouching into a chair. "Can you tell me what's going on?" Jane asked quietly. "I mean, really going on? Between you and me?"

Natalie stared at her hands, unspeaking, and Jane let the

silence go on for a while. "I hated it here at first," she said in a voice so low that Jane had to strain to hear her. "And I know you did too."

"Yes," Jane admitted quietly. "I did. It wasn't easy, moving, for either of us."

"But then I started to like it," Natalie continued, still staring at her laced, nail-bitten fingers. "And you didn't."

Jane processed that for a moment. "And that made you angry?" she finally guessed.

"I… guess." Natalie glanced up at her. "I wanted you to like it. You were so busy in New York – sometimes it felt like you were barely there."

Jane blinked back tears, that old rush of guilty regret surging through her. "I know."

"And the fact that you didn't like it here… it felt like you didn't like us."

"That was never the case, Natalie." Briefly Jane thought of her fantasy apartment, her fantasy life in New York, and cringed. She'd come so close to wilfully throwing away everything she had. "I admit, I had trouble settling into life here – not just to Cumbria and Goswell, but to not working and being a full-time mom to you and Ben and Merrie. Sometimes I missed my job so much it hurt." She took a deep breath. "It still hurts, a little, because I loved what I did. But I love you more."

"I didn't want to make you choose."

"You didn't," Jane said, and reached out to squeeze her daughter's hand. "I did."

Later that night as they got ready for bed, the curtains drawn against the starless night, Andrew came over and put his arms around her.

"You seem a bit preoccupied. A penny for your thoughts?"

"I was thinking about Alice James," Jane admitted. She'd been thinking too about Natalie and her job and the whole crazy adventure of motherhood, but she felt like talking about Alice. "I want to do something for her."

"For her?"

"Only a few people in the village remember her, which I suppose isn't that surprising. She lived a quiet and unremarkable life and yet… she was someone. She was important to someone."

"She was important to quite a few people, I imagine."

Jane twisted in his arms to gaze up at him with a rueful smile. "I probably sound daft, as you British would say."

"Us British?"

She smiled and touched his cheek. "There's something so inspiring about a life quietly lived, isn't there? Without any fuss or fanfare, just simple love and duty. She made a difference, even if no one sees it now, or even cares."

"Is that how you see Alice James's life? Quietly lived?"

"Yes," Jane said after a moment. "It is."

"And what kind of memorial do you have in mind?"

She smiled teasingly. "How do you know I have anything in mind?"

He gathered her in his arms once more. "Because I know you, Jane. Your mind goes a mile a minute."

"Well, yes. I do have something in mind." She smiled up at him. "A garden."

Jane gazed around at the plot of tilled soil that had once been no more than a neglected patch of earth in front of the vicarage. It was finally spring, the sun was shining, and white, wispy clouds were scudding across the sky.

Today they were going to start on Alice's garden. It had

become, in the end, a village effort. Ellen knew someone who specialized in garden design, and Will and Natalie had canvassed for donations. The school had even put some of their coffee morning proceeds towards the cost, and finally they were able to start.

Jane turned to see Ellen, along with a dozen others, coming down the church lane: Simon Truesdell, and Will and his father, a few mums from the school run; even James Welton had come out. Dorothy had arrived last night and was intending to help.

This was how it should be, Jane thought. This was how she wanted it to be, everyone pitching in and working together to make a garden, small as it was, for a person who had lived simply and quietly and still made a difference.

Andrew had, some months ago, dug up some more information on Vera on the internet. "Do you want to know?" he'd asked Jane. "Or will it spoil it?"

She'd laughed and shaken her head. "Nothing will spoil it now. What is it?"

"It was all quite easy once James gave me her last name," Andrew explained. "She went to Cambridge with Alice, as we know, and then to Newnham College. Quite clever, Vera."

"Really," Jane murmured.

"She married in 1954 – to a fellow Cambridge student. He went into the Foreign Service, and they lived abroad for many years. Had four children – I don't know anything about them."

"I'm amazed you've managed to dig this all up—"

"Alice officially adopted her after the war. Vera was an orphan by then. She became Vera James in 1945. And here's the best bit," Andrew finished, beaming. "She's still alive. Lives in a house on Grange Road in Cambridge – Alice James's old house. She left it to Vera in her will."

"She's still alive?" Somehow Jane hadn't considered that.

"Yes – I thought maybe we could write her a letter, explaining who we are? Who knows, maybe one day we could visit."

"One day," Jane agreed, liking the thought of it.

By the end of the day the beginning of the garden had taken shape, thanks to so many volunteers. Merrie had gone round with mugs of tea and plates of biscuits to sustain the workers, and all in all it was a merry and hard-working group.

"You're amazing," Andrew said as he drew Jane into his arms after the last of the volunteers had gone for the day. "To have put this all together—"

"It's not just me," Jane protested. "It's everyone. It's the village. We're all doing it, and I'm so glad Alice is going to be remembered."

"I'm glad too," Andrew said quietly. "I'm glad you discovered more about her life – and all from a shopping list!"

Jane smiled in memory. It seemed like a long time ago now that she'd first found that list, feeling so miserable and lonely and uncertain. Now she felt full of purpose, and happier than she'd ever been.

"I thought I'd show you something," Andrew said, and Jane raised her eyebrows in query. "I saw it in the paper, and I thought of you." Smiling a bit sheepishly, he handed her a newspaper clipping.

"Part-time marketing director required for charity," Jane read. "Based in Workington, twenty hours a week." She looked up at him in surprise. "You want me to go back to work?"

"Only if you do. I feel guilty, having taken you away from your career and your family and friends. I know what a big sacrifice you made coming here, Jane."

"It was worth it," Jane said quietly – and meant it.

"Anyway, I know you've been busy planning the garden and doing all the home stuff, but if you wanted to go back to work… I want to support you in that."

"Thank you." Jane stood on her tiptoes to give him a kiss. "I appreciate that, Andrew. Thank you for being patient with me. I know it took a long time for me to settle into life here."

"Thank you for being patient with me," Andrew returned. "I know it took a long time for me to understand just how hard it was for you."

She smiled and put her arms around him, glancing at the clipping she still held in her hand. Marketing director… the idea held a certain appeal. She'd look into it, she decided as she laid her head on Andrew's shoulder. In this moment, anything and everything felt possible.

CHAPTER TWENTY-SEVEN

Alice
Goswell, May 1943

Alice gazed round the vestibule of the vicarage one last time. Vera was already waiting outside with their cases, and the train for Carlisle left in fifteen minutes.

Alice turned slowly around in a circle, remembering how David had first swept her over the threshold twelve years ago. How full of hope she'd been then, and dreams... and yet she'd felt fear too, and such a terrible uncertainty. She still remembered how, on that first night, she'd huddled in the dining room as the windowpanes rattled and everything had felt cold and dark and awful.

So many days and months and years had passed in this place, days of loneliness and misery and grief, but also ones of peace and love and joy. She blinked back tears as she thought of David in these rooms; she could almost hear the spring of his step on the stair. She took a breath, let it out slowly. The memory of David, the love of him, would be with her always. She didn't need this house to remind her of him.

And perhaps one day this house would be full again, full of people and laughter and children running up and down the stairs, a dog like David had wanted lying contentedly by the range.

Alice longed for the house to be filled the way she had wanted to fill it, to be a home to some distant family in the future. They would never know about her, and the years she'd spent here, although perhaps they would sense her in time's faint echo.

She smiled at the fanciful thought and with one last, lingering look at the home she'd once had, she opened the door and stepped outside into the sunshine, and the rest of her life.